Too Hot to Handle

A Fiona Silk Mystery

Mary Jane Maffini

RendezVous
Crime

Cover art: Victoria Maffini
Design: Vasiliki Lenis

Le Conseil des Arts | The Canada Council
du Canada | for the arts
depuis 1957 | since 1957

We acknowledge the support of the Canada Council for the Arts for our publishing program.

RENDEZVOUS CRIME
an imprint of Napoleon & Company
Toronto, Ontario, Canada
www.napoleonandcompany.com

Printed in Canada

11 10 09 08 07   5 4 3 2 1

Library and Archives Canada Cataloguing in Publication

Maffini, Mary Jane
        Too hot to handle / Mary Jane Maffini.

(A Fiona Silk mystery)
ISBN 978-1-894917-57-5

        I. Title. II. Series: Maffini, Mary Jane.   Fiona Silk mystery.
PS8576.A3385T66 2007   C813'.54   C2007-903838-7

ACKNOWLEDGEMENTS

Special thanks to the ebullient mystery reader Kaye Barley of Boone, NC, for allowing Fiona to kick off this book with her Kahlua Coffee Cake recipe, as well as to Gay Cook for contributing the excellent Sangria Blanca from *Mrs. Cook's Kitchen: Basics and Beyond*, and to Ron Eade of the *Ottawa Citizen* for Grilled Asparagus.

My good friend Lyn Hamilton has been unfailingly generous with recipes, support and camaraderie from start to finish. As always, Mary Mackay-Smith came through with advice and many laughs. The Ladies Killing Circle provided editorial comments and some hilarious recipe ideas, while Linda Wiken keeps me up on trends in the mystery world. I can always count on the Cape Breton Consulting Group for cheerful advice over food and gossip. The members of The Pink Bra Society were fearless in testing many of the recipes, as were Barbara Fradkin, Cheryl and Elaine Freedman.

My eagle-eyed brother, John Merchant, has spotted bloopers as usual, while Janet MacEachen continued to answer bizarre legal questions. This time they survived recipe testing as well.

Special thanks to Dr. Kiley O'Neill for treating Fiona and Josey, to Leona and Jerry Trainer for advising Fiona on her project, and to Chris Knight and Linda Saint for advising me on mine.

I have long coveted the painting that appears on the cover of this book. I am grateful to Victoria Maffini for allowing it to be reproduced and for her guidance on this and many other writing projects. My son-in-law Stephan Dirnberger knows the most amazing and useful facts about fires and police services. On the home front, my husband, Giulio, remains steadfast despite being surrounded by murder and mayhem.

At RendezVous Crime, publisher Sylvia McConnell and editor Allister Thompson have been patient and supportive over the course of seven books. Vasiliki Lenis put her creative talents to making those recipes look good.

Once again, I'd like to remind readers that St. Aubaine is not Wakefield. I've invented the restaurants, businesses, the spa, the good and the bad guys. I've also played fast and loose with the roads and the weather. It's pure fiction and any errors, of course, are my own darn fault. But you knew that.

ch

Suki's Sex and Serotonin

Chocolate Kahlua Pound Cake

Chocolate has long been reputed to have aphrodisiac properties. But even if it didn't, you might still pick this over an encounter with any mere stud muffin. This cake is great on its own, but you can serve it with vanilla ice cream or whipped cream with another dash of Kahlua.

1 cup butter
$1/2$ cup shortening
3 cups sugar
5 eggs
2 cans chocolate syrup (284 grams each) or a 1 lb. can
3 cups plain flour
$1/2$ teaspoon baking powder
1 cup milk
1 teaspoon vanilla

Cream butter, shortening and sugar. Add eggs one at a time, beating well after each addition. Add chocolate syrup and beat. Sift together flour and baking powder. Add alternately to creamed mixture with milk. Add vanilla. Mix well. Pour into greased and floured tube pan or bundt pan. Put in a COLD oven. Set temperature to 325° and bake for 80-90 minutes or until done.

chocolate

chocolate

chocolate chocolate

chocolate chocolat

chocolate

chocolate

Meanwhile, fix the glaze as follows:

1 cup granulated sugar
$^{1}/_{2}$ cup water
2 tablespoons Kahlua or other chocolate liqueur

In a small saucepan over low heat, combine the granulated sugar and water and stir until the sugar is dissolved. Remove from heat and stir in the chocolate liqueur. Cool cake for about ten minutes. Remove from pan and pour glaze over. Take the phone off the hook and enjoy.

ocolate

chocolatechocolate

chocolate chocolate

chocolate

chocolatechocolate

chocolate

chocolatechocolate

One

"They tell me I've been shot." The whispered words slipped from the lips of the man in the hospital bed.

My book tumbled to the floor with a thud. I leapt to my feet and gripped the cool metal sidebars of the bed. I leaned over the pale figure and touched his face. His eyes remained closed. "Yes, you were." My words sounded garbled, the result of the aching lump that squeezed my throat. After eight months of wistful visits to these mud-beige rooms, I had pretty much given up hope for a happy ending.

The poet Marc-André Paradis opened his eyes. They were still the same intense blue that had made my knees buckle the first time I'd met him. He tried to lift his head from the pillow and produced a small but incandescent smile. I patted his hand.

"I cannot say I liked being shot, madame."

"Of course you didn't."

He frowned. "Not that I can remember it. Nothing at all. It is all foggy. *Comprenez-vous?*"

I'm a total patsy for a French accent. But I didn't care for the "vous". We'd been well into the "tu" stage before that bullet had grazed the side of his skull.

"Maybe you are better off without that particular memory."

"Am I?" he said, with interest.

"Absolutely. And you shouldn't try to get up."

"I must move a bit. It is very boring and miserable here in

this…where am I?"

"It's the rehab centre. You were in a…" I hesitated. Was it all right to tell someone he'd been in a hospital bed for months? Should I mention that no one had expected him to survive the bullet that had grazed his head? Or that his memory came back but never stayed long? For sure I wouldn't mention the recent surgery that had set him back to zero.

"And lonely," he said.

"Me, too."

Small beads of sweat had formed on his forehead. They matched the ones on mine. He whispered softly, "It is very warm in here."

"We're having an early heat wave. The humidity is unreal. These hospital rooms seem to be even worse than anywhere else."

"An early heat wave? But it's September."

"Um, June," I said. "We're in June now."

"Really?"

"Afraid so."

He frowned. "June already."

"Time flies," I said with a smile.

We'd been down this road before. In April, May, and two days previously, also June.

"If it is June, then I imagine I will be able to go home soon. That will be wonderful."

"Home? I'm not so…"

"Oui, madame."

No chance of that. He still needed physio and possibly even more surgery. Home was not in the cards. Not now for sure, and maybe not ever. According to the medical personnel, there was a serious possibility that Marc-André Paradis would spend the rest of his days in a care facility.

"I miss using my hands. I am a very good mechanic. Did

4

you know that?"

I swallowed. "I do. You're the best in West Quebec, as well as a poet."

"That's right. High-end imports. My clients must miss me. Are you one of my clients, madame?"

I hope someday you will remember our relationship, I thought. But I managed to hang on to my smile and say, "Sort of. But my car isn't up to your standards."

"I will be back at work soon." He grinned before he sank back onto the pillow and closed his eyes.

"Let's hope."

I whirled at the soft squish of shoes behind me. A burly residents' aide in purple scrubs and chunky white runners bustled through the door and scowled in my direction. Her glance softened as she looked down at Marc-André. A smile hovered around her lips, replacing the scowl.

I'd been visiting for months, and this was a new face to me. Her ID tag said "Paulette".

"Time to let the patient rest." She was one of the many francophones in our region who speak English as well as any anglo. Unlike Marc-André, she had not a trace of a French accent. Probably had gone straight through school in the English system.

I blinked. Had I just imagined her hostility? I'd never seen her before, let alone done anything to merit antagonism.

Her scowl returned full force. It showed off the lines in her fiftyish face.

On the other hand, I could understand. It only takes a few seconds to fall head over sensible heels for Marc-André. I speak from experience. Even so, I didn't want to get into any kind of competition with her. For one thing, she looked like she might toss the javelin for a hobby.

"I've only been here a few minutes."

"Not my problem. Visit's over now," she said.

"But he's speaking today. In fact, a minute ago he was telling me he's ready to go home."

"I hardly think so," she snorted. "Don't go filling his head with that kind of junk."

"But…"

"The patient comes first."

"Of course, he comes first. But he needs company, a familiar face. He says he's bored and miserable."

"He said no such thing. He has been in a coma, and he's a francophone. Who do you think you are kidding?"

"Well, you're francophone and you…"

It didn't help my case that Marc-André was now sleeping, his breathing slow and even.

She rolled her eyes. "Do you really expect me to believe that his first words would be 'bored and miserable'?"

"But they were. He always speaks English to me."

Her eyes narrowed dangerously. "Oh, does he? I don't know what you're up to, lady, but as of this moment, you are out of here."

Assertiveness is not my best thing. Even so, I stood my ground. "I've been visiting him ever since he's been in this facility. I'm here at least four times a week. This is the first time he's spoken about going home. It's an emotional moment. I'm not ready to leave yet."

She crossed her well-muscled arms. "Oh, really?"

"Yes. Really."

"Shall I buzz Security?"

"Security? For me?" I squeaked.

"You got it."

"I'd just like to say goodbye." So much for assertiveness.

Mine evaporated with a slight flushing sound.

She nodded. "Make it snappy."

I leaned over and gave Marc-André a peck on his pale forehead.

He opened his magnificent deep blue eyes again.

"Goodbye," I said.

"So soon, madame?" he whispered.

"I'll be back." I squeezed his hand.

"I know that."

Paulette gave no sign that she'd heard. She gestured toward the door. She mouthed "Security," in case I needed a reminder.

Marc-André struggled to sit up. "Wait, madame."

"Yes?"

"Please, don't leave without telling me your name."

My heart contracted.

"Fiona Silk," I croaked.

"Have we met before?"

I felt Paulette's smirk on my back long after I'd slunk down the hospital corridor. Despite the shimmering heat, I shivered for two blocks until I finally reached my free parking spot.

* * *

Before I began the long drive north from Hull to St. Aubaine, I'd opened all the windows of my overheated Skylark. Even so, my bare legs were sticking to the vinyl seat. The Skylark had recently developed a nervous tendency to stall at low speeds, especially while merging. I'd become pretty adept at a fast restart, but this time it wasn't speedy enough for the guy behind me. He laid on the horn of his hulking black Cadillac Escalade. The blast caused me to yelp and grab my steering wheel. The Skylark stalled again. After fast restart number two, I jerked forward. The driver made an attempt to cut me off as the Skylark leapt like a startled rabbit. When that didn't work, he passed me on the right of the entrance ramp and shot onto Highway 5.

A few minutes later, as I approached the Tenaga exit, I spotted the Escalade again. He was stopped on the side of the road. He glanced up as I passed and made a point of leaning out the window to flip me the bird. I caught a blur of sunglasses and a flash of super-white teeth. He gestured again to make sure I hadn't missed it the first time. Not that I'm ultra-sensitive about road ragers as a rule, but this guy's reaction seemed excessively personal. Worse, there was something familiar about him. Of course, his oversized designer shades didn't help. In my rearview mirror, I caught a glimpse of blonde hair and a laughing red mouth as his passenger leaned forward. She shouted something stunningly unladylike.

I hadn't gone far when the horn blared again. I glanced in the rearview again and saw the Escalade looming right on my bumper. As it rocketed past at roughly twice the speed limit, the laughing blonde passenger tossed a lit cigarette out the window. The smouldering butt just missed my face and landed on the passenger seat. I grabbed it and tossed it into the ashtray. Not quite quick enough, though. The reek of singed vinyl filled the air.

"May you get what's coming to you," I said. It's my favourite curse, although singularly useless.

I didn't know why I felt so shaken by that particular driver. I should have been used to horns blasting and rude gestures. After all, my shuddering old heap brought out the dominant urge in other drivers. It was worse on the highway, and especially with SUVs. This was Quebec, where no one tolerates a slowpoke. Anyway, I had plenty of other problems. I had no time to worry about a pair of jerks in a hundred thousand dollar status symbol.

I knew it was way past time to replace the Skylark, although my bank manager had nearly toppled off his leather executive chair laughing when I'd suggested it. But my mind wasn't on the car or the parts that tended to drop off it, or even whether it would survive the forty-five minute trip. My mind wasn't on any of my money problems or the fact that my writing career, for which I'd left a paying job, had stalled. Instead, I kept reliving the scene with the beautiful, bewildered man in the hospital bed. Was Marc-André back for good this time? Would he ever remember my name? For how long?

A police car with our regional logo whizzed past me. Too bad Mr. Oversized Cadillac Crazyass Jerk was already out of sight. I would have enjoyed seeing him taken down a peg. That kind of speed and the attitude he'd be bound to show would cost him serious dollars and points. The blonde lady wouldn't be much help.

Get a grip, I told myself. That creep is the least of your problems.

*　　*　　*

Sometimes when things go bad, you need some kind of fix. And your dog does too. I pulled off at Tulip Valley and turned right. My best friend, Tolstoy, was suffering greatly from the heat wave. That's the downside of being a white purebred with a Siberian heritage. You're not so adaptable when the temperature hits 32°C, and the humidex breaks local records. As poor Tolstoy was hiding out in my basement, waiting for me to return and the heat wave to lift, I thought some Peanut Butter Dog Delights might improve his spirits. And the stop might take my mind off my troubles. I chugged onto the 105 and drove south again past Les Fougères toward my favourite bakery: La Boulangerie Suki. Inside, the scent of cinnamon, chocolate, vanilla and fresh pastry was enough to lift my mood. Suki handed over a large bag of the doggie treats. I also figured if I nibbled my way through one of those remarkable slices of chocolate Kahlua pound cake, code name Sex and Serotonin, I might be a better driver—in fact, a better human being. It was worth breaking my last twenty.

Slapping that on the counter reminded me that I wouldn't have been down to that last twenty if my ex-husband hadn't been hanging me out to dry on our property split. My friends had been telling me for years that I was a pushover for Philip. I'd been promising myself to stand up to him. I was getting better. He was getting worse.

Once I left Suki's, I pulled out my cell phone to give him yet another call to suggest he quit stalling and just get it over with. Of course, he's a lawyer, and a successful one at that, so there wasn't much hope that I could scare him. But you can't rule out the annoyance factor in negotiations.

Damn. I reached Philip's long-time secretary, Irene Killam, an Olympic-class stonewaller. If she stood between you and Philip, you weren't getting anything but a headache.

"He has an important appointment," she said. It was clear from her tone that talking to me could not possibly be important. Never mind, I've had years to get used to that.

I was still working on an effective approach with Irene. "I need to speak with him."

"He's incommunicado."

"He'll have his Blackberry. I'm pretty sure he even takes it in the shower."

"He isn't in the shower. And I can't reach him."

"You could send him a text message."

"I could, but he won't get it. He'll have the Blackberry

turned off. I wish you would listen to me. You will just have to wait."

We sparred like that for a bit, but she's much better at it than I am. After she hung up, I turned to the slice of chocolate Kahlua cake. My standing up for myself shtick might have needed work, but the chocolate made up for it.

Minutes later, I was back on Highway 5, feeling a bit more relaxed. The slice of cake was just a fond memory and a few random crumbs on my T-shirt. I still had a half-hour drive north through the rugged Gatineau hills. On a normal day, I would have enjoyed the view and the rock formations along the road. This time I wasn't paying much attention, until I crested the last hill near the end of Highway 5 and had to stand on my brakes. The Skylark squealed and smoked. Police cars blocked the road, roof lights flashing. An officer in the green uniform of the Sûreté du Québec stood in the middle of the road, waving traffic off to the side. A dozen cars were pulled over ahead of mine.

I shuddered to a stop, my heart thumping. What a weird place for a speed trap. Ridiculous. The Skylark could barely make the speed limit. What if I'd been going too slow, and there was some kind of fine for that?

But not everything was about me. I stepped out of the Skylark to see what was going on. A long skid mark on the highway showed the path of a vehicle. The bent guardrail on the side of the road hadn't been enough to stop it. That vehicle now lay on its roof near the bottom, like a large dead June bug. Several small trees had been plowed over in its path. Firefighters were unfurling hoses from a pair of fire trucks angled on the side of the road. I stared down at the crumpled vehicle. Even with the covering of dust, I was pretty sure it had been big and black.

Could anyone have made it out alive?

An ambulance screamed along the highway and inched past the row of stopped cars. The wail of the siren sent shivers down my spine. I hoped the paramedics had made it in time. Sometimes these things look worse than they are, I told myself. Maybe the people in the car had survived. Even from that distance, I could tell it wasn't likely.

A pair of firefighters in bulky brown gear and what looked like respirators on their backs made their way down the steep hillside. One had a hose snaked over his shoulder. Two others followed with ropes. As the first pair began to spray foam on the smoking wreck, the QPP officer approached my car and barked at me to get back in. A second officer had just finished setting up cones to close off the two lanes. He had begun to direct traffic back the way we'd come.

"This accident," I said, "what happened?"

"Sorry, madame. We can't really talk about it. You need to get back in your vehicle."

"Please. Was it a black Cadillac Escalade?"

That got his attention. "Why do you ask?"

Of course, I hadn't really wanted to get his attention. "No reason. I just saw one earlier."

"And?"

"He was way over the speed limit. He passed me on the right, when I got on the highway near Hull, driving really aggressively. Then he came right up on my bumper and…so I wondered if it was the same one."

"Can I see your licence and registration, madame?"

"*My* licence and registration? Why?"

"I'd like your name. In case we need to follow up."

I could tell by his guarded expression as I handed over my licence that the crumpled vehicle was indeed the Escalade.

And I knew as I watched the firefighters losing battle below that the driver would never give anyone the finger again. A blue truck from Remorquage Tom et Jerry edged closer to the scene, but I doubted there'd be much left to tow.

"Thank you, Madame Silk. We will contact you if we need to take a statement." He pointed in the opposite direction. "You can turn around and go back the way you came. Take the old highway back to St. Aubaine."

"I don't think I can drive just yet," I said.

He nodded.

"Do you ever get used to this?" I asked.

"No, madame," he said.

He rejoined his colleague redirecting traffic. I sat there feeling sick as a body was unloaded from the smoking wreck.

The
Chez Fred's Special

Poutine

Okay, no one I know actually makes poutine at home. That's why we have restaurants. But its hedonistic qualities make it Quebec's favourite junk food.

2 cups beef gravy (you can make it if that's important to you)
Salt
Freshly ground black pepper
2 pounds Quebec potatoes, peeled and hand-cut into French fries
1/2 pound fresh cheese curd, crumbled
Vegetable oil for deep-frying

Fry the potatoes in hot vegetable oil until golden brown. Remove and drain on paper towels. Season with salt and pepper. To serve, mound the fries into bowls and cover with cheese curd. Spoon the gravy over the fries and cheese curd. Eat immediately! Serves four.

Two

As I drove through the village, I couldn't help noticing the neon yellow banners with red letters screaming EN FEU! HOT STUFF! The banners were strung across Rue Principale. Naturally, here in Quebec, the French words had to be twice as big as the English ones. We have rules. Rules or no rules, the signs didn't mean anything to me in either official language. Every now and then, the village boosters go off the deep end. This might have been one of those times. I was shaking my head as I drove under the banners and past a line of large white trucks parked casually by the side of the road for no reason that I could see. And frankly, at that moment, I didn't care.

I needed an ATM, and I needed it fast. I snagged a parking spot then stood in line for fifteen minutes at the Caisse Populaire. I stared in disbelief at the crowd ahead of me. There's never a lineup in St. Aubaine. And if two people are waiting, they strike up a conversation, or suggest that you go ahead. It's that kind of community.

St. Aubaine is full of aging hippies, old farming families, snowboarders, retired public servants, struggling musicians, blocked writers, starving artists, bad poets and, increasingly, young organic farmers. Oh, right, and tourists. We locals lean toward clothing from Mountain Equipment Co-op, or Tigre Géant, or even Canadian Tire. But this crowd seemed fairly young and oddly urban. Lots of tousled blondes with the kind of hair you see in magazines. Who were these people? Whoever, they weren't inclined to chat with the locals.

Was some edgy new band playing at the Pub Britannia perhaps? Maybe they were attracting the trendy set.

A woman with spiked hair the colour of a freshly polished fire truck pulled up to the edge of the sidewalk in a white Lexus SUV. She hopped out, left it running and raced over to CeeCeeCuisine, the pricey new kitchen supply shop. I was still cooling my jets in line when she returned, carrying a cluster of distinctive green shopping bags with the CeeCeeCuisine logo. She opened the idling SUV and tossed the parcels in. She slammed the door, hustled over and elbowed ahead of me. Stunned as I was by this behaviour, I still couldn't help noticing the startling amount of stretch in her dress and the equally amazing number of rhinestones studding her black glasses. Me, I probably wouldn't have chosen a leopard-patterned headband to go with that look. She sported straw sandals with towering wedge heels, probably the highest I had ever seen in St. Aubaine. Even so, she hardly came up to my chin. She was as stocky as my old washing machine. The wedgie sandals showed off the blood-red polish on her toenails.

I didn't bother to argue over my place in the line. I'm never in a hurry to deal with any bank. When I finally got up to the machine, I popped in my card, pecked in my PIN and picked SAVINGS. I already knew that Mother Hubbard's CHEQUING cupboard was bare.

Oops.

I downgraded my request to twenty dollars.

The hell with you, said the ATM, or words to that effect.

I tried CHEQUING again.

It was not to be.

Well, that's just plain bad when you don't have twenty dollars in the bank.

I yanked back my card before the machine confiscated it. It looked like I would have to dig into my drop-dead emergency fund to get through the month.

Then what?

Nothing but grim days ahead.

I turned to leave and banged into Jean-Claude Lamontagne, my least favourite person on the planet. Too bad he's also my closest neighbour. I might have been awash in perspiration, but Jean-Claude was a vision of dry elegance in his light-weight silk suit, silver grey, of course, one of the money colours.

"Hello, Fiona," he said.

Personally, I thought the salon tan clashed with the cool of the handmade suit, but what do I know? I was wearing my pink flip-flops, my three-year-old jean skirt and a black T-shirt with sparkly white letters that said "Leave Me Alone". I'd lost nineteen pounds since I'd started visiting Marc-André. Maybe it was the smell of all that institutional food. Whatever the reason, it had left me with a limited wardrobe.

Jean-Claude smirked, but then he usually does. Maybe it wasn't the outfit. Had he seen the screen message of AMOUNT REQUESTED EXCEEDS BALANCE? Oh, rats. That was all I needed.

"How are you, Fiona?" Jean-Claude always speaks English to me. I'm pretty sure that's just a dominance thing. He knows perfectly well I can get along *en français*. He makes a point of emphasizing my name.

"*Très bien. Parfait. Fantastique,*" I said. I did my best to look like someone who hasn't sailed past her agreed-on overdraft amount. "I have just been visiting my friend Marc-André Paradis at the rehab centre, and he seems to be getting better again."

"Really? Yet you are…distressed."

"Well, I'm a bit warm, if you must know."

Of course, he could tell that by looking at me. My hair

couldn't have been frizzier if I'd stuffed my tongue into an electrical socket.

"Well, I can certainly understand. Things are definitely heating up in St. Aubaine," he said.

I am always trying to figure out the subtext of what he says. Where there is Jean-Claude, there is always some kind of worrisome undercurrent. Plus, I trust him as far as I could toss him and his shiny new silver Porsche Carrera.

I smiled. "Absolutely."

"Lot of building going on. Boom economy."

Right. Now I knew where we were headed. Same old same old. Jean-Claude has been the driving force behind most of the development in and around our picturesque and historic town. He wasn't satisfied with two monster home developments or his new batch of condos cluttering the waterfront. His latest plan was a grand riverside development just north of the village.

I said, "I'm not planning to sell. Not now. Not ever. Just in case that's where you're going."

"I think you should hear me out. That place you have is a lot of work for a single woman, two acres, a big lawn, that old cottage needing repairs all the time. I couldn't help noticing your driveway needs regrading. I imagine keeping the woods clear of deadfall must get you down. You must worry in this kind of weather. Brush fires, things like that."

"I'm happy there."

"I can't even imagine the state of your wiring." He gave an elegant shudder.

"I love my home. I believe I have mentioned that before. I am sure that my wiring is fine. And if it's not, it can be fixed. I'll never find another place like that."

"Well, it's a beautiful spot, and a lot of waterfront property for sure. But it's not the only nice place in the area. Everyone knows you are broke. I could make it worth your while to sell."

"No," I said, a bit louder than I intended.

The stocky redhead with the towering heels had been lingering by her idling car, maybe counting her cash or even just waiting for someone. She checked her watch conspicuously and scowled in our direction. I was pretty sure that Jean-Claude was the focus of her attention.

Jean-Claude seemed to be totally unconscious of her presence as he turned his back on her. I wondered about that, since he does nothing without a good business reason. He didn't even glance when a couple of giggling teenagers bumped into her. She dropped her purse, scattering the contents. She knew some interesting words, for sure. Everyone around got an earful as she jammed her belongings into an oversized red bag with *En feu!* written on it. Still swearing, she climbed back into the giant vehicle, squealed off down the road, turned sharply and roared up the hill to the old Wallingford Estate, now known officially as Le Domaine Wallingford.

I couldn't help but watch her, but Jean-Claude didn't take his eyes off me. "You could get something a bit more modern, lots of places with nice views a few miles north. Perkins, Kazabazua, Rupert."

"I like the view I have now."

"Continue to think about it," he said. "I will be very fair to you. You'd have money to buy a new place and enough left over to pay things off. Relax a bit. Get some clothes, perhaps travel."

I turned back to Jean-Claude. "Not a chance," I said with a tight smile that hurt my mouth.

Jean-Claude had pressured my late aunt Kit in her final years. She'd left me the little house on the two wooded acres near the water. It came with all the memories of the happy summers I'd spent there as a child. I'd promised her I'd never let him get his manicured mitts on it.

"You wouldn't have to worry about money any more."

"Not happening."

"And you could use a new car as well."

I turned to cross the street.

"Well, give it some more thought and get back to me," he called after me.

When you talk to Jean-Claude, it's as though nothing you say registers. But this time, he seemed even more confident and arrogant than usual. Did he have some way of knowing that I was already worrying about my overdue tax bill? Jean-Claude had a finger in every pie in town. Everyone owes him something, except me, and he's related to half the town. He probably knew the state of my bank account and how little time I had to settle my tax bill before the municipality could take my property.

I kept my head high and didn't notice an object on the ground until I stumbled over it. I bent and picked up a leather wallet with a leopard print design. The red-headed woman must have dropped it.

I opened the wallet and checked for a name. Harriet Crowder would notice the loss of her ID, credit cards and five hundred dollars pretty quickly, I thought. I couldn't find a telephone number. Maybe the people at CeeCeeCuisine would know how to contact her.

The sight of all that cash reminded me that I didn't have a sou. I pulled out my cell phone and called Philip again. This time I didn't even get Irene.

Across the road near CeeCeeCuisine, a huge sign said: *Rafaël et Marietta seront ici!!!* What did that mean? Who were they? Some people with a big budget were getting married? I wasn't the only one who was asking. A small, excited clutch of people were pointing at the sign. Apparently, it was big news.

Not big enough to take my mind off the horrible accident I'd seen, the fact that Marc-André was languishing in the rehab centre, while Phil was stonewalling, my bank account sat below zero, and Jean-Claude was scheming to get my property.

I had hit rock bottom.

That made me crave food with an equal measure of fat, starch and salt. The kind of stuff that you find in small-town greasy spoons. Stuff like poutine. I had just enough change to manage it. I made my way to Chez Fred, my favourite greasy spoon. The Chez has air conditioning, and air conditioning trumps everything. Plus the greasier the spoon, the better the poutine.

I glanced down the street and spotted a rickety bicycle hurtling toward me. The bike squealed to a halt, and fifteen-year-old Josey Thring hopped off and propped it against the wall. She angled it carefully so the homemade sign for her handygirl operation, THE THRING TO DO, showed to advantage. Josey's freckles stood out against her pale skin, and her cowlicks were on full alert.

"Hey, Miz Silk, I've been hoping to run into you." Josey likes to get business out of the way early in a conversation. "You must need a lot of stuff done in your garden. I'll come by and cut your grass. Heat wave like this, you must be up to your neck in weeds. Dust too, I suppose."

"Don't worry about it, Josey."

"It's a pretty hot day. You're looking kind of cooked. I could walk Tolstoy for you."

"Thanks, but it's too hot for Tolstoy to walk right now. He's hiding out in the basement, sound asleep. I'll have to wait until it cools down."

"Oh sure, I can come by later."

With Josey, you have to fight fire with fire. "Shouldn't you be studying tonight? You must have your exams coming up."

"I had a study day today. I guess I should check your gutters too."

"And what exactly were you studying?"

Who was I kidding? Josey never studied for a minute, and as far as I could tell, she rarely went to school. On the other hand, she passed with excellent marks every year, and I did need my grass cut. It wasn't even summer yet, and I'd already given up the war against the weeds. And for all I knew, my gutters did need cleaning. I was a bit unclear on that detail. Josey could provide any kind of house maintenance service you needed. She was clear on details and finer points. Plus she was one of those people who are born knowing how to do things. Too bad I was not one of those people born knowing how to earn enough money to have things done.

"Trouble is, I'm pretty broke, Josey."

"What about your divorce settlement?"

"Still dragging on. That's one of the problems with divorcing a fast-talking lawyer who doesn't plan to remarry any time soon."

"Yeah right, who'd marry him anyway?"

"I did."

Josey shook her head. "Doesn't count. You were young and probably really foolish. Maybe even drunk."

"I wasn't drunk! And I wasn't young enough to fully explain my foolishness. He had a certain attraction, big man on campus, that kind of thing. Good-looking, smart, ambitious. Somehow, over the twenty-five years, it faded."

"Maybe because he expected you to iron his socks."

"I never actually ironed his socks, Josey."

"Of course not, but face facts, Miz Silk, he's a real jerk. Anyway, you're free now, so you have to make sure he doesn't take advantage of you. You need a good lawyer."

"I have an excellent lawyer. Marie-France Sauvé. Unfortunately for me, she works on her own. No back-up. Right now she's on her honeymoon, and she's out of communication range. When Marie-France gets back, she'll fix Philip's wagon but good."

"Get another lawyer and take him to court, Miz Silk."

"That's one of the problems. Philip's really plugged in to the legal community. He made sure I'd have trouble finding a lawyer in West Quebec. Marie-France came up against him in some case and didn't like his tactics. I was lucky to get her."

I wasn't so sure I should take legal or relationship advice from Josey, given that she hadn't quite hit sixteen and her mother had headed out for a pack of smokes some five years earlier and hadn't been seen since. I knew nothing about her father. So maybe her perspective was skewed. On the other hand, my own strategies had been spectacularly useless.

"How about your book writing, Miz Silk? That must make you some…"

I shook my head. "Not going well. I'm hoping something will come up soon, but for now I'm really strapped." I didn't have the heart to mention negative royalty statements to Josey.

"Don't worry about the money, Miz Silk. Your credit's good. You can run a tab. Wouldn't be the first time. Things will get better for you soon. I'll swing by later this afternoon and get started."

"No," I said, firmly. But of course, resistance was futile.

Josey added, "I'm really glad to get this extra work, because I'm saving for my driver's licence. I'm turning sixteen in September."

Of course, I knew that well enough.

"And I need money to take the Drivers Ed," she continued. "If I take it, I can get my licence in eight months; otherwise, I got to wait for a year. They call it your 365, 'cause of the number of days. So you get the idea why I don't want to wait."

23

Absolutely. Josey lives in the back of beyond in a ramshackle cabin with her Uncle Mike, when he's not in the slammer. It's a long, rickety bike ride from anywhere, and Uncle Mike is usually too drunk to stand, let alone drive. Still, I knew better than to badmouth him in front of Josey.

"It's seven hundred bucks for the course," she said. "That's a lot. My dog walking business already goes to pay for my cell phone, and I got other expenses too, you know."

"Um."

"I'll come by later then. You getting poutine, Miz Silk?"

I mentally calculated the money in my purse to see if I had enough to manage a pair of poutines. I didn't want to sit there bathed in guilt while Josey chewed through her savings for her beginner's licence. If I used the parking change in my car, I had just enough for two orders of poutine and a tip. And it would be an early dinner too.

"My treat," I said. "But first I have to check in CeeCeeCuisine to see if they know how to reach the woman who dropped this wallet. Hold on."

"Are you kidding? I love that place. They got such great stuff. I bet they're making a fortune. I'm coming with you."

Josey is never one to miss an opportunity to see someone with a good business model. CeeCee's sure had that. The aisles were jammed. Who were all these people? I tried to get the attention of one of the frazzled clerks. She was coping with some highly focused customers. Maybe there's something about expensive kitchen gear that brings out the beast in us. Not even the soft scent of lavender calmed that crowd.

"Can't help you right now," she said. "If you can come back later, I'll check the credit card slips for a telephone number."

"I'll be at Chez Fred for the next while if she comes in looking for it. I'd be pretty worried if I were her."

I slipped the clerk a piece of paper with my name and telephone number.

"Will do," she said, turning back to the pushiest customer.

One less problem to worry about.

*   *   *

The Chez was jammed too, but then it always is. No matter how many wonderful trendy restaurants open in the village, we locals still hang out at the Chez. There are times when roasted rosemary and exotic salads are not what we need.

As preferred customers, Josey and I bypassed those who were waiting and scored a window booth. We ordered two poutines, which would be prepared in the kitchen, along with the Chinese take-out by the Chilean cook under the watchful eyes of the Lebanese owner.

"What's going on in town?" I said, avoiding eye contact with resentful folks who'd been there first. "Who are all these people?"

"They're here for *Hot Stuff*," Josey said. "I bet that woman who lost the wallet has something to do with it too. It doesn't sound like she's from around here."

"She's definitely not from the village. I saw some banners for this *En feu!* hot whatever. What is that anyway?"

"It's *En feu* if you're French. *Hot Stuff* for us. They're here for the television show. It's the big thing, Miz Silk. The Cooking Channel."

"There's a cooking channel?"

"Sure. On satellite TV. Everyone gets it. You don't know about the cooking channel, Miz Silk? What about reality television?"

I said evenly, "I *can* read, so I do know about reality television. But what does all that have to do with St. Aubaine? We don't even have a television station. Our population is two thousand, including stray dogs. Not exactly New York or LA."

"You really need to get satellite, Miz Silk. How do you think I keep up with what's happening in the world? Trends and everything. Do you know there are even business report channels?"

I shuddered.

Josey wasn't letting go of this idea. "But, you'll have to buy a new TV set first. I can find you one pretty cheap. Uncle Mike knows a guy…"

"No thanks," I said quickly.

"And I can pick you up a dish and receiver at a garage sale. People are always upgrading. Uncle Mike can get you the cheat card, and you'll get hundreds of channels, just like that. Everyone does it. Even if they trace your signal, the worst they'll do is fry your receiver."

I blinked.

She beamed at me. "Easy as pie, Miz Silk. Then you can move into the twenty-first century."

"I don't think so, Josey." Of course, I might have been one or two centuries behind, but I wasn't foolish enough to believe I had heard the last on the satellite issue.

She chattered on. "Anyway, the reason all these people are here…"

I smiled. Josey really cares a lot about Marc-André. She'd be happy to hear that he'd been awake and talking that afternoon. "It's okay. Here's our poutine. And I have good news today. You know what…Josey?"

Josey's fork landed with a clatter. I was so surprised, I dropped mine too. "What?"

Josey's mouth hung open. I followed her gaze. It led to a young man ambling along the sidewalk.

"Holy smokes. That's…"

I stared. "Who?"

"I can't believe it!"

"Me neither. But who is it I can't believe?"

"You're kidding me, right?"

"I'm not. Who is he? And why do we drop our forks when we see him?" I glanced around the Chez. We were not the only fork droppers. Every woman in the place was staring out the window. A few went so far as to rush for the door. From a distance, he seemed lean and hip Quebec stylish, but I couldn't really get a look at his face. He was talking intently to a dark-haired woman with splendid curves and a wide, sexy smile that lit up her face. She put a seductive hand on his shoulder. I wouldn't have been surprised if it had left a burn mark.

Josey lowered her voice. "It's Rafaël."

"Hmm."

"You don't actually know who Rafaël is, do you, Miz Silk?"

I shook my head.

"He's just the most famous TV chef around. He's really, really big in Quebec, and now he's got a new show on English television too. And a magazine. I think he's going to be even bigger than Marietta."

"Who is Marietta?"

"The woman he's talking to. She's big news. She's got books and two shows. She's on magazine covers and even business news. She's what they call a brand. People call her Naughty Marietta, because she's really sexy. I heard she was going to start a whole line of cooking equipment and food too."

"A brand. Unbelievable." I sighed. "Well, I've never heard of either of them."

"Don't take this the wrong way, Miz Silk, but who *have* you heard of?"

Something told me that Homer (not Simpson), Shakespeare and Margaret Atwood weren't going to cut it here.

"Pop culture isn't my thing, Josey. What are they doing in St. Aubaine?"

"I've been trying to tell you, Miz Silk. It's all about *En feu! Hot Stuff!* Rafaël's going to be shooting a special here with Marietta. That's going to be amazing. Even if his lordship did help to make it all happen."

"Oh. Jean-Claude is behind this too?"

"He's involved. Not the only person, though."

"Isn't it enough that he's trying to redevelop the whole waterfront, stick up giant houses and condos and change the character of the village into something…?"

"Snooty patootie?" Josey suggested.

"Exactly. Anyway, when did we stop calling it 'town' and start calling it 'the village'?"

Josey hesitated. "I don't know. It just sort of snuck up on us, I guess. It sounds a bit trendier than 'town'. I wouldn't be surprised. Maybe Jean-Claude was behind that too. He called the new condo development Le Village au bord de la Rivière. That changed the whole look of the place. Did you know that now he's teamed up with those people who bought the Wallingford Estate? They're supposed to be turning it into a world class resort and spa."

"I must have missed that."

"But you keep to yourself, Miz Silk. The grand opening is going to be in a couple of weeks. They're letting the production team use the site free, and they gave Marietta and Rafaël the really fancy rooms. They call them suites. It's amazing PR. Then when the program airs, they'll get exposure across the country. Everyone says Jean-Claude made the connection with the television producers and the new owners of the resort."

I said, "Huh."

"I've never been to a spa."

"I haven't either."

"Not even when you were married to that lawyer?"

"Especially not then."

Time to change the topic. "I guess I missed out on this news entirely. The Wallingford Estate was abandoned when I spent my summers here as a kid. It must have had the best river view in the whole village, from up there on that hill, but even then it was kind of creepy. I haven't heard about the people who bought it."

"You're the only one, then. Her name is Anabel Huffington-Chabot. She's very glamorous, used to be a model. You never met her?"

I shook my head. "Doesn't mean a thing. I know Jean-Claude, and that's enough to put me off the project."

Josey turned toward the window and craned to watch as Rafaël crossed the road. An SUV squealed to a halt and the red-headed woman who'd dropped the wallet jumped out. She appeared to be accosting Rafaël. Marietta jumped back. I watched with my mouth open. A plump young man in skinny white jeans and a form-fitting T-shirt ran up to them and fluttered around waving a clipboard frenetically. I wasn't sure that this was the perfect day to wear cowboy boots, but, as usual, what did I know?

"That's her. The woman who dropped the wallet," I said and started to get out of my seat. Before I'd left the booth, the conversation ended with much arm waving, and Rafaël headed off up the hill, holding on to Marietta's hand. The red-headed woman hopped into her SUV and nearly flattened a few unwary pedestrians as she rocketed out of sight in the opposite direction. The young man in the cowboy boots stood watching with one hand over his mouth.

I noticed a few local women wandering after the famous pair, sort of like a crowd of possessed peasants in a cheesy horror movie.

I said, "Who was that again?"

Josey stared at me with pity. "It's what I've been telling you about. He's Rafaël. She's Marietta. They will be doing a cooking show together. Sort of competition with each other over food. You know. That lady with the ketchup-coloured hair is the producer for the show they're doing together. I forget her name, but I saw her picture in the paper, and she's responsible for a lot of hit cooking shows."

Hit cooking shows? My mind boggled. "How do you know these things, Josey?"

"It was on local TV and even in the St. Aubaine paper. You got to stay on top of things, Miz Silk."

I dug into the poutine. I didn't plan to stay on top of anything that had to do with *Hot Stuff*, Rafaël, Naughty Marietta, Anabel Huffington-Chabot (if that could possibly be someone's name), Jean-Claude Lamontagne or anyone else connected with the whole ridiculous scene.

Hélène Lamontagne's
Sangria Blanca

Makes at least 12 servings
Marinating time: at 3 hours or longer

This is a special wine summer drink to serve for casual entertaining. Red wine can replace the white wine, but use colourful available fresh fruit such as oranges, red apples, berries or grapes.

3 cups chilled dry white wine (750 ml bottle)
1/2 cup (125 ml) Cointreau or brandy
2 to 3 tablespoons (25 to 45 ml) granulated sugar, or to taste
1 each lime and lemon, cut into thin slices, pits removed
1 peach, peeled and sliced
1 unpeeled green apple, cored, cut into thin slices
1 cup (250 ml) green grapes, halved and pitted
Ice cubes
1 1/2 cups (375 ml) club soda

In large glass pitcher, combine wine, Cointreau or brandy, sugar and pineapple or peach, apple and grapes. Chill in the refrigerator for at least 3 hours to mix the flavors.

To serve, add ice cubes and club soda to the pitcher. Serve in large glasses with two or three pieces of fruit in each glass.

Three

"You know what I forgot, Miz Silk?" Josey said when she'd finished her poutine.

"What?"

"Your agent called. She said it was good news."

"How do you know?"

"I dropped in to your house, and I answered the phone because it was ringing, and that's it."

I took a deep breath, then said, "You shouldn't be in my house without letting me know, Josey, and you definitely shouldn't be answering the telephone. Especially when you don't have a key."

"That's okay, Miz Silk. It's no problem."

"It's a problem for me."

"Why?"

"Privacy. You have to learn to respect that."

"Sure, privacy's good, but I'm like your assistant. I can screen all your calls if you want."

"I can't pay you to be an assistant."

"That's okay. You can run a—"

"And I am not going to run a tab for the assistant I can't afford."

"Fine. I volunteer. You need my help, Miz Silk."

"I guess I'd better head home and call her back."

Josey flipped open a small striped notebook with blue pages.

"Don't rush. She's out at a reception now. She's a really neat person. She said she'll call you back tonight. See? I'll take care of the messages, and if it's urgent, I'll get back to them."

"But…"

She snapped the notebook shut and beamed. "In the meantime, I can tell you're worried about this wallet."

"I am. I know that I'd be in a panic if it was mine."

"Not everybody's like you, but anyway, I bet if we went up to the Domaine Wallingford where the *En feu!* production is happening, we could find someone to give it to her. All these extra people you see around town are either connected with the production or they're fans here to catch a glimpse of Rafaël and Marietta."

"Can they do a show in front of an audience?"

"I don't think they're doing that. But Rafaël and Marietta are each supposed to pick a different restaurant every night and have dinner there. So people are trying to be in the right one at the right time. People have driven in from Toronto, Montreal. I heard they're supposed to start production tomorrow."

"Amazing."

"Sure is. That's why Jean-Claude was behind it. It really puts the spotlight on the town, which will help him sell his projects. The cameras will be on Rafaël and Marietta in the restaurants too. And the people at the Wallingford Estate, they offered not only the space, but their big kitchen too. It's going to be great publicity when they open as an *auberge* with a spa and a restaurant. Good business all round. It will be fun to see what's going on up there. What did you say her name was? I forget."

"Harriet Crowder."

"See? You could give her back the wallet and then you could relax. Maybe later we could even go for a swim at Miz Lamontagne's place and tell her about it."

I chuckled. "Hélène hasn't invited us. And I wouldn't want to run into Jean-Claude twice in a day, that's for sure."

"His lordship doesn't spend much time at home, you know that. Miz Lamontagne loves us. And you have to consider Tolstoy in this hot weather."

"Forget the pool. Let's go get rid of this damn wallet."

*　　*　　*

The Wallingford Estate had been imposing even during the many years when it had stood abandoned and crumbling. I'd never fully understood why someone who wanted a relaxing summer getaway would construct a multi-storey home out of granite, on a hill across the old road along the river. But then I wasn't a nineteenth century lumber baron. And I had to admit the place had a certain grandeur, from the Scottish baronial style of the main house to the extravagant flowing lawns and gardens. The only thing that screamed contemporary was the collection of vans and SUVs parked outside. Josey and I were puffing by the time we'd walked from the centre of the village up the long, craggy hill.

Minutes later, when we'd caught our breath, we swept up the wide stone exterior staircase and into the main foyer, a cool, contemporary, slightly Zen atmosphere that came as a surprise. The Zen thing was a bit disrupted by the frantic scurrying of young people in T-shirts and camouflage cut-offs. Most seemed to be carrying mikes, cameras, wires and other equipment.

A young man walked past us and raised an eyebrow. I recognized his white jeans and cowboy boots. He was still clutching the clipboard. Only now he also had an earpiece connecting him to someone somewhere. He also had something twinkly on the side of his nose and was sporting a strange hairdo that seemed to come to a point.

"I'm sorry," he smiled, showing teeth that must have been professionally whitened. "But the facility's not open to the public yet. Is there anything…?"

"We're here to see Miz Harriet Crowder. This is Miz Fiona Silk, and I am Miz Josey Thring. Her assistant." Josey flipped open the little notebook with the blue pages, just in case.

His nose twitched alarmingly before he got control again. "I'm Brady Davies. I'm an assistant director," he said. "All to say, I don't know where Harriet is right now. Is she expecting you?"

I said, "No."

"Ah. Well, um, I can…"

"We have her wallet. Miz Silk here found it," Josey said.

I broke in. "Perhaps you could see that she gets it."

"Are you kidding?" Brady blurted. "I don't go close to the Red Devil. She's mad at me. She'd—"

I interrupted. "Is there someone else I could leave it with? I'd just like to get it back to her."

As this little scene was playing out, a striking woman with shoulder-length blonde hair emerged from an office toward the back of the foyer. She closed the door behind her and headed in our direction. She must have been five nine, with a remarkable bosom, given how slender she was. I estimated the annual upkeep on those blonde highlights could have wiped out my little tax problem. Her crisply tailored cream suit must have been designed for her, then applied with a sprayer. Her expression told me we were going to get the boot, maybe because my three dollar pink flip-flops and the black T-shirt from Giant Tiger weren't in the right league. At the sound of a shrill voice in the distance, she froze, pivoted and hurried up the wide main staircase, tanned legs moving fast, stiletto heels clicking. Whoever she was, she was beautiful, expensively dressed, confident and oddly familiar.

Josey probably has the loudest whisper anywhere. She turned to watch the splendid departure. "That's Anabel Huffington-Chabot. She's the person behind all this. And her husband too, but all everybody talks about is her."

"Um, he's no longer in the picture," Brady whispered back.

I said, "Ah." Sometimes no longer in the picture is best.

"She's the queen now." There was a funny little twist to his mouth. Stories to be told, I imagined, under the right circumstances.

"Oops," Brady squeaked as Harriet Crowder burst into the foyer.

I stepped forward and said, "Excuse me…"

Harriet ignored me, pounded on the office door and yanked it open. We could hear a soothing, almost musical voice from inside. However soothing, it didn't seem to do the trick.

"That looked like Harriet," Josey whispered.

"Sure did," Brady said.

Whoever was on the receiving end of the tirade had my sympathy. Brady shrugged. "I'm sorry. Harriet's obviously in the middle of…"

Harriet Crowder's voice rose like a siren. "You tell that bitch Anabel if I find her before she fixes this, I'll split her down the middle and slow roast her on the barbecue. That'll get the ratings up."

She didn't seem to notice us as she stalked out of the office and back the way she'd arrived. She also didn't glance up the wide staircase, but if she had, Anabel Huffington-Chabot would have done well to dive out the nearest mullioned window.

Doors continued to bang along the corridor.

Josey said, "Wow."

The door to the office closed softly.

"Oh, boy," Brady said. "Poor Chelsea. She doesn't deserve that."

"Who's Chelsea?" Josey said.

I gave her a nudge. "Never mind, Josey. Thank you, Brady."

Brady said, "No problem. Chelsea's Anabel's EA. She's a doll, unlike her boss."

"What's an EA?" Josey said.

"Nothing," I said.

"Executive assistant," Brady said. "In this case, to the world's chilliest woman. But still better than Harriet, the red devil on steroids."

I sighed.

"Executive assistant. Oh, boy." Josey scribbled something in her little notebook.

I was pretty sure I hadn't heard the end of that.

Brady said, "Um, I don't think you should bother Chelsea yet. She just had a rough ride."

Josey answered for me. "Is anybody else around? Marietta or Rafaël?"

I said, "We don't really need to see anybody else."

"Sorry I couldn't help," Brady said. "The thing is everyone's terrified of Harriet. If there's the slightest thing, she goes off the deep end. You just saw a sample of that."

"Do you mind if we try to find her? Maybe she'll calm down."

"Sorry. We're setting up for the production. I can't let anyone have unaccompanied access to Wallingford House. We're having a problem with light-fingered locals, I mean, visitors."

"No! People stealing?" Josey said, scandalized.

Brady chuckled. "Yes. In fact, lots of local shops and suppliers and even farmers are dropping off wonderful gifts to show goodwill for the show. And half of these goodies are walking right out the back door. We've had to put a padlock on the freezer. You could wait here to see if she comes back."

Josey drew herself up to her full height, five three on a good day. "Miz Silk would never steal anything." Not like Uncle Mike for sure.

Brady's eyes widened. "Oh, I'm sure of that, but Anabel Huffington-Chabot owns this facility, and she'd freeze me to death on the spot if I let you in."

Josey echoed, "Facility," slowly savouring the word. I imagined I'd be hearing more of it.

"Can't I just leave the wallet with someone?" I said, feeling exasperated. "I'm just trying to do a good deed. And move on with my life."

"I sympathize, but you picked the wrong person. Harriet doesn't understand the concept of good deeds."

"Fine, I'll just mail it to her."

Brady bit his lip, then said, "Of course, if anything goes wrong and Harriet needed the wallet tonight, she'd think nothing of suing you over it. She tends to win her lawsuits too. But it's up to you. Perhaps you have time and money to spare."

"But that's hardly fair!" I said.

"Fair," he twittered. "Another foreign concept to the red devil."

Josey said, "Maybe we better wait."

I thought I knew her motivation, and it wasn't Harriet. "A couple more minutes wouldn't hurt, I suppose. Don't want to get sued. Do you have a ladies' room I could use while I'm waiting?"

"Sure. Use the staff one right across there. All the prima donnas appear to be offstage." He pointed to a door and scurried off down the hallway in the opposite direction from Harriet Crowder.

In this particular case, I was very happy to avoid the impending catfight between Harriet and Anabel. Conflict is not my best thing. And I really couldn't imagine myself rooting for either one of them.

"I'll keep an eye out, Miz Silk," Josey said, obliquely.

"Before I go in, tell me, Josey. Did Brady have a diamond stud in his nose, or did I imagine that?"

She nodded. "Might have been cubic zirconium, but I'm betting it was a diamond. He's really cute. He had a cool fauxhawk too."

"What's a…oh, never mind. I'm better off not knowing."

As I pushed open the door, I took a deep breath. Since the previous autumn, I'd found ladies' rooms alarming, and there were good reasons for that. Of course, there was no need to be skittish in a luxurious spot like this.

A person could get used to the subdued lighting, dark minimalist woodwork, toilet stalls with tumbled marble walls and dark-stained louvred doors. I had to admire the stacks of real towels and the delicate dispensers for soap and lotion. There was a lingering scent of fresh paint and new wood, two of my favourite fragrances. A pair of smartly dressed middle-aged women passed me chatting on the way out. One of them stopped to pick up a briefcase from the counter.

A minute after I entered a stall, I heard the click of stilettos outside my door. I thought nothing of it. Until I tried to open the door. I flipped the lock and turned the handle. Nothing happened.

Stuck? Not possible.

I turned the handle both ways. I tried again. I pushed and pushed again, a bit harder each time. Nothing. I tried pounding. Maybe the wood had swelled in the high humidity. I tapped the top, middle and bottom. No luck.

By this time, my heart was thundering. As long as you maintain your dignity, that's the main thing, I told myself. I hammered on the door. No response. I banged my fists and kicked. Silence.

To hell with dignity. "Let me out!" I hollered at the top of my lungs.

When that didn't work, I went back to banging. I added kicking to the mix. Suddenly the door flew open, and I tumbled out and landed on my knees on the marble floor. Let's just say I prefer softer materials.

"Jeez Louise, Miz Silk! I'm really glad I heard you yelling! You could have been in there forever."

I picked myself up. "Thank you, Josey. The door was stuck."

"Miz Silk. It wasn't stuck. It was—"

"Let me wash my hands and get out of here. I feel like a fool. Not able to open the door, how ridiculous is that?"

"No, it was—"

"Let's go. I don't even want to talk about it."

"Miz Silk! You have to listen to me!" Josey's freckles stood out in sharp relief against her pale face. Her cornflower blue eyes bulged.

"What?"

"You weren't stuck in there. Someone barred you in."

"Oh, Josey, don't try to make me feel better. I know what happened."

"No, you don't, Miz Silk, or you wouldn't be saying that. Just look at this!" She pointed.

I followed her gesture. "What am I supposed to look at?"

"This chair."

I blinked. It was an attractive chair, but that's all I could say about it.

"It was blocking your door."

"But how…"

"Miz Silk, someone put it there."

"I don't see how that could be. It's not very heavy."

Josey made a soft expression of exasperation. "It was stuck

41

under the knob like this. See?" She grabbed the chair with its thin metal back and tilted it so it fit under the knob.

I stared.

"Now do you believe me? I don't know how you didn't see it."

"I'm sorry, Josey. I was in a panic. Who expects a chair blocking their door? Who would do such a thing?"

She stared back at me. "Well, it has to be one of the ladies who came out of here, doesn't it?"

"A couple of women left when I first got here. But they were gone before I even went into the stall."

"I saw them. One of them is a dog walking client of mine. She's here to talk about a catering contract. She wouldn't pull a mean trick like that. A blonde lady went in right after you, just as they were coming out. She left before you did. That makes sense."

"I don't know. I can't understand why anyone would do such a thing in the first place."

"She was out of there like a bat out of hell. I didn't get a look at her. I was talking to my client about her catering business. Hey, maybe she's someone you used to know. She could be really mad about something you did in the past."

"I can't imagine what."

"Or she could be just a bit crazy. Or doing something on a dare. Although I didn't think adults pulled that kind of stunt. Miz Silk? Are you listening? You have a kind of faraway look in your eyes."

"Hmm? Oh, right. Did you happen to notice what kind of shoes this woman was wearing?"

"Oh, sure. High-heeled sandals, really high. She was used to them, too. She didn't even teeter. Do you think that's a skill a person could learn?"

I shook my head to clear the image of Josey striding around

in spike heels. "I never have," I said. "For what that's worth."

"I know that, Miz Silk. But I was just wondering how come some people can do it and look so natural."

"It's a mystery. What about the other two women? What kind of shoes were they wearing?"

"One had those clunky sandals, and the other one had leather walking shoes. How come you're asking?"

"I definitely heard the click of high heels on the marble floor just outside the door of my stall. I didn't think too much about it. Just figured someone was checking to see if it was vacant. Now it's obvious she must have been pushing the chair up against the door. For whatever crazy reason."

"She can't be that far away, Miz Silk. It's only been a couple of minutes."

"Do you think it might have been Anabel Huffington-Chabot?"

"Oh, wow, Miz Silk. I really wasn't paying attention." Josey radiated guilt. "I was talking to my client and kind of keeping an eye out in case Marietta or Rafaël showed up."

Obviously Josey had not been quite as impressed with Anabel as I had been. I said, "Don't worry about it."

"Never mind, Miz Silk. Let's go find Harriet."

"But Brady said we couldn't have access without… Josey, come back."

I had no choice but to chase after her down the long corridor where we'd last seen Harriet. No one spotted us. It wasn't long before we recognized a shrill voice.

Josey managed to get ahead of me, and before I could stop her, she'd pushed open the swinging doors and barged into the huge kitchen area at the rear of the facility. I'd never seen a kitchen like it. For starters, it was forty feet long, with acres of stainless work surface and a twelve burner stove. Cameras had been set up to face the vast granite-topped island that occupied the centre of the room. Here and there were boxes of groceries and supplies. I could see what Brady meant. A large flowering azalea with a *Bonne Chance! Good Luck!* card sticking out of it sat next to two large green tins of high-end imported extra-virgin olive oil sporting the logo of CeeCeeCuisine. Next to them, I spotted a jumbo jug of my favourite maple syrup from the local sugar bush. Oh yes, and stubby little Harriet had the hapless Brady backed up against the stainless steel double-door refrigerator.

"Wow," Josey said.

"Hello," I said.

Harriet was in mid-shriek. "You can't pull this kind of stunt! We have contractual agreements. We will pull the plug."

Brady managed to squeak out a plea, "I'm on your side, remember. You have to talk to Anabel. She's the one making the decisions about the site."

"If I catch that little tart, I will. And don't you walk out on me, you quivering little wretch. I will find out what's going on."

Brady fled, letting the exterior door swing behind him. Harriet put out her hand to stop it before it smacked her in the face.

"I have your wallet," I called out, a bit too late.

Josey and I watched in astonishment as Harriet stomped out the back door, climbed into her Lexus SUV and tore off down the driveway, spraying gravel in her wake.

"I guess it wasn't the best time for handing over the wallet," Josey said.

"Right. And I suppose we should get out of here before we get accused of pilfering. I think they're serious," I said, pointing to the huge walk-in freezer with the padlock on it.

As we headed toward the foyer, Anabel was descending from upstairs. She glanced around quickly, probably keeping an eye out for Harriet. The blonde highlights swirled as she swept out through the front door and down the long stone steps. The only part missing was the full orchestra.

I decided to try to leave the wallet with her assistant, even if she had been given a rough ride by Harriet. None of this had to be my problem. "What was the assistant's name again, Josey?" I asked. Josey has an uncanny ability to remember people and details.

"Chelsea. And she's an *executive* assistant."

Naturally, Chelsea did not answer when I crossed the foyer again and knocked at the office door. Probably still cowering under the desk, I decided.

* * *

My cell phone rang, and I snatched it up.

"Philip?" I said, continuing to walk back down the hill toward the village.

"*Oh là là.*" My friend Hélène Lamontagne laughed her silvery laugh. "I have been leaving messages at home for you."

"Haven't been home most of the day," I said.

"You are lucky. It will be like an oven at your place now. Why don't you and Tolstoy come over for a swim?"

That was a tricky one. How can I loathe Jean-Claude and spurn his offers, then go take a dip in his oversize pool? Where's the dignity in that?

"The thing is, Hélène, Jean-Claude and I had a little dust-up over my property today. I can hardly…"

"Fiona. I am *not* my husband. I have nothing to do with his real estate business. Nothing. I am your friend, and I am asking you to come to *my* home and keep me company. How can that be a problem? By the way, do you know where Josée can be found? She might like to join us."

45

Josey was looking particularly innocent at the moment, which made me wonder if she'd set up the call.

"I will see the three of you soon," Hélène said. "And by the way, Jean-Claude will be out this evening. He has an important meeting."

"It may take a while," I said. "I found a wallet belonging to one of the *En feu!* producers, and I need to return it to her."

"Ah oui. Who is it? I know a lot of those people."

"Harriet Crowder."

"Oh là là là." I imagined Hélène rolling her eyes.

*   *   *

The level of excitement rose higher every hour. In fact, the whole village seemed to be on the verge of frenzy.

"Wow, no wonder people are excited, Miz Silk. It's Marietta!" She tugged at my hand, pulling me along the sidewalk toward the waterfront.

Marietta turned to us in surprise. A small puff of smoke escaped from her lips. She dropped a cigarette and ground it out. "You caught me. It's naughty, I know, but…"

Josey blurted out. "This is Miz Fiona Silk, and I am her executive assistant, Josey Thring. We're big fans of yours." She snapped open her little notebook with the blue pages, I suppose to drive home the executive assistant point.

Up close, Marietta was a feast for the eyes. Her luxurious mane of chestnut hair did not frizz in the heat and humidity like mine. Her make-up was perfect, the olive skin glowing and flawless. Her full red lips curved in a wickedly conspiratorial smile. The smile went all the way to her dark brown eyes. Every male who walked past us did a double take. I attributed those reactions to Marietta's dangerous curves and her startling cleavage.

Josey said, "We're looking for Harriet Crowder. She's your producer, isn't she?"

Marietta bubbled with laughter. "Oh, my poor Harriet. What's she done now?"

Josey said. "Nothing, except yell at some people. But that's none of our business. Miz Silk found her wallet. We tried to talk to her at the Wallingford Estate but…"

"Her tail was on fire?" Marietta laughed.

"Something like that," I said, cutting into the conversation. "She was pretty fierce."

"Poor little Harriet. She's upset about a few things today. She's really all sound and fury, and one of these days she really should learn to pick her battles. Even so, I don't know why people are so frightened of her. Sticks and stones, right?"

"Perhaps you could give her the wallet," I suggested, not wanting to test the sticks and stones theory. "Since you know her."

Marietta put her soft, warm hand on my arm. "I'm just off to meet someone, or I'd love to. But listen, I'm sure I saw Harriet heading toward the parking lot across the street. We're having a bit of trouble with the air conditioning up at the estate. When she gets too hot, she gets into her SUV to cool off. She doesn't usually go anywhere, so you should be able to catch up with her, no problem." As Marietta sashayed off, a perfectly normal-looking man walked straight into a telephone pole as he followed her progress.

"She was real nice, wasn't she, Miz Silk? And she's so beautiful. Just like on television."

"Right. Let's just get this over with."

I looked both ways but didn't see any combinations of red hair and leopard print. Or any tails on fire. Normally someone like Harriet would have stood out in our community. But today, the population had changed.

47

Josey raised her binoculars. She never leaves home without them. "Oh, Marietta was right. There's the SUV!"

I saw the spiky red head disappearing into the Café Belle Rive.

Josey said, "I can't believe someone would drive down that little hill instead of walking. Come on, Miz Silk."

Sometimes it's a curse to be polite. "Excuse me," I said as we pushed through the crowd on the sidewalk. "Pardon me. Coming through. Excuse me." Talk about a waste of words. I might as well have been invisible. Josey was quite far ahead of me before I finally broke through a knot of chattering young women, but she waited for me to catch up.

"Miz Silk, you'll never get anywhere if you wait for people to let you do what you want."

The story of my life.

The Belle Rive was a venerable restaurant in a restored building teetering on the edge of the Gatineau River. It's a popular spot for tourists and locals. The tourtière and chutney are homemade, and the salads come from a local organic farm. The house wine is very drinkable, and no one there is ever in a hurry. Perhaps there's something romantic about eating French country cooking on the misty shore, because a high percentage of the diners always seemed to be holding hands and gazing with cow-eyed admiration at the person opposite. I followed Josey through the door. Usually at that time of day, the restaurant celebrated happy hour with cocktails and canapés. It was way too late for lunch, and dinner service didn't begin before seven.

A beaming young woman carrying a stack of menus greeted us. "I'm sorry. We're full, with a forty-five minute wait. You might try Oops! across the street."

"Just looking," Josey said, slithering past her. She quickly checked the dining room and scooted out to the outdoor seating.

"We're trying to find an, um, acquaintance," I said. "Do you mind if we check on the verandah?"

Of course, it was a bit too late to ask permission. Josey had disappeared.

"No problem," the hostess said. "Let me know if you want to reserve a table for later."

As usual, every seat on the verandah was occupied. No one looked like Harriet Crowder. But at the far end on the right was a table tucked out of view. I happened to know that spot had the best view of the river. An oversized bag with the *En feu! Hot Stuff!* logo hung over the side of a chair, but I couldn't see the people at the table.

"That must be her bag. Excuse me, pardon me," I said as I eased my way along the narrow passageway toward the end of the verandah, trying not to let my overstuffed carryall knock anything off the intimate little café tables. I couldn't help but note that everyone seemed to be sipping chilled wine and gazing at their partners with something like ardour.

Josey had already reached the end, eager to tell Harriet that we had her wallet, I suppose. I could feel a puce blush spreading up my neck and over my face. A nervous woman grabbed her wine glass as I sped up to get ahead of her.

Josey tapped the woman at the end on her bare and golden shoulder. "Miz Crowder? Oh…"

"Very, very sorry," I said to the two people at the table. "Case of mistaken identity."

Anabel Huffington-Chabot turned and frowned. So did her companion. In fact, he dropped her well-manicured hand as if it were a live grenade. What was he doing there? And more to the point, what was he doing with *her?*

Words almost failed me.

"Please, excuse us. So many people, so easy to get confused

with all the crowds. We found Harriet Crowder's wallet, and I thought I recognized her bag. Can I leave it with you to give to her? No? I suppose not. Sorry."

"But Miz Silk. That's…"

"Come on, Josey. Let's go."

"I think we should…"

"I apologize for interrupting your meeting," I added. I backed hastily down the narrow aisle, pulling Josey with me.

Outside Belle Rive, I took a deep breath.

"Jeez, Miz Silk. Did you just see what I did?"

I nodded.

"I don't know why you dragged me away."

"Oh yes you do."

"Harriet's not here. I don't know where she went. But what kind of a meeting was that anyway?"

"A private one," I said. "It wasn't appropriate to interrupt."

"Well, what kind of business do you think it was?"

"It doesn't matter. She's a businesswoman, and he's an investor."

"It seemed pretty weird to me."

I didn't want to get into a long discussion with Josey over the fact that Jean-Claude Lamontagne had had his tongue hanging out over Anabel Huffington-Chabot. If we hadn't shown up, he might have smothered in that engineered cleavage. I hoped Josey had missed the hand-holding part. "Sometimes it's better to let it go. You've heard the expression 'discretion is the better part of valour'?"

"That Anabel was wearing really high heels. Maybe she was the person who locked you in the toilet stall."

"But why would she?"

"Maybe she knows how you feel about Jean-Claude." Josey goggled at me.

I said, "You were distracted and didn't get a good look at whoever it was. And I just heard the heels. I can't imagine the owner of a place like the Domaine Wallingford would lock someone in the ladies' room. Bad publicity if it got out."

The thin shoulders slumped. "I don't like her much. You think Miz Lamontagne is going to be upset?"

"Upset?"

"Sure, you didn't notice that his lordship was holding his colleague's hand at that important meeting? And staring down the front of her top."

I hesitated. "We won't mention it to Hélène. Maybe we just misinterpreted it."

Josey scowled. "Maybe."

"Let's go hunt for Harriet."

An hour later, after cruising through every street and parking lot in the village of St. Aubaine, we'd still had no luck. We picked up Tolstoy and made tracks for Hélène's.

*　　*　　*

Hélène may be my closest neighbour on our winding semi-rural road, but there's not much in common between the two houses. Her six thousand square foot two-storey custom-built stone home sits on top of a completely man-made hill at the end of a long, winding driveway. Paved, naturally. Each giant blue spruce perfectly placed on the manicured lawns had been delivered by truck and planted by certified forestry types.

My cottage, on the other hand, is the same ramshackle dwelling that my great-aunt Kit inherited from her parents. Well, okay, it was winterized sometime in the early sixties, when Aunt Kit moved in permanently, and she did have a proper bathroom installed. But aside from that, it's not much different. Many of my trees have been there for nearly a hundred years. I'm a lot happier with my glimpse of the Gatineau River than I would be with any landscaper's dream.

Some things money can't buy.

I was damp and sweaty by the time we'd trekked the quarter mile to the Lamontagne's, but I held my back straight and my head high as Josey rang the doorbell. Even the damned chimes sounded pricey. Hélène's Mercedes was parked in front of the house, but as expected, there was no sign of Jean-Claude's silver Porsche Carrera.

"Fiona! Josée! Tolstoy! I am glad you could all make it."

I adore the woman, even if she is married to my nemesis. I don't understand it, but I don't hold it against her. After all, hadn't I spent many long years with Phil? I didn't understand that either. Some decisions are beyond comprehension. An unfathomable swamp of pheromones, desperation and the desire to wear a long white dress just once.

But friendship trumps all that.

She'd obviously been at the pool. She looked stylish in a white eyelet beach cover-up that contrasted nicely with her tan and her burgundy hair. The Gucci sunglasses were a smart touch, as were the bejewelled flip-flops. I'd picked my own sunglasses at the local Giant Tiger. My swimsuit had long ago lost its sproing.

"Come on in for a swim," she said as I followed her.

I wasn't sure how much I would be able to relax, knowing more than I should about Jean-Claude's activities.

Hélène walked ahead through the long marble foyer and the newly renovated designer kitchen, which Josey claimed had cost Jean-Claude close to a hundred thousand dollars. We followed her through the screened porch to the glittering custom swimming pool, surrounded by acres of manicured property. It's magazine quality, but except for the company, I would just as soon be taking a dip on the rocky shore of the Gatineau on my own property. However, Josey loved the pool, and it suited her new status as an EA.

Hélène headed for the sparkling new stainless steel patio bar. "Why don't you get changed, and I'll mix us some sangria. And the Shirley Temple version for you, Josée."

Sometimes it's pointless to argue. Sangria was a great idea.

By the time I managed to get into my suit, Josey had already been in the pool. So had Tolstoy. Hélène had worked some magic with drinks. Everyone was in a good mood, and Tolstoy had found himself a shady spot on the cool slate patio.

"Josée has offered to help me with the organizing for the community logistics connected with *En feu! Hot Stuff!*" Hélène said. "That is very kind of her."

"Oh, indeed," I said. I wondered if any of those logistics would put Josey within swooning distance of Rafaël. "Very public-spirited."

Josey beamed.

"I can use all the help I can get," Hélène said, shaking her artful burgundy mane.

"Mmm," I said.

"So many things to do," she said.

"I suppose," I said.

"Volunteers make for a strong community," she added.

"For sure."

"Sangria?" she said, giving the carafe a playful swirl.

"Absolutely. I love sangria."

"Me too," Josey said.

I raised an eyebrow.

"Without the whatever," Josey said.

I wasn't sure what sangria without the whatever would

consist of, but I was grateful that Hélène had made her the Shirley Temple version. Josey was still clean and sober, unlike the rest of her relatives. And me, of course.

"Ah oui," Hélène said, "I have many happy memories of sangria."

"Right," I said. "I suppose Jean-Claude likes it too."

She shook her head. "No, he does not. Sometimes he is so…"

Josey said, "Pig-headed?"

Hélène frowned, "No, not exactly, I was going to say he is more…"

Luckily, I stopped myself from saying, "Sleazy?"

"Serious," she said. *"Un homme sérieux."*

"Oof," Josey said.

"I suppose he is," I said. A thousand adjectives would have popped into my mind first, but I had to keep in mind the feelings of the lovely person who was handing me a drink in a tall, frosty glass.

"Oui," Hélène said, narrowing her eyes a bit.

Something told me that serious didn't have all that much appeal right at the moment. I had no problem with that. I never understood what a lovely person like Hélène saw in St. Aubaine's version of Donald Trump anyway. All right, better looking, better hair. But even so.

Josey said, "I wonder if Rafaël likes sangria?"

Hélène arched her back. *"Certainement.* He would."

I took a sip, savoured the citrusy sweetness and waited for the little kick. I lay back on the stylish padded lounge chair.

Hélène took the chair beside me. "Fiona, you are gripping that glass so hard, I can see your knuckles. Even Harriet cannot be that bad."

My mind was whirling from everything that had happened that day: the horrible image of the burning Cadillac Escalade,

Marc-André lying in his hospital bed, my empty bank account, my invisible ex-husband, Jean-Claude's attempt to get my property while I was down, and now the guilty knowledge that he might be having a fling with Anabel Huffington-Chabot behind Hélène's back while the village watched and smirked.

I sighed. "Harriet and her wallet are the least of my problems."

Ooh Lola
Ooh Lola Ooh Lola
Ooh Lola Ooh Lola
Ooh Lola

Lola's Contribution

One can of whipped cream, or more as desired.

Technique: Apply whipped cream to selected areas. See what happens.

Ooh Lola
Lola Ooh Lola
oh Lola Ooh Lola
Ooh Lola

la
Lola Ooh Lola

Ooh Lola Ooh Lola
Ooh Lola

Four

When I got home, I checked my messages. Aside from the earlier ones from Hélène, nothing. Nada. No offers of work. No calls from Philip. Nothing at all about that damn wallet. I tried to find a phone number for the Domaine Wallingford, but nothing was listed. I googled it. Nothing. I tried Philip five or six more times. Then I left a message with my new agent, Lola. I hit my office and dusted off a few proposals and old articles. I sent out some emails to long-ago colleagues and editors, checking the waters. I knew that the start of the summer months wasn't the best time to get a bit of government writing or editing work, especially when you've been out of the loop for a few years. But I had to try something. I opened the file with my novel and closed it again.

I distracted myself by rigging up two ancient fans to get a breeze going in the house. Outside was cooler of course, but much too buggy by the river to stay long. Josey had decided to spend the night at my place. In return for the use of the futon in my office, she was making a fresh supply of icy lemonade, using lemons borrowed from Hélène. I had sugar and ice on hand, mint that Josey had planted and a crystal carafe to contribute to the effort. I had left Josey in the small pine kitchen and just started out to take Tolstoy for a walk, when my friend Dr. Liz Prentiss drove up in her Audi Quattro.

"Make yourself at home," I said.

"I will."

Of course, I knew that only too well. But what are friends for?

By the time it took me to get Tolstoy out for his constitutional and back, Liz had managed to ferret out my last bottle of Courvoisier and had already helped herself to two fingers. I was sure I'd hidden it better than that.

I was still feeling the effects of the sangria, so I had some of the lemonade Josey had made. I could hear her humming in the kitchen. I sat in the wingback chair. Liz might be a physician, and she is a close friend, but she is not the kind of person to tell your worries to, so I left out the accident, the money problems and all that. But I had to talk about Marc-André.

"You need to lighten up, Fiona."

Liz had been my friend since kindergarten some forty-one years earlier, so as a rule I cut her some slack. However, there are times when she pushes the limit. This was one of them.

"I *am* lightened up." I eyed her from the wingback chair, where I was fanning myself furiously. The evening mist on the river gave a visual clue to the stifling heat and humidity. The fans didn't really cut it.

"And you need to get air conditioning."

Air conditioning is not an option for me, partly because of the shape of my converted cottage home, mostly because of the cost. "Don't push your luck."

Liz shrugged. She had a talent for pushing her luck.

She peered into her brandy snifter then raised the bottle again. I was too hot to heave myself out of the chair and snatch the Courvoisier from her. I clutched my icy glass of lemonade and said, "I can't believe you told me to lighten up. I am talking about a man I care deeply for. You're a doctor, for heaven's sake. You should be capable of some small amount of compassion."

"Pull yourself together. It's not like he's dead. He was in a coma for months, and now he's coming out of it. Great. But you let yourself get so worked up about every little thing."

Every little thing? I almost choked on that. "He's finally regained consciousness, and he doesn't remember my name!"

"And that's too bad, because you seem to be so besotted with him."

"What is the matter with you? He's a wonderful person, who didn't deserve to die at the hands of a crazed killer. And now he doesn't deserve to live without a memory."

"That's the trouble with head injuries, they have hellish implications."

"But he'll get his memory back, won't he?"

She shrugged. "I'm a GP, not a neurosurgeon. Sometimes they're left with gaps."

"Oh." I knew all about gaps. There had been a serious one in my life since a screaming ambulance had carried Marc-André away from a crime scene.

Liz said, "He's going to need a ton of physio just to be able to walk. And when he was at his best, you only knew him for, what, a couple of weeks? It's not like you were married to him. You have no idea what you'll be taking on. This guy is probably going to have impaired cognitive ability for the rest of his life, and you'll end up taking care of him. I see the impact of that in my practice all the time. Don't take this personally, but you're not that great at looking after yourself, let alone some guy who will be totally dependent. Maybe it's best if you move on. Oh, don't get that look on your face. You're just getting your life together after those miserable years with Phil. Who listened to that sad story? Trust me, I have your best interests at heart."

I scowled at her.

She said, "You'll find the right man. You're still attractive, Fiona. Men seem to go gaga over all that kinky ash-blonde hair. And your eyes are your best feature, that unusual violet blue. I keep telling you to play them up a bit, slap on some make-up. Just don't give up."

I didn't plan to give up on Marc-André, that was definite, or on myself for that matter, although I'm not the type for eye make-up. I felt a surge of sympathy for the patients in Liz's medical practice. Even though I knew she believed she was helping me avoid problems, I searched my mind for a suitably scathing retort but came up empty. Didn't matter, because Liz had changed the topic back to her where it usually was.

"Do these pants make my butt look enormous?" she said.

"First of all, Liz, your butt is in my beanbag chair, which makes everything look enormous, and second, don't interrupt me, you are a size *two*. A cardboard refrigerator box wouldn't make you look…"

"Easy for you to say."

"It *is* easy for me to say. And easy for me to mean too. Anyway, I don't give a flying fig about your butt. I have important matters to worry about."

"Oh sure, you can be offhand and uncaring. I'm alone in the world. You already have a boyfriend."

"But *not* a boyfriend who remembers me."

"Don't be so negative. It could be very, very good from a sexual novelty point of view."

My jaw crashed to the floor and smashed into a… Hang on, that wasn't my jaw, although it might have been. I whirled to face the doorway. Josey stood, white-faced, freckles popping, mouth gaping, up to her skinny ankles in shards of glass.

I said to Liz, "Oh, great. That was my antique cut glass lemonade pitcher. Now look what you've done."

Liz shrugged. "Me? Talk to the person who dropped it."

"She was shocked." I lowered my voice. "For heaven's sake,

Liz. She's an innocent kid. Why would you say something like that in front of her?"

"Don't be daft," Liz said. "Kids are not innocent."

"She is," I said, sticking with the whisper.

"Oh, get over it. She has to grow up some time."

No, she didn't, I thought. Josey's life had been bleak and deprived. She'd never had a chance to be a kid, why should she have to hear about sexual novelty here in my little house? If I hoped anything, it was that Josey would have a glimpse of normal life when she was with me. That wasn't so likely when Liz was on the premises.

"I am really sorry about your lemonade jug, Miz Silk. I know it belonged to your aunt. I'll try to find you another one just like it. I'll check out the antique stores and the pawn shop."

"Don't worry about it. Accidents happen."

"Do you really have a new boyfriend, Miz Silk?"

"No, Josey, I..."

"What about Marc-André? It hasn't even been a year."

"Don't move your feet, Josey. There's glass all around your sandals. Let's watch out for Tolstoy."

In his corner, Tolstoy raised his handsome Samoyed head, struggled to his feet and headed down to the basement again. I think we were too much for him.

"And don't worry. I'll be there for Marc-André," I said.

Josey beamed. "Well, that's the best news. Because, if there's going to be any of that sexual novelty stuff, don't you think it should be with him, and not some new guy?"

*   *   *

If you drew up a ledger for my life, with columns headed "positives and negatives", Josey would be at the top of the positives, and not just because for a small fee she could mow my lawn and fix my sticky windows and ferret just about anything out of the local library, including the reference department. In the time I'd known her, she'd become like family. Like the child I would never have. Tolstoy, being a dog, naturally would make the plus side, darn near tied for first place with Josey and Marc-André. My friends Liz and Woody could be on the positive side, depending on their moods. Also a plus, along with the house, the garden and the village, was the Colville painting that Aunt Kit had left me. I loved it more than any other object.

On the negative side was my financial situation. Negative meaning, in the red, out of credit, here comes trouble, what now, dear God, that kind of thing. And my career as a romance writer, since I hadn't earned out my last advance. I suppose we shouldn't forget my car, which was gasping its last. And definitely, you could add the phone, which was now ringing, and which never brings anything good.

I let it shrill on and on until I heard my agent, Lola, on the answering machine.

"Pick up, Fiona, darling. You'll be glad you did."

I picked up. As a rule, I put Lola on the positive side. Even though she was calling at nine in the evening. After the day I'd had, I might have already gone to bed, except that Liz was still there and showed no sign of leaving.

Lola takes a little getting used to. By getting used to, I mean three things: first, don't expect her to actually listen to anything you have to say and second, do expect to be startled by almost every word that flies out of her mouth. For a third, don't be surprised that she calls everyone darling, even, say, police officers attempting to give her speeding tickets.

Lola had what she thought was a great idea.

"I should write a what?" I said, predictably startled by her opening gambit.

"An erotic cookbook. Isn't that too perfect? I told your assistant this afternoon. I hadn't realized that you had an assistant."

"Sorry?" I said again, thinking I must have heard wrong. Something that happens quite often with Lola.

"Never mind, darling. It's none of my business if you have an assistant when you're too broke to breathe."

"Listen, Lola. Your confidence in me is gratifying, but there's no way I can write an exotic cookbook."

"Erotic!" Lola shrieked.

"What? Erotic? Are you insane? That's even worse. That's not even possible."

"Bixby and Snead are keen to have you do one. They'll really play it up on next fall's list. There's a spot, and the topic's hot."

"What do you mean they're keen to have me do one? Do you think maybe they have me mixed up with someone else? Say, for instance, with someone who could write an erotic cookbook? Hang on! What did you tell them?"

"This is no time to be overly fussy, darling. We have a chance at a terrific high-profile project. You'll get tons of media and better yet, money. Let me remind you, you can use it."

I started to say that I hate media, but Lola was too fast for me. "Stop resisting. You need this deal desperately, and I mean that in the kindest possible way."

"I can't cook."

"You can read, can't you?"

"Of course, I can read."

"If you can read, you can cook."

I was pretty sure that wasn't true, but I tried another tactic. "I have no sex life. None whatsoever. Don't you think that might make things difficult?"

"Pay attention, darling. I represent a couple of crime writers. They don't go around bumping people off or solving cases. Get with the program."

I was about to say, I'm not turning out to be much of a writer, when it occurred to me I shouldn't remind my agent of that. "Aside from my unsuitability, I wouldn't even know where to start a project like that."

"Start with research."

"I don't know anything about…"

"A bit of erotic lore, aphrodisiac foods, seasonal variations, recipes. Whip it all together, ha ha. A few anecdotes, memories. Nothing to it."

I said, "Wait a minute, I have to know, why me for this project? Is it because of what happened with Benedict?"

"Perhaps you shouldn't dwell on that."

"That was murder. And now they want to splash my name all over the papers again? I'm not the kind of person who can deal with that kind of attention."

"What you *are,* darling, is not the most solvent of my clients. And in this business, that's saying something. So yes, it was my idea and, yes, the thing with what's his name is a fabulous hook. Especially the bed part. It means you've got name recognition."

"Because my lover was found dead in my four-poster, and everyone in Canada saw a clip of me on the news? That's supposed to be a good thing?"

"Don't complain. You know your career's tanking. Lots of writers would kill to have this problem."

That Lola. What a way with words.

I took a deep breath. "I don't even get the idea of food being sexy. I can't imagine a single sexy food."

"Don't be silly, darling. Food is very sexy. What about a can of whipped cream? Who doesn't find that sexy?"

"Whipped cream? I don't. Listen, Lola, thanks a lot, but I don't believe I can do this project."

"Think again, darling. I've got you a good advance too. I told them you have a desperately sick relative, and they coughed up a cheque. That doesn't happen every day. Up front on signing. The contract's on its way. I sent it yesterday by XpressPost. I'm surprised you don't have it already."

"Yesterday? But you hadn't even spoken to me."

"You should answer your phone more often. You'll get a cheque on signing. I told them you'd be thrilled."

"You told them what? Lola? Lola? *Lola!*"

I returned to the living room, somewhat dazed.

"I wouldn't want you to break a rib, laughing like that," I said to Liz, who seemed unable to catch her breath, once I told her Lola's plan.

"Arrrotteeecogggbkkkk!" Liz howled before falling out of the beanbag chair with a thump.

"How can I do an erotic cookbook? It's out of the question. Stop snickering. I mean it. You know, that's a really unbecoming position you're in," I said.

She continued to wheeze.

I added, "And it does make your butt look big."

Josey popped her head in the front door, clutching a fist full of envelopes. "What is that exactly? What she said?"

"Nothing," I said.

Tolstoy had emerged from the cool of the basement. He greeted Josey by thumping his tail on the floor.

Liz wiped her eyes. "Now I've heard everything. It would be like asking SpongeBob SquarePants to head up the UN."

"That's so uncalled for, Dr. Big Butt."

"But what is it, Miz Silk, that's so uncalled for?"

"It's just a mistake, Josey. A project that's not going to happen."

"Sure, whatever. It's after nine. I picked up your mail. You shouldn't leave it in your mailbox at night. People could steal it."

"There's nothing worth stealing, Josey," I said.

"You never heard of identity theft, Miz Silk? Where do you want me to put this stuff?"

I held out my hand. I find it's best to be brave with mail and face it squarely, no matter if FINAL NOTICE is stamped in red on the front. Of course, if I were brave, I would have picked up my mail in the daytime like everyone else.

"I'll open it for you," Josey said.

"Thank you, but that's not necessary." Of course, that was pretty well drowned out by the sound of the letter opener doing its thing.

"Oh boy, Miz Silk. Disconnect notice from Hydro Quebec. That's bad. You wouldn't want to be without your electric fans this summer, that's for sure."

"People's bills are private, Josey. I believe I've mentioned that on a previous occasion."

"Well, sure. But I didn't think you meant private from me. I can understand if you don't want Dr. Prentiss to see them, but I'm staff."

Liz said, "Hey. I'm the best friend, remember? Through thick and thin for more than forty years. Anyway, what's that kid doing here at this time of night? She can't be biking all the way up those back roads in the dark. Too dangerous."

When Josey doesn't go home at night, there's always a good reason for it. I don't push her to tell about it. I know she's proud. And I also know that Uncle Mike spends a lot of time in the local hoosegow. When he's home, some of his friends leave a bit to be desired. "She's spending the night here. She'll give Tolstoy a couple of extra walks to make up for the ones he's missed."

Liz shrugged. "Your life."

Josey went back to the mail. "And what's this one? Oops, that doesn't look good either. But here's an XpressPost."

I snatched the mail from her. Looked like I was going to have to tackle that ridiculous cookbook after all.

*   *   *

The next morning, Josey was gone before I got out of bed. Her note said: "Tolstoy had a nice long walk. Your coffee is made and in the thermos."

The day was soft and warm, still comfortable, although the mist rising from the Gatineau hinted at lurking humidity. That was the perfect time to take a stroll by the river's edge with Tolstoy. I ambled along and thought about the cookbook project. It was the kind of day when anything seemed possible. When I got back, well before Lola would be at her desk, or even out of bed, I left a message telling her I'd signed the contract and would get it back to her pronto. Then I poured myself a cup of French roast. I took the mug of coffee out on to the porch, where I could watch the river and take note of what my flowers had managed in twenty-four hours. I am a flower person. Outdoor flowers. Call me hopeless with herbs or grass or indoor plants. Let me add that I like to ease into the day watching for passing cardinals, jays and finches. And I figured the soothing atmosphere on my porch might awaken my cookbook muse. Lola was right. I did need to do this project. My main hope was that, unlike the previous day, today would be tranquil. I sat there imagining what an erotic cookbook would look like, or at least what the kind I might write might look like. I stared through the trees to the water, hoping for inspiration from nature.

A bearlike man lumbered around the corner of the house. I jumped, spilling my coffee. There are people you don't want to see in your backyard in the morning. Sgt. F. X. Sarrazin of the St. Aubaine police, for example. Everything about him reminded me of the events which had led to Marc-André's current situation. Scenes flickered through my mind like a bad reel of film.

"Madame Silk," he said.

No point in staying outside and having Sarrazin ruin the view. One bright note, at least Josey had already cleaned up after herself and departed, leaving no indication she'd ever been there. Possibly she'd even gone to school, although that would have been a surprise. At any rate, she and Sgt. Sarrazin were not a good mix in an enclosed space, so I was thankful. I pointed toward the sofa. But as usual on these visits, he chose the delicate Queen Anne chair. I was sure I heard it squeal as he lowered his bulky body onto it. I took the wingback.

Tolstoy loved Sarrazin, for some reason. He had his head scratched and lay down at Sarrazin's size thirteens, smiling.

Sarrazin glanced around at the sad philodendron, another relic from my aunt. He reached over and picked off a couple of leaves.

"I'm better with outdoor plants," I said.

"I understand," he said, in his completely unaccented English, "that you observed the vehicle that was involved in the crash on Highway 5 yesterday."

"Yes."

"I'd like you to tell me what you saw."

"Was it a fatal accident?"

He nodded. "Yes, madame."

"I wasn't sure. The ambulances were…"

"You told the officer you had encountered the vehicle earlier."

"I did."

"Can you tell me what you observed?"

I said, "Okay. On the Hull ramp onto Highway 5, a black Cadillac Escalade passed me on the right."

Sarrazin nodded. "Is that it?"

"Not exactly."

"What else occurred?"

"First, he came shooting right up behind me, well above the ramp speed, and laid on his horn."

"Why?"

"I have no idea."

He raised an eyebrow.

"Well, my car might have stalled getting onto the highway. But it re-started right away. These things happen. It's not like I did it on purpose."

Sarrazin gazed out the window at the Skylark, then turned back to face me. He raised his inch-thick eyebrows. "And?"

"And he gave me the finger. And he shouted at me."

"You heard him shouting?"

"His window was open."

"Was the driver swerving at all?"

"Swerving?"

"Yes."

I thought for a couple of seconds. "No. I'm pretty sure I would have noticed swerving."

"Anything else?"

"Isn't that bad enough? I was unnerved by it."

"Happens all the time."

"I've never seen a fatal collision before. The weird thing is, I feel responsible somehow."

He narrowed his eyes. "Why should you feel responsible?"

"I swore at him."

"That's it?"

"Well, it's not like me."

He chuckled.

I said, "I'm not that kind of person."

He nodded. "Don't worry about it. You're probably okay under the Criminal Code on that one."

"Funny."

Sarrazin met my eyes. "Did you know him?"

I shook my head.

"Think about it."

I said, "I didn't know him."

"Take your time."

I stared. "I just told you I didn't know him."

"You want to close your eyes and relive the scene? You might recognize him then."

"I really don't want to relive that scene."

"Take your time. Break it down into frames. Maybe it will come to you."

"Why? Who was he?"

"Sorry, madame. We will not be able to release the name until the family has been notified."

"Oh. But…"

"Is there a particular reason you want to know, madame?"

"Because you are asking me about him, even though I keep telling you I didn't recognize him. And, all right, I'll admit there was something familiar about him. I just don't know who he was. And everybody looks familiar lately. But what happened to the woman?"

"What woman?"

"His passenger."

Sarrazin frowned. "There was no passenger."

"Sure there was."

He blinked first. "I am certain of it. There was only one body found in the vehicle."

"Maybe she was destroyed by the fire. Maybe her body was…"

"It doesn't work that way. If there had been another person in that Escalade, we would have known."

"But I saw a woman. I'm positive that—" I stopped myself. "Well, I sure don't want to hope that someone else was in that crash."

"You were under stress from the hospital."

"You knew I was at the hospital?"

"I am a police officer. Everyone in the village knows that you visit Marc-André Paradis several times a week."

"They do?"

"People think it's nice. They know he's in bad shape. They know what happened to him. They hope that he gets better. Anyway, it must have been difficult for you, that particular visit."

"Surely that hospital aide didn't…"

"No madame. Just…"

"Gossip?"

"We call it intelligence. Anyway, you were rattled, the way the guy intimidated you. He gave you the finger. He was driving aggressively. Most people would find that upsetting."

I nodded.

He said, "So, it would be easy to be mistaken about seeing someone else."

I cast my mind back to the scene. "I hope you're right."

But I knew he was wrong.

Spotted Dick Canadian Style

Contributed by Woody Quirke of L'Épicerie 1749

¹/₃ cup butter	Pinch of salt
¹/₃ cup white sugar	¹/₃ cup milk
2 eggs	1 tablespoon water
1¹/₂ cups self raising flour	¹/₂ cup sweetened dried cranberries
1 teaspoon baking powder	Grated zest of one large lemon

Cream together the butter and the sugar, before gradually adding the eggs, while beating. Carefully add the flour in small amounts, along with the baking powder and salt. Beat in the water, followed by milk to get a smooth creamy consistency. You may need to add a bit more milk.

Stir in the cranberries and the lemon zest. Transfer the mixture to a greased pudding bowl, approximately 2 pint capacity. Cover with double layer of waxed paper tied with string (or a shoelace) around the outside of the bowl and place in a large Dutch oven or similar pot with enough water to reach halfway up the exterior of the bowl. Simmer for 2¹/₂ hours, covered.

Serve with custard sauce:

3 egg yolks	2 cups scalded milk
¹/₄ cup sugar	1 teaspoon vanilla extract
Pinch of salt	

Beat egg yolks, then add the sugar and salt. Add scalded milk slowly while stirring constantly. Cook in a double boiler until thickened slightly and the mixture coats a spoon.

Five

Later I wondered why one of the *enquêteurs,* as we call detectives here in St. Aubaine, would waste his time dropping by to ask me about a traffic accident. What had he really wanted? Why had he kept asking me if I knew the driver? I needed an activity to take my mind off that.

I picked up the phone and dialed. "I know you're there, Philip." It still seemed sort of weird to be saying that, since I've spent years ignoring his calls. I left a message. "We need to finish up this settlement business. You know that as well as I do. Let's just get it out of the way. Pick up your phone, and I'll get out of your hair faster that way. Life will be sweet without me."

I slammed down the phone. A new behaviour for me. Thanks to Philip's stonewalling, I was learning fast that there was more satisfaction in being the slammer rather than the slammee, which up until that moment had been the pattern in our relationship. I knew what he was up to. Wait me out, wear down my resistance. Over the years of our marriage, he had built up a stock of real estate and investments, not to mention what the legal types call "the matrimonial home". I still thought of it as the place where I'd spent my paycheques for years. Anyway, I was much happier in my humble cottage. Nevertheless, the law said I was entitled to a serious chunk of Phil's nest egg. Without a doubt, Phil would manage to prevaricate and hide assets, many of which I had contributed to myself. That was fine. I just wanted to pay my taxes and my hydro bill before something very bad happened.

Of course, I'd been pussyfooting around. But Philip wasn't one to tiptoe. He knew I had assets too. The tumbledown cottage, the two-acre lot. When my Aunt Kit had owned this land, it had been in the back of beyond. Now it was prime real estate. Phil had calculated that value at the current market price, using what Jean-Claude could get for it, as far as I could tell. Of course, he hadn't bothered to subtract the cost of upgrading the house to bring it up to contemporary standards. Not surprising, since that was something I probably would never do. That was all I had, really. I'd already pretty well blown through part of my RRSPs trying to make a go of writing, without going back to the not-so-wonderful government day job. I had years before I could access my pension, and I'd made sure the rest of the RRSPs were locked in. Aunt Kit had left me some crystal and china, which I loved, but even with the inflated estimates from Phil's lawyer, it still wasn't much. Luckily, Phil had never thought much of Aunt Kit's taste in art.

I had to do something to take my mind off that. I drifted into the kitchen, which is pretty and pine, but not actually large enough for pacing. I stared around at the rustic cupboards and the wheezing old fridge. The open shelves looked pretty enough with the Fiestaware that Kit had collected. She'd sought out all the colours—ivory, cobalt, light green, turquoise, yellow and red—at second hand stores and garage sales over the years. The dishes didn't get used enough, but I loved the look of them. The kitchen served mostly as a bar and dog food storage area. The fridge did a pretty good job of keeping my hummus fresh. The freezer section held ice cubes and a stack of diet dinners. Except for the microwave, the kitchen was the same as my childhood memories.

No matter how I looked at it, I couldn't see too many erotic food possibilities coming out of this. Unless there was a market niche for an erotic cookbook using microwavable, pre-packaged food. That I could manage.

I opened a few of the lower cupboards and poked around. I had a vague recollection that Kit had owned some cookbooks. Where would they be? Stored away? In the attic crawlspace? It was way too hot to climb up there amid the boxes. A person could die.

A new plan was needed.

I'd given up on Phil phoning me back when I finally bit the bullet and headed to the village. I opened the door to the basement and yelled goodbye to Tolstoy. He'd prefer chilling out in the cold storage room. And I figured I'd find support at the health food store. The owner, Woody Quirke, was the only person I've ever been close to who actually made his living from food. Granted, he was an old draft dodger, reputed former biker and resident English rights curmudgeon. But he was my friend. I picked up the contract to mail it, and before I reached the front door, Tolstoy bounded up the stairs. His Samoyed instincts are pretty good. He must have figured out where I was going.

Just as we were getting into the car, I remembered Harriet Crowder's wallet. Why hadn't I thought about that when Sarrazin was there? I could have unloaded the damn thing onto the police. Oh well, I hoped Harriet had gotten the message that I had it. If not, she might be cancelling her cards and getting new ID that morning. I knew how much I would hate that. I grabbed the wallet and hopped into the Skylark. Tolstoy joined me.

"One quick stop before Woody's air conditioning," I told him.

*　　*　　*

I parked in the shade of a spreading maple tree, told Tolstoy to stay on a shady part of the lawn and trotted up the stairs to the Wallingford Estate. I glanced around the huge cool foyer for someone I knew.

No sign of the plump, friendly Brady with his twinkling nose stud and fauxhawk. Nor of the cool, blonde glamourpuss Anabel Huffington-Chabot. Neither Marietta nor Rafaël was to be seen. Probably they were all behind the scenes doing whatever you do when a hit cooking show goes into production. Naturally, Harriet Crowder was not in sight either.

I asked a few scurrying helpers if they knew where I could find her. I got shrugs, plus a few muffled comments that told me she might not be the most popular person on the property. No one wanted to find her for me. No one gave a flying fig about her wallet.

I couldn't leave Tolstoy long. I headed for the office and knocked.

The door was whipped open by a sweet, smiling young woman, about twenty-five, with soft honey-brown hair. At last, someone looked like a normal human being.

"Can you help me find Harriet Crowder?" I said. "My name is Fiona Silk. It's very important and…"

She smiled at me, uncomplicated and friendly as any girl next door. She had a firm handshake and musical voice. Her brown eyes were meltingly warm. I felt a rush of relief as she waved me into the office. "I'm Chelsea Brazeau. I'm Anabel's executive assistant."

She must have been the person Harriet had savaged the evening before. That seemed a shame, because unlike Anabel Huffington-Chabot-Homewrecker, this Chelsea was lovely and welcoming. How did she manage to keep that warm smile while working for the Ice Queen and having to fend off the Red

Devil? Didn't seem fair, all those extremes in temperature. "Oh, right," I said, glad that Josey wasn't there. "Executive Assistant."

"It's a catch-all phrase," she chuckled. "I'm doing the PR for the Wallingford Estate, and that means everything, including watering plants and unpacking boxes. And on one spectacular occasion, fixing a leaking pipe in the kitchen. You probably know that we'll soon be reopening as InnCroyable. It's going to be the best spa and restaurant in the region. Not that we're bragging," She gestured toward a wall with plans, plaques and photos prominently displayed.

"I didn't know that."

"You're about to hear plenty about that and the shoot for *En feu! Hot Stuff!* You can't imagine how exciting this is for me. I'm from a small town in northern Saskatchewan. I can't believe I'm working right next to these big names in this beautiful place. But I'll try to find Harriet for you. I warn you, though. Her bite is worse than her bark, and her bark's awful. She hates me because I'm working with Anabel. That reminds me, I have to connect with her in..." she glanced at her watch, "Ohmigod, two minutes."

"Don't worry about it," I said.

"I'm so sorry. Let's see. Harriet, Harriet, where can you be? I'm really scattered. We've been overwhelmed getting ready for all this plus our grand opening. Anabel's got some promo shots on the putting green shortly." She gestured vaguely at the bag of golf clubs in the corner.

I watched as she dialed number after number.

At the sound of heels clicking on the marble floor, she grimaced. "No luck. And here comes Anabel. We never, never, never want to keep Anabel waiting."

"Do you have Harriet's cell number?"

"I wish. Harriet doesn't give it to anyone. She likes to be the caller."

"I should have explained. The reason I'm trying to locate her is that I found her wallet, and I'd like to return it. Can I leave it with you?"

Chelsea opened her mouth.

I whirled at a voice behind me. The chilly presence of Anabel Huffington-Chabot. Up close, she was even more formidable, from the frosty blonde tips of her hair to her designer stilettos. Standing next to friendly Chelsea with her soft, pretty face didn't help Anabel much. Just made me wonder how much Botox had filled that immoveable visage. She knew who I was, all right. She'd seen me when I'd blundered across her and Jean-Claude at their *tête-à-tête* yesterday. "Sorry. We can't take responsibility for the wallet. Harriet's such a loose cannon. Who knows what she'd accuse us of? You'll have to find her yourself. Are you ready, Chelsea? We don't want to keep the photographer waiting."

Chelsea shot me an embarrassed glance and a helpless shrug. "I'm so sorry," she mouthed. Before I knew it, I was on the far side of the oak door. It closed behind me with a soft yet insulting click.

Several minutes later, I had left messages with every person I encountered on the property. As I left the Wallingford Estate and headed for the post office to XpressPost the contract back to Lola, I thought about Harriet Crowder. I had the feeling that not a single person she knew would toss her a life preserver if they saw that she'd been washed overboard.

*   *   *

"A what? You're going to write a what?" Woody twirled in his custom-made power wheelchair, the tires narrowly missing a customer's feet near the organic baked goods section. The panicked customer hustled her Birkenstocks to the far side of the bulk product bins, near the organic quinoa. I was pretty sure she was hunkered there, giving us her full attention. But in case she or anyone else in the newly renovated and enlarged L'Épicerie 1759 was not totally tuned in to our conversation, Woody bellowed with laughter. It worked, for sure. All eyes were now on us.

"Shh," I said. "I don't want everyone in town to know. Please don't make today any worse than it already is." I was already regretting sending off the signed contract.

"Why the hell are you telling me then?"

"Because you're my friend."

"Are you out of your freakin' mind? What were you thinking?"

"I thought you could give me some useful information. You own a health food store. You know about food. Josey's too young. Anyway, I don't want to talk to her about erotic recipes and aphrodisiacs and all that. I'm not even sure *I'm* old enough. You're right, I probably am crazy."

Woody chortled and shook his head, spewing a little bit of Jolt Cola. The silver braid swung back and forth. Woody is the faux hippie to end all faux hippies, and he's always careful to look the part.

"Do you actually think I would keep a secret?"

"Oh, I did, yes. But now I see that I might have been a bit off-base with that assumption."

"Yeah, especially with an erotic cookbook! Everyone will want to know about that. My business is going to boom."

I maintained my dignity and hoped the Birkenstocked customer, who had sidled toward the cash, hadn't heard.

"I wouldn't be doing it at all if I wasn't desperate for the money."

"Yeah, I heard that too. Taxes in arrears. Hydro getting cut off. That's rough, kiddo."

"I'll survive." Who had squealed? The mail carrier or Josey?

"Well, sure you will. Squeeze something out of that useless ex of yours. I wish I'd known earlier. I could have helped you out a bit. But I just settled up with my contractor for my renovations. Cleaned me right out. I'm in serious overdraft."

"Don't worry about it.

"Try Liz. Nah, on second thought, don't bother. She's the stingiest woman I ever met, and I've known—"

"Thanks anyway, Woody, but I don't want to borrow money. I'd just be postponing the payback. Until I can get my share from Phil, I'll have to make it myself whatever way I can."

Woody lit up a cigarette under the DÉFENSE DE FUMER sign. "But you got to admit, that cookbook idea is just plain hilarious, kiddo. Plain freakin' *high*-larious."

"I'm glad you think so," I sniffed. "My new agent has arranged the deal, and it's an offer I can't afford to refuse. It's not like it's an idea I would dream up myself. They'll pay the first part of the advance on signing. I've already mailed the contract."

"You sure you heard right? Any chance she asked you to write a neurotic cookbook? That would make more sense."

"Okay, that's it. Tolstoy, we're out of here," I said.

Tolstoy was slow to move. He loves Woody and Woody's store, since Woody has no problem with him. Of course, Woody doesn't enforce any regulations on general principles. Tolstoy was standing underneath the INTERDIT AUX CHIENS sign. It means no dogs, but then again, Tolstoy doesn't read French, and Woody doesn't believe in it.

"Come on, kiddo. Where's your sense of humour? I'm stunned anyone would think of you for a job like that. You sure this Lola's playing with a full deck? When did you ever cook anything? You live on take-out. If it weren't for the hummus and pita here in L'Épicerie, you'd have starved."

"Well," I said.

"Although I don't know how anyone can eat this stuff. Give me Mickey Dee's any old day. I can't wait until the Golden Arches comes to St. Aubaine."

I glanced around. No one was paying any attention. For some reason, Woody's customers see no incongruity in his personal lifestyle and opinions and the high-end organic products he sells.

Woody held up his hand. "I know you make great coffee, but in no way does brewing java count."

"That's not fair."

"Tough luck, kiddo. The irrefutable fact is that cookbooks almost always include solids."

"I look after Tolstoy."

"Do you make his food?"

"I open the tins and mix it with his kibble. He really likes the way I do it." Tolstoy's tail thumped on the wooden floor.

"But any examples of cooking for, say, human beings?"

"I can't remember. I made food when I was still married to Phil. I'm sure I did. I must have. I've tried to blank out those years. But that's not the point."

"Oh right, so for the erotic cookbook, the point is your exciting and varied love life?"

"You are being just plain mean, Woody."

"I'm merely pointing out that any guys I know you to have been associated with are either dead, suffering from head wounds and amnesia, or you've just divorced them. Well, I guess I'm leaving out agents of the police, but that's different. Aside from me, of course. But hey, there's an idea."

I said, "In no way is that an idea. And this is just a cookbook, not an autobiography. I don't have to provide the erotic realism. They just need recipes and text. I suppose. And photos. Oh, maybe not photos."

"Haven't you been complaining about your books tanking?"

"I just couldn't get the right romantic mood going in the last two. The novel I'm working on is, um, coming along slowly, and my proposals have been generally sneered at. So, I take your point. But I'm still going to try." I wasn't sure how, but I couldn't say that to Woody. He'd never let up then.

"You were in the news not long ago. Right across the country. TV, newspaper headlines. That'll help. It was pretty steamy. I imagine any cookbook you produce will just fly off the shelves."

I reached for a container of hummus and a package of whole wheat pita bread, which was what I'd come for. "I'm sure that's what's behind the whole deal. Put this on my tab, will you?"

Woody still chortled. "You're the only person I know who runs a tab in the health food store, kiddo. I shouldn't let you get away with it, but you always give me my daily smile."

I ignored that. "I'm heading home to get started. I've got nothing but time on my hands, I need the money and, anyway, in spite of your mean-spirited comments, how hard can it be?"

"Hey, don't get all bent out of shape. I'm just being friendly. I can help you."

Oh, right. Woody's pushing sixty, with a pot belly and receding hairline and a long grey braid to take your mind off that. He spends his days in his chair guzzling Jolt Cola or Red Bull, eating cheeseburgers and blowing smoke in your face. He loves to terrify the locals when he barrels through St. Aubaine in his specially-built van. It has an unusual combination of hand controls inside and custom flame designs decorating the exterior. Woody's loud, opinionated and inclined to run over your foot with his wheelchair. He's a great and loyal friend when he's in a good mood, and even if he's not. But Woody's no heart-throb. Maybe it's all those Grateful Dead T-shirts.

"Don't get that look on your face, kiddo. There's life in the old guy yet. Women love me."

"I'm sure they do," I said, watching a middle-aged customer pivot and scurry off as fast as her Mephistos could carry her.

"And I have ideas."

Yes. And I didn't want to think about them.

"Aren't you going to ask me what ideas?"

I sighed.

He yelled, "Spotted Dick!"

I stood rooted with horror. "What is the matter with you, Woody?"

"Nothing. Spotted Dick. It's a traditional English dessert. Come on. You mean you never heard of it?"

"Really? It sounds more like a…" I was about to say an STD, but of course, everyone in the shop was eavesdropping.

There was no point wasting time explaining to Woody the difference between eroticism and boyish double entendres.

"I'll take it under consideration," I said, meaning I would never give it another thought as long as I lived.

"And there's…" he said.

"Not to change the subject," I said, "but since you are the gossip epicentre of the village, have you heard about the man who was killed in that accident on Highway 5 yesterday?"

"The cops are keeping quiet about that. No details yet about the guy."

"I thought you might have found out anyway. Sgt. Sarrazin told me it's because they haven't informed the next of kin yet."

"Bunch of killjoys. The cops I mean, not the dead guy. And, hey, do you have time to come in back and see my big renovations? My living quarters are finished. I blew a bundle, but it really rocks."

"Later," I mumbled. Although I was sure I would have found Woody's newly done apartment fascinating and no doubt quite surprising, I had an overwhelming need to go home.

"It's quite the pad," he said, waggling his eyebrows.

"I bet."

"Hot tub."

"Huh."

"Mirrors."

"Oh."

"Media room."

"My, my. Maybe I'll get the tour another time."

But Woody had already lost interest in me. Perhaps because Marietta had entered L'Épicerie 1759. I was lucky I wasn't flattened when he rolled forward to intercept her.

*　　*　　*

As I pulled into my driveway, I spotted the battered bike and the familiar sign. Josey was back.

"Hi, Miz Silk. I fixed that leaky tap in your bathtub," she said, waving a wrench triumphantly. She must have brought it with her. I was pretty sure I didn't own a wrench.

"You really shouldn't just let yourself in."

"Why not? I'm staff. We've discussed all that. Right? I think an executive assistant has to know everything about the executive. Are you just jumpy because of this cookbook?"

"The cookbook? Of course not."

"Okay, okay, don't get upset. It's just that everyone is saying…"

"What? What are people saying? What is the matter with this place? Can't a person have a single thought or action without the whole village commenting?" I paused for breath, and Josey stared at me. She ripped one of the blue pages out of the notebook and crumpled it into the wastebasket.

I said, "All right, I'm sorry. What exactly are people saying?"

"Today I heard you are going to have to sell your house because you can't pay your taxes, and you can't pay your hydro, and Jean-Claude Lamontagne has made you an offer you can't refuse."

"Not true."

"Oh boy, Miz Silk. I would hate it if you had to sell your place. I love this house. It's the only place I really feel at home." A guilty look flashed across her freckled face. "Except at home, of course."

I'd seen that cabin in the woods, seen Uncle Mike passed out. "I'll manage to hang on."

"But things are bad for you right now, aren't they?"

"They are. I'm stuck with this icky project."

"That project sounds like fun, but if you really hate the idea, I have an idea for how you can get your hands on some serious cash."

No point in trying not to listen. I would just get worn down. "How?"

"Sell that picture of the woman in the boat. The one over your desk. I know you really like it a lot, but—"

"Josey, I can't."

"Sure you can, Miz Silk. That picture's worth a bundle. I checked out that artist, Alex Colville, and his stuff sells for a lot of money."

"I am not selling the painting. End of conversation."

"One of his pictures went for more than $400,000 at an auction, last year. Do you know how much that is?"

"Well, of course, I do."

"So, maybe they're worth even more now. It's just one little picture. It's worth more than the whole property and everything on it."

"The painting means a lot to me. And I'm not going to sell it."

Josey folded her arms. The freckles stood out, almost three

dimensional. "You could get a lot of special paintings for less than that, Miz Silk. And pay your taxes and all your bills and get a new car."

"Won't be happening, Josey."

"You could even build a ramp so that Marc-André could come and visit. I'd help with that. I even got a set of plans."

A ramp for Marc-André!

"It would be wonderful to have a ramp like that, and I know how much you want Marc-André to get better and get out of rehab, but I will never sell that painting, Josey. I'm not even going to discuss it any more. We'll have to come up with some other solution to this latest cash crunch."

Josey shrugged. Of course, I wasn't dumb enough to dream that I'd heard the last about selling the Colville.

"I'm trying to find a way to make my, um, cookbook project work."

"Pretty hard to do a cookbook in the state of that kitchen."

"What does the state of my kitchen have to do with it? Don't I just have to find a few recipes? I'm a whiz with the microwave. My aunt had some cookbooks. I think they might be in the attic. I'm going to crawl around up there and find them. I might get some ideas for the framework of the book."

"Jeez, Miz Silk. Cookbooks have to be up to date. They have to have food that's in style, the latest ingredients, techniques. They have to look right."

"There are styles in recipes? You're kidding, right?"

"No way. People follow trends in the food world. I can't believe you don't know about that. You better get that satellite dish."

"Forget it."

"There's fashionable food and unfashionable food. You got to have clear glass bowls for your ingredients. All sizes."

Clear glass bowls? That made no sense. "You're kidding. Anyway, what kind of food goes out of style?"

She frowned. "I'm not really sure. But turnip, I hope. And Brussels sprouts."

"I hear you."

"I'll get you some recipe books from the library."

"You don't have to do all that, Josey. I can look after myself, you know."

"It's okay, Miz Silk. Remember, I'm saving up. I got a lot of expenses and more coming. I need all the odd jobs I can get. You got until I turn sixteen to settle your tab."

I said, "Well…"

"You should ask Miz Lamontagne if she has any food magazines."

*   *   *

What was this thing everyone had with trying to solve my money problems? Everyone except the one person who had a legal obligation, namely Philip.

I picked up the phone. While I was out, Josey had thoughtfully programmed Philip's home, office and cell phone numbers into the speed dial. First, she'd found a phone set for me that had a speed dial, back when I still had a few dollars. The phone rang on and on, as it had on my previous seven tries. Finally, blessedly, it was snatched up.

"Philip," I chirped, "let's agree to get this settled once and for all. Imagine how much happier we'll both be. Freedom from each other at last! How exhilarating would that be?"

"Look, Fiona, you have to stop hounding me."

"Hounding you? You mean my phone calls this week? You've been artfully stalling for months."

"Hardly. I'm a busy man."

"Right. You're a busy man with property and assets. All I want is my share. I realize you'll cheat me, and I don't even care. Let's just get it finished. "

"Sure, now that you're not making it as a writer, you want to plunder my assets. Get the rewards without working for them. If you wanted the good life, you should have stayed married."

I was proud of myself. I didn't let him get to me. I didn't bleat that I had put him through law school working multiple jobs when he didn't have two cents to rub together. I didn't mention that I'd spent the entirety of our marriage in dreary but well-paying employment that had sapped my spirit.

He knew that just as well as I did. There was no point in bringing it up. I wanted to rid myself of Philip, not plunge back into the unwinnable situation of two people who never should have hooked up together in the first place.

Move on, I breathed to myself.

"No problem," I said. "You can talk to my lawyer next. Or your lawyer can. Of course, that'll cost you."

"That's easy for you to say. Hit me when I'm down. That's just like you, Fiona. Take advantage when I'm distraught."

There was so much wrong in that statement, I hardly knew where to begin. I started with, "What do you mean down?"

"You haven't heard?"

I bit back irritation. "Heard what?"

"You're just doing this to get to me."

"You know what? You're getting to me. Take care of the settlement and make it snappy."

"My partner's dead."

"You don't have a partner."

"Not a law partner, but I had business dealings with him, investments," Philip yelled.

"Did you say dead?"

"Yes. Killed on the highway near St. Aubaine, yesterday. Don't you even listen to the radio? What do you do all day?"

"What do you mean, don't I even...never mind. That's terrible. Dead. I'm sorry."

"That's right. Danny's dead. So you'll understand I have other things on my mind beside your money grab."

I stood there with my mouth open.

After a while, Philip said, "Fiona? I'm a busy man. Hello? Are you there?"

I was there all right.

What's more, I had finally figured out why the face of the man in the Escalade was familiar. I'd met him with Philip, without the sunglasses. He'd given me the finger then too. Metaphorically, of course.

Danny Dupree.

Grilled Asparagus

Courtesy of Sgt. F. X. Sarrazin

1 bunch of asparagus, the nice thick kind, not the skinny ones
Wooden skewers soaked in water for twenty minutes
Olive oil
Sea salt, the best you can afford

Pre-heat BBQ grill to medium. Snap asparagus at their natural breaking point. Discard woody ends. Attach asparagus, four or five at a time, with skewers (across, not lengthwise). Brush asparagus with oil. Season with sea salt, to taste. Grill just until nice grill marks appear.

Live a little.

Six

Luckily, I still had Sarrazin's telephone number from the troubles of the previous fall. I dialed it before I lost my nerve.

"I know who he was now," I said.

Sarrazin simply grunted on the phone. Of course, he'd already known the answer.

"Daniel Dupree. A colleague of my husband."

"And you just figured this out how?"

"I told you before that there was something familiar about him. When Philip mentioned this morning his friend had been killed, I realized where I'd seen the driver."

"Hard to believe you wouldn't recognize him right off."

"Shouldn't be. I met him at some business reception a couple of years ago, when I was still married. I probably saw him a few times at fundraisers and cocktail parties. He wasn't wearing sunglasses then and whipping past me in a vehicle."

"And?"

"And what?"

"Do you have anything else you want to tell me?"

"What else would I want to tell you?"

"You never spent any amount of time with this guy?"

"I didn't even like him. He was sort of a blowhard. Anyway, I wasn't his type. He always seemed to have a beautiful young woman with him."

"You didn't like him. Did he have a problem with you?"

"I'd be surprised if he even remembered my name. I don't think he even noticed me."

Sarrazin paused before speaking. "Are you sure? You *are* the kind of woman that men notice."

"No, I'm not."

"Sure you are. Just your hair alone is enough to get attention. And how many people have violet eyes? Maybe he just pretended."

I wish people wouldn't talk about my hair. I have nothing but trouble with it, and I don't get what the fuss is about. "Trust me. There's a type of man who doesn't register your existence if you're over thirty. Or maybe even over twenty-five. He was definitely that type."

"Oh, come on. You were the wife of a colleague. He must have been polite."

"I'm telling you, he never acknowledged my presence. He didn't say hello. He didn't shake hands. He looked right through me. I felt invisible. Of course, I disliked him instantly."

"Did your husband get upset about the way he reacted to you?"

"You mean the way he didn't react to me. No. Philip would be absolutely oblivious to anything like that."

"Huh. Maybe you complained."

"Are you kidding? I wouldn't have wasted my breath. First of all, Philip would have told me it was because I was wearing the wrong clothes or standing the wrong way or being generally unworthy of notice. I don't know why you are asking these things, but you're definitely barking up the wrong husband."

"Could be. The scene on the highway as you described it has a personal feel to it. Don't you agree?"

"Yes, I do agree. It felt personal at the time. I was kind of shaken. But I don't believe it was. I drive a ten-year-old Skylark with timing problems. I'm used to jerk behaviour aimed at me."

"Maybe."

"I bet you don't encounter it in your full-size police vehicle, looking like you do."

"What do you mean 'looking like I do'?"

"I mean a large man who carries a gun. And anyone could tell you're a cop. I'm pretty sure that would be a good deterrent. So you don't comprehend how the rest of us live. By that I mean non-cops, non-men, old car drivers."

"Okay. You don't have to get huffy. So you think he gave you the finger because you were a woman driving an older model car? Because there are a lot of people who fit that description. You know what bothers me, as a cop?"

"No, what?"

"The coincidence that you actually knew him."

"Speaking of being bothered, any word about the woman in the Escalade with him?"

"That woman who wasn't there? No, madame. There's no word about her."

"Well," I said, with all the dignity I could manage. "Thank you very much, Sgt. Sarrazin. Goodbye now."

He wasn't ready to hang up. "Listen, about that cookbook of yours."

I didn't recall mentioning that project to Sarrazin.

He kept talking. "It's still officially spring, so you have to include asparagus. I do mine on the grill with really good olive oil and sea salt. I can write out the technique for you."

It was hard to decide which was less erotic: asparagus or Sarrazin. "I'll take it, I said."

*   *   *

I'd been stuck for hours in front of my computer working on

a plan for the book. Let's just say the screen was still blank, and it matched my mind. Finally, I had the slightest glimmer of an idea. I picked up the phone and called Lola.

"How about this? I'll do a little back story of a couple who meet, and I'll set up the meals they make as their relationship deepens."

"Oh, blech! Stay away from romance, Fiona. Just make it sexy with beautiful, lively food. Come up with something that has a lot more sizzle than that. And remember, time is short."

I was alternating between staring at the blank screen and at a piece of paper, when the front door banged.

"Okay," Josey said, "if we are going to make this work, we have to do our homework."

"Speaking of homework, how's the exam preparation going?"

"Piece of cake. It's time to get serious about your book."

"I am serious about the book, Josey. See, I've started to work on it." I pointed to the piece of paper in front of me. So far, the only word written on it was "asparagus". But it was a start.

"We gotta go beyond print. We need television to sell it. I've been looking into this. All the chefs on The Cooking Channel have lots of cookbooks. And sometimes magazines. The show sells the books. Books sell the show, and the show sells products. Business, Miz Silk."

"I don't know, Josey."

"You see all the fuss about *En feu! Hot Stuff!* and the number of people in town just because they're going to be shooting it. Food is big business, and not just the food you eat. It affects everything. If Rafaël or Marietta buys something at CeeCeeCuisine, everyone's going to want it. Every restaurant in the village will be competing to get them to come for dinner."

"Really? I find that hard to…"

"Oh, believe it. TV chefs are real stars. They get a huge

viewership on The Cooking Channel, on W and Life and other channels too. You should check it out. Woody's got cable and digital and the movie channel and everything."

"Woody would never watch something like The Cooking Channel."

"You're wrong, Miz Silk. He's hooked on *Extreme Sauté* and *The Slam Dunk Chef* and *Close This Restaurant! NOW!*"

"You're making up those programs."

"Nope. He likes *Killin' on the Grill* too. Trust me."

"I despair."

"Don't despair. You should try to make it work for you. If we get you a television show, think about what will happen with your cookbook. Into the stratosphere."

"Couldn't happen."

"Sure it could. There's no one on now with your type of looks. I think the camera would like you."

"What?"

"That's what they call it."

"Who calls *what* that?"

"TV people. Doesn't matter. The thing is people like you. You have sort of a way about you. Sympathetic. Personal. All that kinky ashy-blonde hair."

"It's very nice of you to say that, Josey, but…"

"I read somewhere that Naughty Marietta gets ten thousand emails a week. Or maybe it's ten million."

"People email television chefs?"

"Well, sure. This new book could catapult you into full-time celebrity. You'd have to have a blog."

"I don't believe this. I am a writer, not a cook, not a cookbook writer, not a celebrity. And the last thing I would ever want is ten thousand emails a week. What's a blog? It sounds disgusting."

"Okay, forget the blog. But this is a pretty big opportunity."

"Sure. What would they call the program? *Shoot This Chef?*"

"Come on, Miz Silk. They'd come up with something. Maybe *Romantic Recipes with Fiona Silk*. Or *Fiona's Feel Good Food* or something sexier. S*ilky Sensations* or hey, how about—"

It was time for a counter-attack. "When do you watch all this television with school and homework and your business?"

"Not the point. They're on all the time. Everywhere. You can't miss them. And I need to find new business opportunities if I'm going to get my driver's licence. That takes cash. Your project is perfect. And the main point is these people are in St. Aubaine. You have a chance to meet them."

I must have turned pale, because Josey said, "Don't worry about it. I can do the background work. First you have to be a bit professional. You have to learn who's who and what's what. You have to catch on to the personalities and the language. When I was making the list for your supplies, I noticed you don't have any wooden spoons or spatulas or any of those nice little clear glass bowls in different sizes. You need to get your kitchen stocked up to test your recipes."

The bowls again. I said, "I was planning on very simple foods, nothing at all complicated to make. I don't imagine people will be reading an...I mean a romantic cookbook for the cooking instructions."

Josey said, "Have it your way. But you're still going to have to jazz up your kitchen. Even if I do the prep work, I don't even know how the food stylist would manage."

"The what?"

"Never mind. I'll just take stock, okay? You need equipment. You've got no time to waste before you lose your house in order to hang on to that old picture."

"Be my guest," I said. "I can't buy any equipment right

now, and I'll have to pay you for these jobs later."

She sniffed. "Not everything's about money, Miz Silk."

"I'm glad to hear it."

"I'll try the Roi du dollar first. You can settle up later. Maybe we can get some product placement deals."

I would have said something sensible, but of course, the door had already banged behind her.

*   *   *

"I *do* think it's great news," I said to Liz. I wasn't sure how much work I could get done on this ridiculous project if people kept dropping by in the middle of the day. Not that Liz would care what I thought. She watched me from the beanbag chair and wiggled her toes. I added, "But good news or not, we're not having Courvoisier."

She pouted, because pouts still look good on her. We'll see how that goes in another ten years.

She said, "Is that because you're jealous that *I* have something to celebrate for once?"

"No, it's because it's the middle of the day."

"Maybe you're pissed off."

"Well, I am pretty ticked off, actually. I know this is a huge thing for you, and you're really happy to purchase a property. But how come you didn't think to mention it to your best friend of forty-one years, which would be me, until the day you're taking possession?"

"Actually, it's the day I'm moving in. I knew you'd disapprove. For someone so passive as a rule, you have to admit you are pretty tight-assed about development in the village."

There was so much to react to in that sentence. I took a deep breath before I responded. "It's your money, and quite a chunk of it too. If you want to sink it into one of Jean-Claude's condos on the waterfront, what business is it of mine?"

"That's what I mean about tight-assed."

"I'm trying to be a supportive friend," I said. "I can understand you were tired of renting."

"I know what you're thinking. Environmental factors, damage to the waterfront, changing the character of the community, lining Jean-Claude's pockets. Yada yada yada. Did I leave anything out?"

"How about going into debt to accomplish those other things you said?"

"I can manage the mortgage and condo fees easily. I *do* have a medical practice." She glanced at her watch and frowned.

"But you just told me that you were dead broke because of all the expenses. Did I hallucinate that?"

"Cash flow, that's all. Down payment, land transfer, that kind of thing, otherwise I would have helped you out with your own taxes and hydro until Old Cheapskate comes through. Plus I had to order some new furniture."

"Absolutely."

"I needed to put a serious deposit down on that stuff. You think I could borrow this chair?" Liz patted the beanbag fondly. "I always like sitting here. I have a great view of the Gatineau now from my balcony."

"Hey, why not? Take all three chairs until you're settled."

Liz leapt on the idea.

"Great," she said.

"I was joking. You can't take all my furniture."

"Don't start whining. You'd still have the sofa, and if I came by for a visit, you could sit on one of the pine chairs from the kitchen. It's only for a couple of weeks."

Right. The lumpy sofa. Lucky me.

"I can get the beanbag and the Queen Anne chair in my car now. Maybe we can get Josey's uncle to bring the wingback chair over in his truck. Assuming he's sober enough. Hmm. I wonder if I should just send my movers."

"Whatever. On another matter, do you know anything about a guy named Danny Dupree?"

She frowned. "Wheeler-dealer."

"I wouldn't be surprised."

"Slippery customer."

"That was my impression too."

"Trust him as far as you could throw that wingback."

"He's the guy who was killed in the crash of the Escalade on Highway 5. The one I saw yesterday."

"Live fast, love hard, die young," she said with her usual dose of doctorly sympathy.

"He was involved with Philip somehow. A partner in some business deals."

"Ouch," Liz said. "You want to watch out for that."

"Phil is really upset."

"Maybe so, but don't let him use this guy to snow you."

"Do you think it would be possible for someone to die in a crash like that and for the investigators not to find the body?"

"That's a bizarre question even for you, Fiona."

"I saw a woman in that car. I saw her clearly. Sgt. Sarrazin thinks I might have just been upset. But I know she was there. However, they only found one body."

"It couldn't happen, Fiona. Sarrazin's right: you imagined it. Or she got out somewhere along the way."

"That's what I think. But where could she have gotten out? They were on the highway."

"What difference does it make?"

"I'm bothered by it."

"You said he was a jackass."

"Even so. It was a horrible way to die, and…"

Liz shrugged. "Forget about it. Obviously, this woman wasn't in the car, and she didn't die. You don't have to worry about her. Or him for that matter. He was a sleaze. No use crying over spilled milk. That reminds me: the movers dropped my china box."

"What?"

"Maybe the price was a little bit too good. They were a disaster. They have to pay up, but in the meantime, I need to borrow dishes and something to drink out of. When I arrange for the wingback, can I just take what I need?"

"Not the Fiestaware," I said, standing up for myself for once. "You could have some of the Spode for a while, I guess. But don't let those movers do it. It would be really hard to replace. Even if you could. This stuff—"

"Belonged to Kit. Yeah, yeah. Do you think I don't remember that, Fiona? I'll pack them myself."

Beggars may not be choosers, but they can sure be snippy.

*　　*　　*

Josey found me staring around my empty living room just after Liz departed. "Don't let Dr. Prentiss get you down, Miz Silk."

For some reason, I felt like I was living in a turnstile. "She doesn't get me down. I'm used to her."

"But she's so mean. And taking your chairs from right under your nose. It's just not right."

"A couple of points. First, I said she could take the chairs. I know you two don't always get along, but please remember, she's my friend, and she isn't always mean."

"Anyway, whatever, I have this proposition for you."

"I can't pay you, Josey."

"You can pay me wh—"

"I owe thousands of dollars. I need kitchen stuff that I don't even know the name of and—"

"But Miz Silk, you'll get paid for your book that you don't want to talk about in front of me, and you'll get your settlement at some point and then you can reimburse me. I don't even need the money until September. Anyway, I didn't even tell you what my proposition is. Why don't you listen first? Do you want to be part of the problem or part of the solution?"

Tolstoy felt the rising tension in the room. He got to his feet, stretched his hot, fluffy white body and headed for the basement.

I wilted under the steady stare from her round blue eyes. If Josey started spouting business aphorisms on a regular basis, I was doomed.

"Well, Miz Silk?"

"Fine. I'll hear your proposition."

"Oh, boy, that's great. You won't regret it. We have a unique opportunity here—"

I flinched at the sound of unique opportunity.

"—to talk to these chefs, Naughty Marietta and Rafaël."

"What?"

"It's simple. They could each contribute a recipe to your book."

"But why would they?"

"Because it's good advertising for them. They have cookbooks too. You would mention that when you credit them for the recipes. Anyway, I think they love to talk about themselves."

"Absolutely not."

"Leave it to me. Oh, and by the way? CeeCeeCuisine will allow you to use their stuff in return for a credit in the book. I'll talk to Boutique Rejeane about a wardrobe thing. And you should really get your nails done."

"Wardrobe? No," I said, firmly. "Please don't go around town trying to get me free stuff. It's bad enough everyone knows my business. I don't want to be looking for charity."

"I've already told you, Miz Silk. Not charity, product placement."

"Absolutely, unequivocally no."

Josey stared at me wide-eyed. "Hey, not a problem." Now why did I think there would be? "I'll start getting those recipes lined up," she added.

*   *   *

I walked a very reluctant Tolstoy briefly on the shady side of the road and got ready to head for Hull and the hospital. I came back to find that Liz had returned and was lazily eying the Spode while muttering about how busy she was and how she needed to get to her new place and settle in.

"Don't you have patients today?"

"Nope. Moving day. We shuffled all the appointments. But I need to get everything settled. I could use some help."

"Sure. I'll give you a hand after I visit Marc-André."

"What's your big rush? It's not like he's going to remember that you came."

"In case that's what you were trying for," I said, "congratulations, you'll be pleased to know you've hit a new low in empathy."

"Just being practical," she said. "We can't all be woolly-headed romantics like you."

"Since you're being practical, there's an empty cardboard box in my office," I said. "Help yourself."

I was damp and distressed by the time I found free on-street parking two blocks away from the rehab centre and raced into the building to Marc-André's room.

I stopped and stared. The bed was empty. Thoughts raced through my brain: blood clot, hemorrhage, fall from bed. My heart was thundering. Where was he?

I whirled and smacked into the burly aide, Paulette. She was wearing blue scrubs today. Blue was definitely not her colour. Of course, purple hadn't been either.

"What happened?" I said.

Smirking was obviously her hobby. "You're late."

"What? Late? I don't have a schedule. I come here during visiting hours." I stopped talking. Why did I feel the need to explain myself to this woman? I hardly knew her, and what I did know, I didn't like.

"Patients like regularity. It calms them."

"Where is he?"

"Gone for physio. And I believe he had to have some scans done."

"Oh. Well, when will he be back?"

"They're really backed up today. Not for hours, I'd say."

She was enjoying this. A smile flickered on her upper lip. I thought she could have done with a bit of a wax job, but I told myself not to be mean. It's not like I'm a beauty queen.

"Hours?"

"You snooze, you lose."

"Can I join him? Keep him company?"

She just loved telling me no.

*   *   *

The Skylark behaved well on this trip. I got onto the highway easily. I took my time and pulled over whenever anyone swooped up behind me. I was one hundred per cent certain I had seen the woman in the Escalade yesterday, just before I'd turned off at Exit 13. The Escalade had shot past the exit. That was the last one before the accident. I kept an eye out on the side of the road for a place she could have gotten out. But I'd been right the first time. There were no houses, no exits, no access roads, nothing but rock face and gravelly, sloping shoulders.

It wasn't really safe to stand on the side of the road and wait for a lift. There was simply nowhere she could have gone between Exit 13 and the ravine where the Escalade had crashed and burned. I had come by again less than a half-hour later, and there had definitely been no pedestrians or hitch-hikers on the highway.

Just to be on the safe side, I made the loop back to Hull a second time and drove the route again.

But as Liz had pointed out, it had nothing to do with me. Why couldn't I let myself believe that?

strawberries
strawberrie strawberries
strawberri strawberrie
strawberries

Strawberries and Cream

Recipe contributed by Marc-André Paradis (more or less)

2 cups fresh strawberries in season
2 cups whipping cream
1/2 cup sugar
A generous splash of Cointreau or Grand Marnier

Wash and hull strawberries. Place in a clear glass bowl. Whip the cream and, when it begins to thicken, add the sugar, then the Cointreau or Grand Marnier. Whip until quite thick. Serve with the strawberries.

strawberries
strawberriesstrawberries
strawberrie strawberries
strawberri strawberries
strawberries

strawberries
erriesstrawberries
wberriesstrawberries

strawberrie strawberrie
strawberries

Seven

It seemed strange having a conversation with an appliance, but I gave it my best shot. Of course, since I couldn't get into the kitchen, I spoke from the door. "Please stop fussing about the living room chairs, Josey. Liz will bring them back eventually."

Josey's disembodied voice drifted up from behind the stove, which had been pulled slightly away from the wall. "Did you know she was going to take all that other stuff? That china cabinet sure looks weird without anything in it, Miz Silk. And what are you going to drink out of?"

"Everyday glasses will be fine."

"You mean the blue plastic ones you got from Le Roi du dollar?"

"They have a certain cheerful charm, and the price was right. Don't worry. Liz will take care of the crystal snifters. But to return to the matter at hand. What exactly is wrong with the stove?"

Josey popped up from behind the appliance, a spider web dangling from her front cowlick. "I think maybe something chewed on the wires, Miz Silk. It's a real good thing you never turned this stove on. You could have been fried like a piece of bacon."

Tolstoy's tail thumped. He loves bacon, although he has to go to Woody to get any.

I said, "Oh."

"And it's extra bad, because now you'll be spending more time in the kitchen, because you don't have any furniture in your living room. I don't know why you let Dr. Prentiss treat you like a—"

"I like it here. I have the table and chairs. And I have a better view of the garden. So do you think this old clunker can be fixed?"

Josey eased her way out from behind the stove. "Wow! See what I found! What is it? A walking stick?"

"Thank you, Josey. That's my Aunt Kit's. I've been searching for that for years."

"Boy, it's heavy. It's nice, though."

"Made of chestnut, I believe. If I remember correctly, she brought it back from a trip to Ireland. She always used it for hikes. I can't imagine how it got back there, but I'm glad to have it. It's like a family heirloom."

"Well, you better be careful Dr. Prentiss doesn't take it. Anyway, speaking of family heirlooms, how old is this stove?"

I shrugged. "Been here as long as I can remember. Even when I was young and visiting. Maybe it goes back to the thirties. It could be older. Aunt Kit might have bought it secondhand. She found a lot of stuff at garage sales. Like the beanbag chair, for instance."

"Don't take this the wrong way, Miz Silk, but maybe it's time for you to get a new one."

"I love those old chairs. I'm not really into décor. You know that."

"I meant the stove."

"You know the monetary situation. Minus zero and all that."

She said. "I could try to fix it for you, but it's 220 wiring, and you need a licensed electrician to mess around with that. You have to do something, Miz Silk. You could catch fire."

Josey might still be short of sixteen, but she knows way more about such things than I do at forty-six. Or than I want to. 220 wiring? I wasn't exactly sure what that meant. Except danger. Even though my insurance bill was actually paid, I wasn't too keen on fires.

"A lot of these converted cabins, their wiring's in real bad shape. Yours too, Miz Silk. You need someone to bring it up to code. Probably need to replace the electrical panel."

"I have an electrical panel?"

"Sure, Miz Silk. It's in your office. I wouldn't put it past his lordship to call the city and ask them to check it out."

"He couldn't do that." Of course, he could. He'd pretty well insinuated that when we spoke.

"He can do whatever he wants. You know my uncle Mike is a licensed electrician."

I must have blanched.

Josey raised a dusty eyebrow. "He's real good at it when he's sober."

"I'm sure he is," I said, "but didn't you just tell me that he's back in, um, for disorderly conduct?"

She looked miffed. "Not disorderly this time."

"Sorry, public drunken…"

"No. No. Uncle Mike's trying to get sober. It was a dispute over this television set he picked up at the Britannia. Some guy claimed it was stolen, and I guess it had some security number etched on it."

"Huh." I didn't mention that if you were trying to go sober, maybe you shouldn't hang out in the worst booze-pit in West Quebec.

"Uncle Mike didn't know, but the judge didn't believe him. He couldn't get bail, but he'll be out again. I'm pretty sure he'll get two for one for time served. He's got a pretty good legal aid lawyer."

I felt a throbbing in my temples. Uncle Mike talk can bring

that on. But for all his faults, he is Josey's family, if you don't count the institutionalized senile granny, the missing mother and the father no one knew. I said, "I seem to have no choice. I'll get it fixed."

"Okay, I'll see if I can find someone for you. But, if you don't mind me saying so, if you're going to start cooking stuff and trying recipes, you're still going to need a lot more stuff."

"Like what?"

"Maybe measuring cups and spoons. You could consider a frying pan."

"I have a bowl and a wooden spoon. And Kit had some Tupperware measuring cups and spoons. Avocado green. I remember them distinctly. I'm sure they must be here somewhere."

"I already found them. They're pretty neat and retro. I can find someone to sell them on eBay for you and make a few bucks. But you'll need more than that, and you need it now. The stuff has to look good too. Even with the product endorsements, you've got to spend money to make money. That's a basic business principle. And if you don't mind me saying so, Miz Silk, a lot of people have spices in their kitchens too."

Spices? Apparently I had a lot to learn.

"The thing is, Josey, I can't run a tab all over town. The advance will take a while. So will the book, since I don't even have an idea how to do it yet."

Josey offered a bit more guidance. "You have to think positive, Miz Silk. We can beat this thing."

I'm not proud. I'll admit that I needed that pep talk from the kid who'd had more trouble in her life that I'd ever had in mine. Even so, facts were facts. "I'll work with you, and I appreciate everything you do. But I can't pay for anything else, Josey."

"Why doesn't Dr. Prentiss help instead of just taking things?"

"She's got a cash flow problem because she just bought that condo. And the same with Woody. He's sunk a bundle into renovating his living quarters and the store. They'd help if they could."

"So would I, Miz Silk."

"You are more help than anyone."

"Sure. I know that," Josey said. "You're the writer. I'm the executive assistant, remember? But you can help yourself. I picked you up a bunch of cookbooks from the library. Sort of like homework."

"Speaking of homework, how is your exam preparation coming along? You're spending all your time on my project and…"

Of course, you can only get so far explaining yourself to an old stove. I tucked the walking stick in the kitchen corner and headed for the phone.

*   *   *

I lowered my voice in case my fifteen-year-old executive assistant, and now apparently career coach, home renovator and financial advisor, heard me on the phone.

"All I can say, Lola, is that this erotic cookbook idea is turning out to be a disaster. How about if I write a book about brain-damaged people getting their memories back and living happy, fulfilled lives afterwards. That would be worthwhile. That could be really heart-warming. People would—"

"Don't be crazy, darling."

"Or what about people who love brain-damaged people and stay with them and try to have some kind of life, even though—"

"Fiona. Pull yourself together. We have a winning formula with this idea. By the way, I have a title for you: *Too Hot to Handle!* We'll come up with a subtitle later. Don't worry about that."

"The lack of a subtitle is the least of my problems. The lack of recipes or ability is key. Pay attention, Lola. I'm getting nowhere."

"It hasn't even been two days, darling. You need to cut yourself some slack."

"You don't understand. I'm the wrong person. I don't have a single sexy thought. I can't remember one event in my life that ever connected food and sex in any kind of successful way."

"Now you listen to me. Get out of that mindset, because I have gone way out on a limb for you on this one."

"What? Why?"

"Because, as I keep trying to tell you, it's a moneymaker. It's an easy moneymaker. I've already told them you'd do it, and you've signed the contract Let me remind you that we need to make this work. So pull yourself together, get out there and start mining your contacts."

"Mining? What contacts?" I said in a distinctly panicky voice.

Lola sighed, grandly. "Really, Fiona. Speak to the people you know. Ask everyone for ideas, suggestions, the sexiest food they ever had, erotic encounters involving food, meals that turn them on. You know. People love to be involved in projects like this. You can thank them in the acknowledgements or keep their names quiet, if they'd prefer."

Oh, boy. I couldn't imagine asking the people I knew about any of those things, not because I was afraid they wouldn't tell me. I was far more afraid they would. In fact, they'd already started. I thought about it: I spend most of my time alone with Tolstoy, and the rest with Liz, Josey and Woody. Woody had already offered suggestions, so had Sarrazin right out of the blue. I shuddered just thinking about them. And Lola herself, if you count the whipped cream suggestion. But really.

"Not possible," I squeaked.

"Make it possible," Lola said. "Find people to help you. You're funny and non-threatening. Everyone likes you. You have to take advantage of that, darling. Be ruthless."

*　　*　　*

Lucky me. The burly and smirking Paulette was nowhere to be seen when I arrived back at the rehab centre that evening. Outside of Marc-André's room, I ran into Luc, a good-looking nurse I often saw on my visits.

"We're glad to see you, Fiona. Marc-André's been a bit restless today. It happens when they regain consciousness."

"I was worried about that, but he wasn't here when I came in the afternoon. He was having some kind of scan."

"He was?"

"Yes. And I couldn't go with him."

Luc frowned. "I don't think so."

He flipped through the clipboard and shook his head. "No. He was down in the sunroom for a while. That's all."

I stood there, mouth hanging open. Was it better to be a liar or a dupe?

Luc raised an eyebrow.

I said, "One of the residents' aides told me he was. She chewed me out for not showing up, and then she said I couldn't see him. Are you sure?"

"I'm sure. Who told you that?"

"Paulette something. I think she's new."

He narrowed his eyes. "She's new, all right. And I hope she doesn't last long. Anyway, that's too bad you had to make the extra trip, but I'm glad you're here now. Someone else will be happy too."

Marc-André's eyes were open as I moved close to the bed.

113

"Ah," he said. "You again."

My heart hit the inside of my skull. "You remember me?"

"But of course, madame. You were here yesterday."

"Oh. Yes, I was."

He frowned. "There was some kind of...problem."

"I'm not sure what that was about."

"It doesn't matter," he smiled.

I nodded. Sometimes, I can't manage to get words out.

"What is your name?" he said.

"Fiona Silk."

"Fiona Silk. I like that name. *Très beau.* Thank you for coming to visit me."

Talk about your snakes and ladders games. This relationship had its slippery slopes.

Marc-André was in the mood to chat. I sat forward in the chair and held my breath.

"Are you one of my nurses?" he said.

"No."

He looked puzzled. "Well, then why do you come here?"

"I'm a friend," I said. What else could I say? I am your almost-lover? I might have become much more than a friend, if only...

His face lit up. "I am glad I have a friend."

"You have lots of friends."

"Really? That's good. Where are they?"

"They come by."

"And my wife? I can't remember her name."

I bit my lip. "Carole. Her name was Carole."

"Was? Oh."

"You were very happy."

He nodded. "Thank you."

"You missed her a lot after she, um..."

114

"Then I will have some good things to remember."

"Yes."

"The doctors say I will improve, but I have to work at it. How am I supposed to do that?"

"I'll try to help."

"It's no good. I have a big empty head. I wake up with nothing."

"You're able to speak English and French. That's good. You haven't forgotten two entire languages."

"But to forget my wife. That is unbelievable. And I couldn't recall your name, even though…I remembered your hair. It's unusual." He reached up to touch it for a brief moment then sank back onto the bed.

"You'll get better. Your old friends will start to visit now that you are awake again."

"I'm a mechanic. Did you know that?"

"I do. You're a poet, too. An award-winning poet."

"I don't remember any of that either." The pain on his face was unbearable to me. I could only imagine how he felt.

I had nothing to lose. I said, "Here's a tricky question for you. How about food? I am writing a book about recipes connected to…well, anyway. Do you remember anything wonderful you loved to eat? Something connected with love or romance?"

Tears filled his eyes. I had blown it again.

But the incandescent smile lit his face again. "I do. I do remember something. Strawberries. Strawberries and cream. Yes. I remember eating that with…" The smile faded.

"I'm sorry," I said. "I should never have asked."

"No, no, madame, don't be sorry. *Merci beaucoup.*"

"But why are you thanking me?"

"For the memory. You cannot imagine what it means to me. To recall those strawberries, the scent of them, so fresh, and the cream, so sweet, so smooth, and something else. Grand Marnier, I think, or maybe it was Cointreau. Yes. Yes! I can taste it now. It is the first time I have a memory of food, something so intense. It is wonderful. I believe that someday I will remember the rest of my life."

I looked up to see Luc in the door. He gave a little wave and vanished down the long hallway.

Marc-André squeezed my hand. "You have given me hope, madame."

"Me, too," I said in a strangled voice.

As I headed out from the rehab centre parking lot once visiting hours had ended, I jumped and yelped at a squeak of rubber behind me.

The young nurse, Luc, looked even more shocked than I was. *"Pardon,* I thought you heard me calling you."

"My mind was elsewhere," I said, trying to get my heart rate under control.

"That was a beautiful moment, back there with Marc-André. I hope he continues to regain his memory."

"At least he has the sensual memories now. That was really something."

Luc looked down at his feet. He flushed a bit. "I didn't mean to listen in or anything, but if you need more recipes, my partner and I have a special way of doing oysters. We find that romantic. Let me know if you need that, and I'll write it out for you."

"Oysters. Of course. I need it. And thank you."

"Next time you're here, I'll give you the recipe."

Things were definitely looking up.

* * *

The next morning, I started off groggy, most likely because I'd tossed and turned all night. I'd stayed up later than usual looking at the cookbooks Josey had dropped off. *More Than You Ever Asked About Pies* and *The Skewer Encyclopedia* were glossy and larger than you could ever imagine. *Icing! Icing! Icing!* looked small but sweet. I went through them trying to figure out how to structure my own project. My night had alternated between hopeful thoughts of Marc-André and nightmares about cooking. The worst one was treading water next to a bad-tempered goose in a giant pot of stock that was slowly coming to a boil. I was not too groggy to see the significance.

I had just stepped out of the shower and was standing dripping wet when the doorbell rang. Times like that, it was really handy to have the door-answering machine Josey had rigged up for me the previous fall.

"Leave a message after the beep," I thought merrily as I twirled my hair into a damp ponytail. I wasn't worried. Philip wasn't likely to show up so early on a work day, if ever, and all my friends appeared to be able to walk through walls.

But the doorbell kept ringing. The message kicked in: *I can't come to the door right now. Leave a message after the beep and I'll get back to you.* Josey's voice is on the recording, as mine lacks authority. I rethought that strategy when I heard the voice of Sgt. Sarrazin.

"Answer your door, madame," he said, in that curiously flat delivery that the police seem to have perfected.

One point to him. I wrapped myself in a towel and shouted from the other side. "Give me a minute."

Three minutes later, I was dressed, but my fresh cotton T-shirt and my Bermudas were already clinging, not in a good way. Tolstoy had preceded me to the door and was parked there, tail drumming musically. Visitors! One of us really loves them.

When I yanked the door open, Tolstoy nuzzled up to

Sarrazin, who patted him on the head then pointed to the box on my door. "That stupid contraption is a terrible idea. Why would anyone stick an ugly box like that on their front door ?"

I said, "It works for me. Usually."

He actually shivered in the heat. "Well, it gives me the creeps."

"Really?"

"I have no idea where you would get something like that."

"A friend made it for me. After all that trouble last year when I needed to be left alone by the media and all that. I'm sure you remember."

"I'll never forget it. Who made it?"

What kind of inquisition was this? I couldn't see any harm in the answer. "Josey Thring. But she made it for me as a special gift. She doesn't make them for... Is there a licensing issue or something?"

"No. I just wondered where you'd get one. And why you'd want one. You don't have the media chasing after you this year. I should have known it was that Thring kid. Comes from a pretty bad family."

"I'm a writer, and I always need to protect my time. I don't want distractions."

He glanced at my mop of wet hair. "And were you writing?"

"Are you here to see how I spend my time?" Was this some new tactic by the tax people? Find out if people are really doing what they claim in their deductions? Use the local cops as moles?

He glowered at me. He had the eyebrows for it, and the seventeen-inch neck added impact. "I'm here to find out what your relationship was with Daniel Dupree."

"I didn't have one. I explained that when I called you yesterday. Why do you keep asking about that?"

Again with the bearlike look. "Here's the way it works: I am the cop. I ask the questions, madame. It's the law."

I didn't ask what exact law that was. Instead I said, "You may as well come in. It's still a bit cooler in the house."

He followed me through the door and into the living room. "You weren't really straight with me about that relationship. Try again. Get it right this time. It will be easy. Then I'll leave."

"I have it right. He had business dealings with my former husband. I don't think I ever talked to him."

He stopped and blinked. "Didn't you used to have some chairs in here?"

"My friend borrowed them. Try the sofa." The sofa was lumpy, so maybe it would cut his visit short. I didn't offer coffee or lemonade.

He plunked himself down. I swear the sofa groaned. He said, "He was your ex-husband's partner?"

Tolstoy climbed up next to him on the sofa. I didn't care.

As I walked toward the kitchen to get a chair, I said, "In some business dealings. Philip's not…"

"Gay?"

"Not really sexual at all. At least, I never really noticed it. Now you've made my head hurt."

"That's all this Daniel Dupree was?" He held up his hand. "Let's review this: you don't need to know why I'm asking. You just need to answer. Did you see him often?"

"Maybe twice or three times. I told you that."

"Are you sure, madame?"

"Of course, I'm sure."

"Did you have a reason to be angry with him?"

"No!"

"Take your time, madame."

"My ex is taking quite a while to liquidate his assets as part of our divorce settlement. I was angry at *him*. But he's still alive. I never thought about this Dupree. That is the truth."

"Hmm. Your divorce settlement. I'd heard about that. I hear you were pretty upset about it."

That's the trouble with living in St. Aubaine. There's a very good chance that everyone in town knows your business. Financial problems are a preferred source of local chatter, running a close third to fractured love lives and extramarital flings. I was pretty sure that Sarrazin had done his homework and knew that I was behind on my municipal taxes and a few bucks short of paying the Hydro bill.

"Maybe you blamed Daniel Dupree for your financial problems."

"Are you listening to me? I was angry at Philip for stalling. I still am, not that I see what that has to do with anyone but me."

"And this Dupree was involved too?"

I massaged my temple. For some reason it felt like I might have a migraine coming on.

"Only in that he and Phil probably still had business dealings."

"But he was contributing to your financial problems?"

"It's really just a cash crunch," I said.

"Did you hold Dupree responsible for this, madame?"

"What? How could he be responsible?"

"Uh-uh-uh. Who asks the questions?"

"He has nothing to do with it because…" I paused. Hang on. Maybe he did. If Philip was having trouble getting my share of the community property into my hands, was that because of Dupree?

"Yes, madame? You have something to add?"

"It's possible that one of the reasons Phil has been slow to settle is because of the business dealings they have together, but I'm not aware of it. You'd have to ask Philip about that."

"I plan to."

"Oh. Well. Good."

"But I am talking to you right now."

What was the question? "No. I didn't blame him. I prefer to blame Philip. It's familiar, and it just feels right. Danny Dupree was in that accident. That's the one fact I am sure of. I didn't have anything to do with that."

"You know I hate coincidence."

"But I can't explain it. I was going home from the hospital at my regular time when he hassled me on the road. The next time I saw him, the Escalade was upside down in the ravine."

"Did you pursue him on the highway?"

"In the Skylark? That would be funny if it wasn't so…"

"Did you?"

"Of course not."

He leaned forward. The man gives new meaning to the word menace. And he's supposed to be a good guy. "So, let's see if I understand. You were following him, and…"

"Well, actually, let me correct you there. He was preceding me. He passed me just before Exit 13 and…"

"Yeah, okay. You made that point. So he was ahead, and you were behind and then…?"

"Quite far ahead. He must have been doing one-fifty. Maybe more."

"And you were doing?"

"The speed limit. Probably less."

"Okay. That's not possible, is it? It takes awhile for the first responders to get there. It took a few minutes to close the road. You would have been there minutes afterwards. Not a half hour later."

I stared at him, perplexed. I'm not so good with time and

space calculations at the best of times. "I was a bit shaken up. I got off at exit 13 and drove back on the 105 to get some chocolate Kahlua cake at Suki's."

"You never mentioned that."

"Why would I mention it?" I squeaked. "I went to get a slice of cake and some dog treats. It never occurred to me that it was important, if it is, which I doubt."

Tolstoy's tail tapped on the floor.

"And you can prove that?"

"Prove it?"

He watched me wordlessly.

My voice went up an octave or so. "There was a person I knew very very very slightly who acted like a jerk, even though I didn't recognize him. He got in an accident, probably because he continued to act like a jerk. I came along afterwards and was stopped by the police officer. I told the officer about the earlier incident, and that's all there was to it. It was a horrible accident, but it has nothing to do with me. You have to stop…persecuting me."

He cleared his throat. "Three points, Madame Silk. One, I am just doing my job. Two, it was not an accident. And three, it appears it does have something to do with you."

"Not an accident?"

"No, it was not."

"Suicide? But he was such a…"

"No, madame. Doesn't look like suicide."

"But that leaves murder."

Champagne Breakfast

Contributed by Miz Josey Thring, EA

4 homemade or frozen waffles—prepared
1 peach and 1 nectarine, pitted and sliced
1/2 teaspoon lemon zest
1/2 cup fresh blueberries
1/4 cup blueberry syrup
1 teaspoon maple syrup

Heat syrup, zest, syrups and berries. Place two waffles on each plate. Top with fruit and syrup. Serve with chilled champagne and orange juice.

Eight

Y es, madame."

"Well, he was alive and obnoxious the last time I saw him. Oh. Did someone shoot at him from the side of the road? A rifle? Because…"

He shook his head. He reached out and picked a shrivelled leaf from the poor old philodendron that Aunt Kit had left behind.

"Please leave my plant alone and tell me what happened."

"Preliminary tests indicate the presence of drugs."

"Drugs? He took drugs?"

"GHB. A date rape drug. I suspect he didn't know he was taking these."

I stared at him. "You can't think I had anything to do with it. I barely knew him. And what about the woman who was with him? Maybe she—"

"There was no woman."

"Believe me, I don't hallucinate women. What if someone gave her drugs too, and she was injured or shocked, and she crawled into the woods."

He shook his head. "You saw the vehicle. No one would have made it out of that."

"Perhaps she was thrown from the vehicle on impact. That happens. Doesn't it?"

"Sure, but there's a body when it does happen. Based on what you said, we did a very careful search of every centimetre of that ravine. Believe me, no one crawled away from that accident."

"I can't believe you suspect me."

"I don't."

"Are you asking everyone in St. Aubaine if they blamed Danny Dupree for their problems? How about my neighbour Jean-Claude Lamontagne? I bet you're not asking him."

"You are right, madame. I am not. I'm just doing—"

"Well, I'd like to be doing my job too, but the police won't leave me alone. This situation isn't the same as the last time. I actually *had* a relationship with Benedict, but Danny Dupree meant nothing to me. Hardly even an acquaintance. There would be hundreds of people more involved with him than I was."

"We got a tip."

"A tip? What do you mean a tip?"

"A tip. Everyone knows what a tip is. Someone called the station and suggested that you had something to gain from Danny Dupree's death. I have no choice but to follow up."

"I have nothing to gain from his death. I keep telling you, we're not connected. He held some of my husband's investments, that's all." I thought about my words. Unfortunately, it was too late to call them back.

"That's what our caller said. You want your husband to settle your property division, and he's stalling. Dupree was helping him with that game."

"Game?"

"Sure. Men play it all the time. Maybe women do too. But mostly it's men. This Dupree was your husband's ally. So, poof, you even the odds."

"That's ridiculous."

"You do need money, madame."

"Lots of people need money. Most of us don't bump people

off to get it though."

He shrugged yet again.

"The woman saw me. She even tossed a cigarette out the window. Oh wait, *she* must have called in the tip."

He shook his head.

I said, "Well, none of it makes sense. Who else would call in a tip like that about me?"

"Someone who has a grudge against you and wants suspicion deflected from them?"

"I don't know who that could be."

"Your ex-husband perhaps."

"No. Trust me, Philip is a jerk, but he's not a crook."

"We'll be checking him out."

"Oh, boy." That's all I needed—Philip, distracted from the business of settling up with me, liquidating everything he owned to fight false charges, weeping because the laundry services in the local slammer didn't put the right amount of starch in his shirts.

Sarrazin unbent from the sofa. "And madame?"

"Yes?"

"This plant is in the wrong place. If you don't move it so it gets more indirect light, it's just going to get worse."

Tolstoy was sorry to see him go.

* * *

Josey showed up so soon after Sarrazin's departure that I could only surmise she had been hiding out behind a tree. Perhaps studying since, once again, it turned out to be a study day. Where were all these sunny June study days when I'd been chained to a desk at school?

"You know what I think would be sexy, Miz Silk?"

"What?" I gulped.

"Breakfast in bed. With homemade waffles and maybe peaches. And fresh orange juice with champagne. Wouldn't that be great?"

"It would. Of course, I have no idea where you'd start with something like that."

"Try here," she said and handed me a fresh batch of cookbooks from the library. I took them to the lumpy sofa as she headed into the kitchen with a package to install a spice rack. I didn't like to ask where she'd gotten it. What do I know about product placement?

I was working my way through the latest pile of cookbooks and looking forward to *The Wacky World of Waffles*. A tap on the window caught my attention.

I looked up from my spot on the sofa to see Hélène Lamontagne's attractive nose pressed against my living room window. She doesn't bother with the door since I rarely answer it, but Hélène is one of the few people I am always glad to see.

I hoisted myself off the lumpy sofa and headed for the door.

"Fiona!" she said, sweeping into the room. *"Oh là là."*

"Oh là là?"

She wiggled her shapely eyebrows. "I heard."

"Um, heard what?" Did she think I was a murderer too?

"About your book."

"You mean the…?"

"Of course. Is there another book?"

Certainly not my great Canadian novel mouldering quietly in the middle drawer of my battered desk. No one would ever *oh là là* over that.

"No. Where did you hear about it?"

"It is all over the village, Fiona. Spreading like a *feu de forêt*. In both official languages. You have almost but not quite replaced Rafaël and Marietta as the most interesting topic of the day. Why didn't you tell me yesterday?"

I flopped onto the sofa again and groaned. "Because I didn't want to talk about it. It's a new project, and I'm not wild about the idea. What do you mean it's all over the village?"

"Well, what did you expect? In a town like this…" She shrugged beautifully, being French and all. "Surely you remember the last time. Oh *mon dieu*. Where is your furniture?"

"It's been borrowed. Are you sure? All over the village?"

"*Certainement*, by now it will be halfway to Hull. Or Ottawa."

"And I only told three people."

"And I noticed that I was not one of them. That was not very nice of you, Fiona. I like to be on top of things in St. Aubaine."

"Next time I'm not telling anyone anything."

"But why are you not happy? The timing for this new book could not be better."

Josey stuck her head around the corner. Hélène smiled fondly at her.

"Hi, Miz Lamontagne," Josey said. "Miz Silk has to write a sex cookbook. But she doesn't have anything to cook with."

Hélène flashed me a glance.

"Not my fault," I said. "She was here when the call came in. She spoke to my agent. Anyway, it's not really that."

"I believe it's an erotic cookbook," Hélène said. "So much more elegant, *n'est-ce pas?*"

"I guess so," Josey said. "Does it make a difference what you call it?"

"But of course, Josée. Every woman has her little secrets to keep some spice in her life."

"Hélène," I whispered, "have you forgotten that someone is only fifteen?"

"Someone is standing right in front of you," Josey said.

Hélène tsked. "Fiona, Josée is almost a woman."

I stared at Hélène in unqualified amazement. I suppose up until that defining moment, it had never crossed my mind that the freckled girl with the bony frame and the goggling blue eyes and the cowlicky hair that looked like it had been cut with the garden shears, which it probably had been, could ever turn into a woman.

I barely stopped myself from asking where anyone would get such a harebrained idea.

"That's right," Josey said. "I'm pushing sixteen. I'm saving for my driver's licence. I'll be looking for lots of odd jobs. Let me know, Miz Lamontagne, if you have anything when you-know-who is not around. Miz Silk is really broke, but she's running a tab, and that's all right, because I know she's good for it. She'll pay up when she gets the first part of the advance for the sex, I mean, erotic cookbook. But it's not getting off to such a good start."

"Don't worry about that. *Bien sûr,* I will help her. Anything you need, Fiona. You can count on me."

"Thanks, Hélène," I said, hoping the conversation would end soon.

"Help her how?" Josey's cornflower blue eyes were the size of ashtrays.

Hélène smiled in that sensuous secret way that French women seem to be so good at.

"Will you tell her your little secrets, Miz Lamontagne?"

"I think I will, Josey. Jean-Claude and I have been married more than twenty years, and it's important to keep the romance in the relationship."

I spotted the expression of horror creep over Josey's face and hoped my own reaction didn't seem quite so obvious. Secrets with Jean-Claude? Sex? It made the blood run cold.

Fortunately, Hélène seemed oblivious. "A man like that,"

she said, "I make it my job to keep his interest, to make him happy and excited to come home at night."

Josey gasped. I felt faint.

Hélène said, "Candles, music, flowers, the right lingerie. It all matters. And then something to stimulate the taste buds. *Ah oui,* I will have some suggestions for your cookbook, Fiona."

"Awesome," said Josey in a shaky voice.

Hélène smiled at me. "And is there anything else I can do to help?"

Josey leaped in. "Miz Silk should get to meet Rafaël and Marietta. We've seen them on the street, and we've been up to Wallingford Estate, but it's not the same as a proper introduction. They could give her recipes. She could have her picture taken with them."

I said, "Oh, I don't think…"

"Quelle bonne idée! Jean-Claude worked very hard with the new owners of the Domaine Wallingford and with the executive producers to bring this in. He got funding and sponsors and provincial government grants. He made contacts. I will see what I can do."

"That's great," I said, politely. "But I don't want to put you to any trouble."

I made sure I didn't glance at Josey. He'd made contacts, all right. And I didn't want to be the one to tell Hélène about them. Josey made tracks back to the kitchen.

"More than great, Fiona. It means that everyone he contacted will listen to him."

"Oh."

Josey popped back in again. "But Jean-Claude wants to buy Miz Silk's property, and she doesn't want to sell, and she doesn't have any money, so she'd be in a bad situation there, Miz Lamontagne. You can see that."

"Of course, Josée, I don't know anything about Jean-Claude's real estate business. I would never think to interfere there. But he is much too busy with everything to be involved in this little meeting. So I will make the arrangements. *Moi-même.*"

Josey said, "Oh, boy. That's better. You've got the connections. Would Rafaël and Marietta each give Miz Silk a sexy recipe? Miz Silk wouldn't really feel comfortable asking them. When we were up at the Wallingford Estate the other day…"

I shot her a warning glance.

She kept going. "No one paid any attention to us."

"But I will ask them. Fiona, you really shouldn't be…how do you say that?"

Josey interjected. "Woody says she's a doormat."

"Oui. C'est ça."

"Listen, you two. I am not a doormat. I am merely practical."

Josey grinned. "I told you it could really work for you, Miz Silk."

I said, "What if they don't want to? I mean, it is a bit of a bother to help someone out with their cookbook, isn't it? Aren't they all very busy? What would they get out of it?"

Hélène laughed. "That is so sweet, Fiona. They will not do it themselves. That is what sous-chefs are for."

"You see, Miz Silk."

"Mais oui," Hélène said. "Marietta and Rafaël will show up for the photo shoot and whatever promotion is planned around this project."

Photo shoot? My ears buzzed.

Hélène nodded, her artfully made-up face rapt, her burgundy hair aglow. "You could be at the centre of *En feu!*"

"Sizzling," Josey said.

*   *   *

It was past time for me to get moving on this cookbook, but thinking about Jean-Claude fuming triggered a thought. Something about smoke. Something I should have remembered. What? It was only after Josey had headed out for dog walking duties and Hélène had hurried off to a committee meeting that I remembered what. Of course. Danny Dupree's passenger had tossed a cigarette out the window, and it had landed on the Skylark's passenger seat. I'd moved it to the ashtray. Now why hadn't I remembered that useful tidbit when Sarrazin had made his early morning visit?

I hustled out to the car. Sure enough. There it was. A half-smoked cigarette with a lipstick smear on the filter. Perfect. I picked it up and put it in a plastic bag. I mean, it's not like I'd never seen a crime show on television.

Better late than never.

I settled Tolstoy in his basement retreat, climbed into the Skylark and took off for the village. I was getting pretty familiar with the interior of the Sûreté. Although that wasn't something that had ever been on my wish list. Sarrazin uttered a small sigh when I was ushered in past the bulletproof glass at the entrance.

"Remember the woman in the Escalade?" I said.

"The woman that wasn't there?"

"The woman who tossed a cigarette out the window. It flew into my car and landed on the vinyl, still burning. I put it in the ashtray and, well, here it is." I held up the baggie.

He blinked.

"It proves she existed. I didn't imagine her."

"You didn't mention it before."

"It was such a small detail, and I was a bit rattled when you said it was murder. The drugs and everything."

"Maybe Dupree tossed it."

I passed him the bag. "Look at the lipstick."

133

"Are you familiar with the phrase 'chain of evidence', madame?"

"I guess I can figure out what it means."

He handed the bag back to me. "Then you will understand that we can't use this at all. You could have picked it up off the street."

"I didn't do that! Why would I?"

"I'm not really suggesting you did, but you could have. So we can't use this item in court."

"Okay, fair enough, I just want you to know that she was there and that she must have had something to do with the crash. You said he'd been drugged. Maybe that accounts for his weird behaviour. Either she's involved, or she could be a witness. Or she could have—"

He shrugged. "It's a cigarette butt. That's all."

"Fine. But listen to me. I've been thinking about this. They went past me at exit 13, and she was still in the car. I drove that route. There was no place for her to go."

He raised his shoulders in that familiar shrug. "Maybe she hitchhiked."

"Why would she get out of the Escalade to hitchhike? Unless she knew it was going to crash. That would explain a lot."

"Maybe she'd been hitchhiking in the first place. Maybe Dupree picked her up."

"I don't think so. Just from the glimpse I got, she looked fashionable. Expensive."

"Hmmm. But you can't describe her, because you just caught a glimpse."

"Okay, I admit that sounds goofy, but women have a sense about these things. And if you'd had the same glimpse, you would understand my point."

"Which is?"

"Obvious. Where did she go? She didn't have much time to stand around. At the speed he was travelling, the accident must have taken place within ten minutes of the time I last saw the Escalade. I came along shortly afterwards. She definitely wasn't on the side of the road."

"And…"

"Exactly. Even if she'd been picked up by someone, they would have had to stop for the accident. I saw a police cruiser go by just a minute or two after the Escalade. I was hoping he would have spotted the road rager, but Dupree was already out of sight. He stopped the traffic to make way for the emergency vehicles."

Sarrazin frowned and nodded. "He was on his way back from court in Hull. Someone had already called the accident in from a cell phone, but he came upon the scene right afterwards."

"You're probably thinking maybe he noticed the blonde woman with red lipstick in one of the cars."

"I'm thinking he had other stuff on his mind beside women."

"And she might have been smoking."

"You aren't going to give up, are you?"

"I probably will. I'm not much of a fighter. But there's one more weird little bit."

He sighed. Loudly.

"Right. Well, the strangest one was that I think this woman happened to be in the same ladies room as I was. Hear me out. I didn't see her there, but she must have seen me and thought that I would recognize her, so she locked me in the toilet stall. Before you ask how, she placed a chair under the door."

He coughed suddenly.

"Go ahead, laugh. I realize how incredibly silly it sounds, but it did happen. There has to be some reason for it."

"Forgive me, madame. But forgetting about why anyone

over the age of twelve would do that, if you were locked in and you didn't see this woman, and you don't know what she looked like in the first place, then where do you think we can go with this?"

"It was up at the Wallingford Estate. Josey spotted a woman with blonde streaky hair. I think it might have been Anabel Huffington-Chabot. My point is she could have locked me in because she knows that I know that she was in that Cadillac with Dupree just before he died. And she doesn't want that information to get out."

He scratched his ear and shook his head. He lowered his eyebrows. He sighed for good measure. "Well, madame, if you see her again, you can tell her not to worry. Even if this information, which doesn't make sense, does get out, I have a reputation to uphold."

"I'll keep that in mind. And while I am here, can I hand over this wallet that I found? It belongs to a woman called Harriet Crowder. She's some kind of producer with *En feu!* I just can't track her down."

"Try the front desk, madame."

Right.

I would have had a bit more luck with the front desk if two officers hadn't been wrestling in a pair of belligerent drunks just as I arrived. One of the drunks managed to throw up over quite a wide area. Somehow, it seemed better to just keep going. I tossed the baggie with the butt into the car and drove to the Wallingford Estate.

Bananas flambé

Contributed by Hélène Lamontagne

2 bananas, split into 3 equal parts (lengthwise along the stem), cut into 2-inch pieces
1/3 cup halved macadamia nuts
1/3 cup rum
1 tablespoon butter
1-2 tablespoons brown sugar
2 martini glasses
French vanilla ice cream

1 fire extinguisher

Heat a medium skillet over high heat. Add the butter and swirl to coat the pan. When the butter shimmers, add the bananas and the macadamias and reduce heat to medium. Sauté, stirring, until golden brown, about 8 to 10 minutes. Sprinkle brown sugar until just melted. Deglaze the pan with the rum then flambé the bananas and the macadamias. When the flames are extinguished, remove the pan from the heat. Scoop ice cream into martini glasses. Top with flambéed bananas.

Keep fire extinguisher handy. Do not attempt this in other people's homes.

Nine

Okay, so no luck ditching the pesky wallet at the Sûreté. Plus I couldn't get near the Wallingford Estate that morning. Cars and pedestrians were being turned away from the driveway of the building. According to the two people I asked, the place was off-limits because they were shooting *En feu!*, and the previous day, they'd had problems with overzealous fans.

I tried to talk my way in anyway, but Harriet Crowder's wallet wasn't enough to get past security. Strike two, and it was barely noon. I arrived home to find an urgent message from Hélène asking me to come over at once. Tolstoy preferred to remain in his cool basement space, so I headed down the road solo.

She met me at the door. "But, Fiona, I do not understand why you didn't tell me yourself that you were so worried about this little book." Hélène Lamontagne looked down her elegantly restructured nose at me.

It wasn't hard to figure out that she was offended. Not just because of the nose thing, there was also the tapping of the designer shoes. The foot reminded me of the high-heeled blonde who might be undermining both of us. "Because I… Who told you I was worried?"

"Oh, no one."

"Josey, I suppose." My first clue was the sight of Josey standing behind Hélène and looking remarkably innocent.

"Josée is just trying to help you."

"It's a bit embarrassing."

"I can see that. You are already blushing."

"Right. It's the curse of my life."

"But why are you embarrassed?"

"I don't have the vaguest idea of where to begin. I'm reading these piles of cookbooks, and so far I have no idea where to start. Lola can really put on the pressure."

"I am offering to help you. Sometimes, as Jean-Claude would say, you present quite a challenge."

"Jean-Claude says that about me?"

"No, no. He says it about situations that present challenges. I would never discuss you with him."

"For reasons that are obvious to both of us."

"Malheureusement."

Unhappily, for sure. "I'm not trying to present any kind of challenge, Hélène. I just really need the money, and I hate the idea of doing a book like this. It's so not like me. But I have no choice. And I can't really concentrate. I keep thinking about Marc-André and that accident I saw on Highway 5. The police think I am connected with it in some way. "

Hélène's face clouded.

I continued. "Maybe that's just an excuse. I know it's a matter of getting my head around the fact that some foods are supposed to be sexy or even aphrodisiacs, then getting some recipes that use those foods and linking it all together with a bit of text."

"That sounds all right, Fiona."

"No, it's really not all right. I have to get cracking before the municipality seizes my house or Hydro cuts off the power or my car conks out. Or I need to eat dinner."

"Mais, voyons donc. You are my friend, and I will be happy

to help you. I left some messages today, and I expect to hear from Rafaël and Marietta soon."

"I appreciate that."

"She also needs practice cooking," Josey said, her head held high. "And she doesn't have any equipment. Or ingredients yet. Plus she needs to, um, ease into the situation. Get her confidence up for when she's talking to them."

"I am standing right here while you two are discussing me. Maybe I'd be better off at home in the basement with Tolstoy."

"Do you have a recipe that would fit in Miz Silk's cookbook?"

"Oh là là."

"Come on, Hélène. You're a gourmet cook. You must have."

Hélène shrugged modestly. "Well, I have always loved anything flambé."

"Flambé?" I squeaked. "That sounds really complicated. Don't you have anything that involves opening two cans?"

Hélène shuddered. "There's no such thing as a flambé of canned mushroom soup and flaked tuna."

"Huh. Maybe there should be," Josey said.

Hélène merely said, *"Des bananes!"*

Josey's eyes were like huge blue saucers. "You're kidding, right?"

"No, I am not kidding, Josée. This is a very elegant dish."

"But is it sexy?"

"Mais oui! Think of the symbolism."

Don't! I thought. Please just don't.

"What symbolism?" Josey said.

"Never mind," I said.

"It is very sexy when it is done right, in the proper atmosphere. I used to make these for Jean-Claude, on very very special romantic occasions."

Josey said, "Ew." I thought the same but managed to keep it to myself.

Luckily, Hélène missed Josey's comment because she was checking through the zillion cupboards. I gave Josey a look that was supposed to mean, *try to self-censor your comments given where we are.*

"I have everything we need," Hélène said. "Bananas, rum, macadamia nuts, brown sugar. *Allons-y!*"

This was exciting. I had never witnessed Hélène's kitchen in use. It was more like something you'd see in a high-end photo shoot. There was the black granite countertops. Then there was the custom glaze finish on the cabinets, subtle and hand-done, a luscious grey-green that defied description. I couldn't even imagine what that work would cost, or why you would spend that kind of money. It hadn't occurred to me that Hélène actually prepared food in this dream room.

"What are macadamia nuts?" Josey said, seizing the moment.

"Think expensive," I muttered.

Of course, Hélène had to give Josey a sample of macadamia nuts. Hélène is as kind as she is elegant. She makes up for the fact that Jean-Claude reacts to Josey like he found a scorpion in his shoe. Jean-Claude is the only person I've ever met who could take such a dislike to a young girl. Especially one like Josey, industrious, cheerful, loyal and honest in the things that really matter.

Perhaps that is why Hélène bends over backwards for her. She never refers to Josey's impoverished background or criminal relatives. Packages appear for Josey from time to time. Clothing that Marie-Eve, the Lamontagne daughter, has outgrown. Food that might go to waste. Sporting gear. Even Josey's now-rickety bicycle had come from Hélène at one time.

I've tried to get Josey to stop calling Jean-Claude "his

lordship", but she still automatically curls her lip when she spots him. But Hélène had said Jean-Claude was off at a shareholders meeting, so the mood was light.

Josey and Hélène got the ingredients assembled as I stood there, useless as a garden gnome. Still, it was fun to watch them, and possibly even educational.

"Can I do anything?" I said.

"Better not," Josey said.

"I feel a bit guilty, since this is all to help me."

"*Oh là là.* Just sit over there. Perhaps you can take notes."

Taking notes sounded good to me. Hélène extracted a non-stick pan from a drawer that held dozens of pots and pans. She measured out the brown sugar into one designer measure and the rum into another. Josey poured the macadamia nuts into a third one.

"*Voyons.* What can we serve this in? Oh, I know!" Hélène selected four long-stemmed martini glasses from a glass-fronted cupboard. "This will be elegant."

"Are you sure I can't do something?" I said plaintively.

"We're sure," Josey said.

"Can you get two tablespoons of butter, Josée?"

Josey scrambled over to the French-door fridge and opened it. She picked out a pound of butter, unwrapped it and flipped two tablespoons into the non-stick pan. Absolutely nothing went wrong.

I sulked. I could have fetched the butter.

"Don't look like that, Miz Silk," Josey said. "You said yourself that cooking is not your best thing."

"True, but I can't believe the two of you don't trust me to get the butter. I have to start small."

Hélène glanced up. "Did you write everything down?"

I hesitated. I hadn't, of course. "I'll remember."

She reeled off the few ingredients this recipe required. "You might not. What if you forgot the rum? It won't *flambé* without that."

Josey shook her head. If her expression was anything to go by, this *flambé* experience was a big hit with her. "Are we really putting it in those fancy glasses, Miz Lamontagne?"

"As soon as it's ready. We have to flame it first."

"Right."

"And because this is supposed to be romantic, we will put it on a tray with something pretty." She bent down and opened a drawer filled with table linens. She pulled out a piece of sheer, sparkly fabric.

"C'est beau," she said, arranging the fabric on a black lacquered tray. She set the martini glasses amid the folds, pulling them here and there to make a pleasing backdrop. A trip across the room, and three crystal candle holders with votives were added to the tray.

"That's neat," Josey said. I imagined she was working out a plan for using that sort of thing in THE THRING TO DO. Romantic desserts on request. "Do we put the glasses on that too?"

"And before that, we have to put the ice cream into the martini glasses. Here's the ice cream scoop. I have wonderful French vanilla ice cream, and this scoop makes a nice shape."

"I can do that," Josey said, racing back to the refrigerator and opening the lower freezer.

"Hang on," I said, "are you telling me that you two don't trust me to carry a container of ice cream?"

"Take good notes!" Josey said. I did my best not to roll my eyes. She added, "Really good notes. I want to be able to do this again."

I wrote down *Get ice cream from freezer.*

Even though Hélène trusted Josey to get the ice cream, she

clearly thought that scooping appropriate scoops was a higher level job. I had to admit that Hélène did that as well as everything else she put her hand to. That is to say perfectly.

Josey lit the candles instead.

Hélène poured the rum over the bananas and swirled it around the pan. I was pretty sure I could have done that too. She took a barbecue lighter from a drawer and flicked it. Nothing happened. At last, something that Hélène didn't get right the first time. Three more attempts and still nothing.

"*Oh là là.* They are supposed to be child-proof. What does that make me?"

"I'm really good at that, Miz Lamontagne! Let me." Josey reached for the lighter and relieved Hélène of it. "There's a trick to it. You hold it here and then you press this, and presto."

"*Et voilà!*" Hélène said.

Josey leant forward to light the rum mixture. The sauce and bananas caught and flamed beautifully. "Wow!" she said. "This is cool!" She held the flaming pan in her hand.

"What the hell is going on here?"

I jumped from my perch at the sound of Jean-Claude's booming voice. Josey leapt sideways. Her arm hit one of the martini glasses, which toppled the next one. That crashed into the third. I raced across the floor as I saw the domino effect about to happen. Splintered martini glasses one, two, three.

Hélène stood still, her eyes wide, her hand over her mouth.

Josey hung onto the handle of the pan with the still-flaming mixture.

As I sprinted toward the tray, the third glass hit the first candle and knocked it over. The candle tipped, in slow motion it seemed. The gauzy fabric ignited in a whoosh. Flames snaked across the granite counter. Others shot up, licking at the cupboard doors. One leapt and caught Josey's sleeve. She yelped and dropped the pan. Sauce, bananas and flames rippled across the floor.

Hélène shrieked.

I grabbed a pair of decorative dish towels and smothered the flames on Josey's sleeve. There were tears in her saucer-sized blue eyes. I slapped the towel at the rest of the flames, which were leaping up the cupboard surfaces. I shouted. "Where's your fire extinguisher? And someone call 911."

Jean-Claude reached under one of the many sinks and extracted an extinguisher. He sprayed foam on every surface in reach. Josey grabbed the phone and dialed 911, gasping out where we were and what was happening.

Hélène still stood, hands still on her mouth, burgundy nail polish stark against her ashen face.

Jean-Claude hadn't lost his command of the situation. "What the hell are you doing? Trying to destroy my kitchen? Well, you are damn well not going to get away with it. *Tabernac.*"

Hélène gasped. If you add up all the swear words in the English language, they might equal *tabernac* in shock value. But probably not.

I said. "We are trying to stop Josey from being burned alive."

"Exactly," Josey said. Her eyes were still a bit teary, which told me that the burn on her arm must hurt like hell.

"Well, you had no damn business being in my house in the first place."

I reached deep into my small store of courage. "Get a grip. We were all having fun here, and an accident happened. I'm sorry about the damage. We'll be leaving now. Josey should see a doctor."

"You are not going anywhere until the police get here."

"Wrong," I said. "She needs medical attention fast."

He sneered. "Let's let the police decide who needs what."

"But Miz Silk. Maybe we should have stayed. You heard his lordship. He's going to press charges because we left the scene of the crime. What if he uses that against you to get your house?"

I gripped the steering wheel of the Skylark as we rocketed along Chemin des cèdres toward the village. "It's all right, Josey. There was no crime. And you need medical help. Please don't make any snippy remarks to Liz. We're lucky she's back in the office after her move."

"What happened to your eyebrows?" Liz said as we bypassed the patients in her waiting room and hustled in. "You look—"

"Nothing. We're here about Josey. You have to check her arm. Josey, climb up on the table please. I'll help you," I said. "It's a bad burn. I thought about the emergency department at the St. Aubaine hospital, but I figured you'd be faster."

"Hard to be slower. But seriously, Fiona. What happened to your eyebrows?"

"Miz Silk got singed putting out a fire. It was all my fault."

Liz snorted. "Why does neither of those things surprise me in the slightest? You know what? There are easier ways of shaping your eyebrows."

I bit my tongue. After all, we had jumped the queue in the office. "It was not her fault. It was an accident. No more arguments, Josey."

Liz said, "I despair of both of you. Looks like she has second degree burns. That's a lot better than third degree. Essentially, there's not much we can do except to keep the wounds covered and apply antibacterial ointment to prevent infection. Fiona, you'll have to watch out that it doesn't get infected. If it does, then you get her in to me pronto for antibiotics. Josey, you listen to this. If you ignore the signs of infection, you can end up needing IV antibiotics, probably in the emergency department. The same goes for you, Fiona. I'll give you antibacterial ointment too. Use it and watch for infection. Keep your hair off your forehead."

Josey said, "We'll watch out for each other. Thanks, Dr. Prentiss."

Liz loaded us up with antibiotic cream samples. "Stay out of trouble. Just this once," she said as we left.

The impatient patients in the waiting room probably got a thrill when they saw the local cops show up looking for the two people who had elbowed their way ahead of them. I heard one woman mutter something that translated roughly into "pushy English people getting what they deserve."

Sgt. Sarrazin regarded us with a frown. "Are you really that surprised to see me, madame?"

I was, actually. In fact, the whole day so far seemed like a weird variation on *Groundhog Day* in that Josey, Sarrazin, Liz and Hélène just kept turning up and nothing ever got any better.

Josey said. "We've been expecting you. It's just that Miz Silk's eyebrows got a bit singed."

"Josey has a bad burn," I said. "Anyone else but Jean-Claude would have driven her for medical help rather than calling you."

"That explains it," he said, whipping out his little white notebook.

"It was an accident," I said.

"My fault," Josey said.

"Let's start at the beginning. Is there a place here we can talk?"

Liz had stuck her head out the door to see what the discussion was about. She said, "Not here, there isn't. Not enough chairs for the walking wounded as it is."

I shot Liz a look. "I don't think Josey's in any shape to go to the Sûreté. Anyway, she hasn't done anything. I can go with you."

"Neither of you has to go to the Sûreté," Sarrazin said. "I just need to ask you some questions about the fire."

Josey leaned over and whispered. "They always say things like that, Miz Silk. Then when they get you behind bars, watch out."

Sarrazin sighed. "Now that the secret's out, I guess I won't get to work you both over with my rubber hose."

Josey raised her chin. "I want my lawyer."

"Get lawyered up if you want. Or just tell me what happened." He glanced at Liz scowling in the doorway. She was probably his doctor too, so maybe that was a factor in his decision. "We can go to the Chez."

"We're broke," Josey said.

"The Chez will be great," I said at the same time.

"I'll try to minimize the brutality," Sarrazin countered. "I'll even buy the fries."

"How about poutine? Miz Silk really likes poutine."

"Don't push your luck."

As the door swung closed behind us, I pictured everyone in the waiting room yanking out cell phones to spread the latest news.

*   *   *

The Chez was great, if you didn't mind having two dozen witnesses to your police grilling. Lucette, everyone's favourite server, zoomed right in. Sarrazin ordered three large fries and three Pepsis, without consultation. It's hard for a normal person to polish off the towering plates that they serve at the Chez. But Tolstoy adores fries, so I'd be popular when I finally crawled home and enticed him out of the basement with the leftovers.

"Make mine with gravy," Josey called after Lucette.

"Let's talk about the fire," Sarrazin said.

"Do we have to?" I said.

"It *is* why we're here. We're only here because you both are obviously injured. So let's get started. I am puzzled about why you would be at the Lamontagne residence. Everyone knows that you and Jean-Claude don't get along."

"Hélène is my friend. I don't have to get along with Jean-Claude. Usually, I avoid him."

"It was the cookbook. Miz Silk has to write one because of her taxes, and it has to be," she glanced at Sarrazin, "romantic. Otherwise Jean-Claude will get his filthy mitts on her house."

"I've already explained about the cookbook, Josey," I said, not wishing to discuss it in detail with Sarrazin.

He rumbled, "And I'm not sure how it connects to the fire at the Lamontagnes' house."

"Miz Lamontagne was showing how to make a flambé. I guess his lordship likes them. We were testing it in her kitchen, because Miz Silk's stove isn't working too good. It's completely my fault," Josey said.

I interrupted. "It's no one's fault. It was an accident. If you had to blame it on a person, it would be Jean-Claude himself. Hélène and Josey were just flaming the rum when he showed up without warning and started shouting. A candle was knocked over. The decorative fabric just ignited. Whoosh! A tower of fire."

Josey said, "In the future, we might want to change how we make that recipe."

Sarrazin rubbed his forehead. "M. Jean-Claude Lamontagne seems to believe there was malice aforethought."

"Malice aforethought?" Josey snapped. "What exactly did his lordship say happened?"

"He implied it was done deliberately to damage his recently upgraded kitchen."

"Deliberately?" I squeaked.

"He claims the damage is over fifty thousand dollars."

Josey inhaled. "That's crazy. Jeez, it was just a small fire. He put it out with the extinguisher."

When I caught my breath, I said, "And it can't possibly be that amount. They're cupboards, not the Sistine Chapel."

"What did Miz Lamontagne say about it?"

"Not much. She was very quiet. I think she might have been in shock about the whole thing."

Josey narrowed her eyes. "I bet she's afraid of him. Everyone else in town is. He's a real bully."

"Is that a fact?"

"For sure. And somebody in the tax office must be working with him, because why else are they trying to take Miz Silk's house for unpaid taxes?

One inch-thick eyebrow rose. "That's interesting too," Sarrazin said.

I said, "Jean-Claude does want my property for the new development, but I don't think he'd actually…." On the other hand, maybe I did. "Josey listened to Jean-Claude accuse us of something that simply wasn't true at all. She's had a bad fright, and these burns really hurt. And then the police show up."

He said, "Yeah, and buy her fries and soft drinks. Make sure you add that to the list of brutal tactics."

"It's just unfair. We're not criminals."

Sarrazin cleared his throat. "Back to what happened in the kitchen. Lamontagne says at the very least it was careless and negligent use of fire."

I shrugged. I might have caught it from him. "You can choose to believe me, or you can choose to believe Jean-Claude." I shot Josey a look intended to stifle a snort.

He said, "You know what I think? I think we'd be laughed out of court if we tried to prosecute you for this."

Josey said, "I knew that."

I felt a wave of relief. "And that's the end of it?"

Sarrazin picked up a fry. "The end of it, as far as I'm concerned. But you might want to keep your eye on—"

Josey narrowed her eyes. "His lordship, right?"

Sarrazin said. "I'd be asking myself why a man who could have a perfectly good insurance claim for an accidental kitchen fire would make such a big deal over it and jeopardize his insurance claim by accusing you of deliberately damaging his home."

I stared at him. "Could he come after me in court? That's just ducky. I can't afford to fight him on this."

Sarrazin gave one of us famous shrugs. "If I were you, madame, I'd be careful."

*   *   *

I was feeling vague and distressed. The best antidote for that is to take my dog for an amble. I waited until just before sunset. I brought along Aunt Kit's walking stick for fun, and we moseyed from the house through the woods to the water's edge. You could just see the water from the cottage. Since it was built in the 1930s, the trees have grown and blocked some of the view. That's okay with me. I love the walk to the shoreline. I never fail to be astounded at the power of the river to move me. If I could see it from my window, I'd never get anything done.

The shore is rocky. It's also shallow enough to dip your feet in. That suited me too, after a long and sticky day. I was wearing my waterproof sport sandals. Tolstoy keeps his distance from water, but there was plenty to interest him in the woods.

The last of the evening sun glittered off the little waves.

The river is wide and powerful at this curve, flanked by green hills. Just the occasional rooftop can be seen peeking through the cedars or maples on both sides of the bank. It's pretty much unchanged since the days when logging fueled the local economy. You can almost feel the brawling spirit of the French and Irish loggers who settled the area.

For me, every tree had a memory attached to it. There was the maple where Liz and I had our first tiff. Liz had stomped off in a snit and smacked her head on an oak branch, knocking herself out. I still felt a bit of guilt about that. She was not above bringing up the subject when she wanted something. Then there was the cedar where I used to smooch with Phil, just out of Aunt Kit's sight.

We'd spent our prom night on that beach, with bare feet in the water, drinking Blue out of the bottle and discovering that cigarettes were not really for us. Liz's boyfriend from that time was long gone, and eventually Philip would be too. But Liz and I still had a lifetime attached to that shoreline. We'd had our issues from time to time, but they always passed. I shivered at the thought of giant homes hunkered on treeless lawns that stretched to the shore, where huge docks would jut into the river.

I turned as a branch cracked behind me. Josey emerged. Tolstoy bounded toward her, tail waving with joy.

"Oh, boy, Miz Silk. You can't let his lordship take this away from you."

I nodded, a lump in my throat.

"This is where I first met you. Remember?"

"Who could forget?"

Josey had been selling lemonade during a heat wave. Or maybe it was selling lawn mowing services. Or possibly dog walking. Whatever it was, it hadn't taken her long to become part of our lives.

153

Tolstoy leaned forward to get his ears scratched.

"How can he do it, Miz Silk? It will ruin this whole stretch of the river. Doesn't he value anything?"

He values money, I thought. And power. And making people bend to his will. "I don't know."

"There must be some way to stop him."

"I'm sure there is a way, Josey," I said, staring out over the glittering water, "but I don't know what it is."

"Yet," she said.

I spotted the quiver in her lower lip and averted my eyes. Josey is nothing if not proud.

"Yet," I echoed.

Fig Salad

Contributed by Marc-André Paradis

2 figs
2 thin slices of imported Italian prosciutto
2 ounces fresh mozzarella
Crusty baguettes

Honey lemon dressing
    2 tablespoons extra virgin olive oil
    1 tablespoon lemon juice
    1 teaspoon honey,
    Salt and pepper

Split the fresh figs at the top with a cross, cutting less than halfway down the fig. Now pinch at the base to force the fig flesh through the split skin. Put the figs, ham and sliced mozzarella on a plate.

Whip dressing ingredients together until they thicken.

Drizzle the dressing over split figs, mozzarella and ham. Serve with sliced baguette and wine.

Ten

Despite everything that had happened over the past three days, I was smiling as I hurried into Marc-André's room. Once I was there, my trouble seemed to melt away: wiring, taxes, insurance, divorce, disaster. At least there was one thing getting better in my life. Someone with no price tag attached. Someone with much bigger problems than I had, even if he didn't know it. Someone unwavering, even if he didn't remember why.

The smile that flashed across his face made everything that was bad in my life recede further.

"Madame! How are you?" He recognized me! His smile vanished. "But what happened to your face. You look…"

"Ah, yes, well, I lost my eyebrows in a dessert-related accident."

"I don't understand."

"Why don't we talk about you instead? You're sitting up. That's terrific."

"And I am glad to see you, even without your eyebrows. You still have your smile. Of course, that is the best part of Fiona Silk."

"You remember my name!"

"The specialist was in today. He says I am recovering well, and now I am starting to remember. These last few days were a setback, but I am getting better. He told me not to worry too

157

much about these setbacks." He leaned a bit forward. "But there is something else wrong, isn't there?"

"No, no, no."

"You can tell me. I am your friend."

I nodded, feeling that damn lump swelling in my throat.

"You have been visiting me, thinking about me, worrying about me. Is that right?"

"Yes."

"Friendship cannot be one-sided."

"Of course not."

"You are thinking that I am in this bed and you need to be sympathetic to me and my problems, but I need to be a friend too."

Okay, I knew I shouldn't have blurted it out. He was the one who needed help and cheering up and ongoing support. He didn't need to have me melt down in his fragile presence. But I did, and the whole sordid story spilled out: the overdue taxes, the stalled settlement, the threat to my little property by Jean-Claude and his development plans, and this problem with the thousand dollars for the wiring, which all started with an innocent check behind the stove. I felt a flush spread over my cheeks as I explained about the cookbook.

He laughed out loud at that.

"It's not really funny," I said. "I'm quite hopeless at it. It'll be a spectacular failure."

"Perhaps not, madame. But let me help you."

"With recipes?" I said stupidly. "I am already using your strawberries and cream."

"And I remember I used to make a terrific fig salad. Oh, that is a wonderful memory too. I can taste it! But never mind that now, I meant I can give you the money for your taxes and whatever else you need."

"But I couldn't accept it."

The brilliant turquoise eyes met mine. "Why not?"

"It just wouldn't be right."

"Because I am a prisoner here in this hospital bed? Is that it? Because you feel sorry for me?"

"Of course not."

"Why then? Am I not a man who can help a woman?"

"I just wouldn't feel comfortable about it."

"Fine. Don't just take it. I can make you a loan. Interest free. It's no problem for me. It's not like I have anything else to do with my money while I'm here."

"All this medical attention, the rehab. It must be costing you so much."

"I had a good medical plan. After my wife got sick, I made sure I was covered for everything you can think of. See? Today I remember Carole too."

"That's wonderful about your memory. But I don't think I can accept any money from you. For one thing, who knows when I could pay you back. And the way my ex-husband's behaving, he might find a way to keep me from getting my settlement."

"I would forget the loan then."

"But that's the problem. *I* wouldn't forget it." I reached over and squeezed his hand.

He squeezed back. A good sign neurologically, I imagined. "I suppose not, madame. And I am not surprised. Did you forget to keep an eye on my home? To pick up my mail? To make sure my car was stored properly? You didn't forget to visit me in the hospital? Did you?"

"No. But that's different."

"It is not different, madame," he said. "This is just one more thing you can do for me: to allow me to help you. Let me feel like I am capable to give again, not just receive."

I smiled back at him. It seemed easy enough to say yes, and yet what kind of slippery slope was it?

"I will write you a cheque," he said, "for whatever you need. And you can pay me back whenever you want."

I shook my head.

"Don't think you'll get away with that for one more minute." I jumped at the angry voice behind me.

"What?" I stared at the beefy aide, Paulette. She looked large and dangerous in her rumpled scrubs.

Marc-André's eyes flashed. "This is not the business of the hospital. It is between me and my friend."

"*Au contraire.* There are laws against trying to extort money from vulnerable patients. It's called fraud. And there are policies here as well."

I said, "But I haven't accepted anything from Marc-André."

"Tell it to the judge."

"What judge?" Marc-André said. "This is ridiculous."

She turned to me, triumph on her face. "You will leave this facility immediately. And once I have made my report, you will not be granted access to it again."

This reaction didn't even make sense. I didn't even know this woman, yet she was as vindictive as Jean-Claude for no reason I could imagine. Unless, of course, the reason was Marc-André.

I said, "I haven't done anything. I'm certainly not extorting money. Which you would realize if you weren't jumping to conclusions."

But she was already on the phone to security. I got one last glance at Marc-André's stunned face as they bundled me out the door, down the long corridor and out of the hospital.

Security made sure I knew I wouldn't be allowed back. In both official languages.

*   *   *

I got home to two messages. Hélène's said that she'd found us an electrician. Lola had left the second. Liz had arrived at the same time I did. She made herself at home, meaning she poured herself a walloping drink from my Courvoisier while I listened to Lola's message.

"Fiona! Lola here. Great news, darling. I got the contract you sent. So it's a go. Of course, they might want changes, possibly a diet version. We're still talking about that. So in the meantime, watch the calories in those recipes. Anyway, I got the first part of the advance cheque. I've XpressPosted it to you. That sick relative story worked. Remember that if you're talking to anyone from the firm. You'll have it tomorrow. Go crazy, girl! But stay on top of the project. We have tight deliverables! Well, gotta go. I'm getting ready for BookExpo Canada. Get busy, and I'll talk to you next week."

I hung up and did a dance of joy around my living room.

Liz peered at me from the lumpy sofa. "You need a new sofa. This one is horribly uncomfortable. What are you dancing about?"

"Money is coming! Just when I thought I was living in a Victorian melodrama, now I can pay my tax bill! It's going to be all right."

Liz stayed seated but raised her blue glass in the direction of Jean-Claude's house. "Take that, you bastard," she said.

Josey arrived back from the village, entered without knocking, and joined me in a little jig. I couldn't stop dancing. Even poor old sweltering Tolstoy got in the mood and jumped around with us, his white tail waving.

"Hey, Miz Silk. After you pay your land taxes, you think there will be enough money to get an air conditioner here? I think Uncle Mike knows a guy who can get you a great deal on one."

"Hey, I had that idea first," Liz said. "It's always so hellishly hot here."

"One thing at a time," I said. "At least we're out of the woods. I mean at least we can stay in the woods."

"Anyway, I've been in town," Josey said, "and I ran into Marietta and Rafaël when they were going out to dinner. They heard from Hélène. They'd really like to talk to you."

"That's great, Josey. And another good thing. I got a message from Hélène."

"She called? What did she say? Is she upset about her kitchen?" Liz said, "Whoa."

"Take a breath, Josey. Everything's good. Hélène knows we weren't responsible for the fire. She called to see how we are. I think she's embarrassed about Jean-Claude's behaviour. She said that he won't be taking legal action against me. She also has a line on an electrician. So that's good. And even better, our friendship is still intact."

"No thanks to his lordship."

"Never mind him. I think we're on our way out of this situation."

* * *

Although I knew it rankled, Josey showed her sporting side when Hélène was able to locate an electrician before she did.

"Face it, Miz Silk. We need to get this wiring fixed, no matter what it takes. And Hélène's got the connections through his lordship. No wonder this guy can come right away. Ordinary people don't have that kind of clout."

Josey was waiting at the door when the electrician's mud-covered pick-up pulled up near the door. Luckily, I spotted the handsome German shepherd accompanying him. I tossed one of Suki's special dog treats down the basement stairs to distract Tolstoy. The last thing we needed was a turf battle.

"Do you play basketball?" Josey said as she led him into the kitchen.

It was a fair question. He must have been six foot five. He was lean without being lanky. His shoulder-length dark blond hair was caught back in a loose ponytail. A gold stud twinkled from each ear. He wore faded jeans and a T-shirt featuring Che Guevara, who was in turn wearing a Bart Simpson T-shirt. The electrician seemed to be in a heck of a fine mood, which might have been because he looked so damned good. Or maybe it was because he'd had the benefit of an excellent dentist for most of his life, which I estimated to be about thirty-five years.

"What about football?" Josey added.

He grinned and ducked to avoid whacking his head on the door frame. "Nope. Just tall. So what seems to be the problem, ladies?"

I stuck out my hand and introduced myself. "Thanks for coming," I said and meant it.

He gripped my hand in his huge paw and said, "My pleasure. Arlen Young."

The dog checked us out. She remained aloof and cautious.

Josey said, "What's your dog's name?"

"Sweetheart."

"Good name. Hey, I think I know you from somewhere." Josey entered something in the little notebook.

Arlen grinned down at her. "I been a lot of places."

"The Britannia?"

He said, "Aren't you a bit too young for the Brittania?"

"They let me in when I have to collect my uncle. You some kind of musician?"

"I play a bit of guitar. The band's called Nowhere To Go But Oops."

"Hmmm. That could be it, but I've never heard you play." She nodded and ripped out the page. Another crumpled blue page landed in the wastebasket. Just as well. If Josey acted on everything she wrote in that tiny book, we'd all be exhausted.

"Could be. I'm from just up the line. I bet you're Mike Thring's family, right? I think I've seen you with him."

I decided to re-assert my role as homeowner. "The wiring in the stove seems to be bad. And in back of it too, the what do you call it."

"Two twenty," Josey said. "A mouse must have gotten it. I know, you fish a lot up the river from here?"

"You got it. I live to fish." He showed his incandescent teeth. "So you got mice here?" He grinned again. Possibly he'd never stopped grinning. With those large and perfect teeth, maybe that was a default state for him.

"All these converted cottages get a few mice every fall. You'd know that if you were from around here," Josey said haughtily.

Arlen laughed out loud. "And I guess we get our mice up the line too."

"I'll bet you do," Josey said darkly.

Time for me to butt in. "Maybe you'd have a look at the rest of the kitchen wiring while you're here. I don't want to take a chance if the mice have been busy. And the stuff in my office too."

"It's a great old stove," he said. "They don't make 'em like this any more."

That was excellent news, because the last thing in the world I wanted was to go out and buy a new stove that I would use for this one cookbook. If luck was with me, I'd never have to cook again once I finished.

Josey watched Arlen's every move. There was good money in the trade. I thought perhaps she was considering it. It took him next to no time to scout out the electrical situation in the kitchen. Of course, by then, Josey had managed to win the heart of his dog.

"You were lucky," he said. "Two twenty's tricky. This stuff's in real bad shape, all gnawed out. You could have been killed just checking it."

"Huh," I said.

"How much?" Josey said.

"Everything's doable if you got the time and money. It can cost a bit to fix up these old cottages, but since you're a friend of Mrs. Lamontagne's, I'll give you a good price. And here's my card."

"Make sure it's a real good price," Josey said, folding her arms.

"Sure, won't be much more than a thousand."

A thousand? Might as well have been a million from where I stood.

Oyster Stew

Contributed by Luc Sauvé

1 cup minced celery
1 cup butter
3 tablespoons minced shallots
1 quart half-and-half cream
2 (12 ounce) containers fresh shucked oysters, undrained
salt and ground black pepper to taste
1 pinch cayenne pepper, or to taste

Melt the butter in a large skillet over medium heat. Cook the celery and shallots until shallots are tender.

Pour half-and-half into a large pot over medium-high heat. Mix in the butter, celery and shallot mixture. Stir continuously. When the mixture is almost boiling, pour the oysters and their liquid into the pot. Season with salt, pepper and cayenne pepper. Stir continuously until the oysters curl at the ends. When the oysters curl, the stew is finished cooking.

Open a bottle of white wine, turn the lights low and serve.

Eleven

The next morning, I jumped out of bed at six and stared at myself in the mirror. I didn't like what I saw. For once it wasn't just the wild corkscrew curls, ash blonde mixed with bits of silver. It wasn't even the blistering forehead or the missing eyebrows. I saw a Grade A malingering coward.

I straightened my shoulders. "Today," I told the coward, "would be a good time to start relying on yourself. Settle Phil's hash, and if that's not possible, find a way to make your own money again. Get that damn wallet back to the woman everyone loves to hate. Convince the police about the woman in the Escalade. Find the money for the wiring, even if you have to plead with the bank manager for a mortgage. Get started on the book, go see Rafaël and Marietta. Just stop futzing about and whining over this project. And most important, get yourself back to that rehab centre and clear your name. While you're at it, don't forget Tolstoy has an appointment at the V-E-T this afternoon for his shots."

Of course, it was too early to do any of those things. The Caisse Populaire didn't open until ten a.m., Marietta and Rafaël were probably snoozing, Philip refused to answer any of his phones, and the day admin staff wouldn't have arrived at the rehab centre. So Tolstoy and I tumbled out of the house for a long walk. With the weather still in record heat condition and my long list of chores, it was the last opportunity to take him for a cool stroll. He needed it, and so did I. I planned to shower and shampoo and get going right after the country walk, so I caught up my out-of-control hair with a scrunchie and hoped I wouldn't see anyone I cared about.

We ambled down the driveway and set out along Chemin des cèdres. Lucky for us, there are few Ottawa-bound drivers on this road, so no need to leap into ditches to avoid coffee-swilling commuters. The air was already warm, but not unbearable. I listened to the hum of insects and the cheer-cheer-cheer from the forty-foot cedar at the end of my driveway. I glanced up to see the brilliant red flash of a male cardinal making his morning rounds. His peachy little mate swooped after him. The past few years, we'd had three breeding pairs of cardinals in our little enclave. Later in the season, I could expect to see the young ones along for the family outing. How would any of them survive Jean-Claude's plans?

An hour later, we had made the loop along the road and were panting towards the house. We were feeling great and planning to dip our feet in the river. A black Buick Lesabre sat idling, windows closed, air conditioning running, as I approached. The engine stopped, the door opened and my insurance agent stepped out, a sheepish half-smile on his pale, freckled face. He must have been well past sixty-five, but Faron Findlay's not likely to retire, ever. He's been my agent as long as I've been in St. Aubaine, and before that he was Aunt Kit's. He's always been helpful and gentlemanly about any small embarrassments over bounced cheques. I am always glad to see Faron, but doubly so because I didn't owe him anything at this point. My insurance was up-to-date and paid.

"Hi there, Fiona," he said, extending his hand. Tolstoy growled. Faron stepped back. His few sprigs of white hair stood up.

"Sorry about that," I said. "Don't be rude, Tolstoy." Tolstoy bared his teeth. "I don't know what's wrong with him, Faron. It's not like him at all. He's the friendliest dog in the world. You know that."

Faron stayed flattened against the car. Maybe he didn't know that.

"Tolstoy, behave."

Another, deeper growl. I was shocked. I had so many things on my mind, and the one creature I could always count on for good behaviour was letting me down.

"Maybe he has a burr stuck between his toes or something. I'll just take him inside and check. Want to join me for a coffee on the porch? I can make iced coffee for you if you like. Might as well enjoy the best part of the day. Even though I still can't afford whatever it is that you are about to propose."

He shook his head, sadly. "Can't stay. I have a couple of early appointments. I just needed to get this out of the way."

I blinked. "Get what out of the way?"

"It's hard for me, Fiona. I've always liked you. I remember you way back when you were just a wee girlie visiting here."

I grinned at him. "I remember you too. I think Aunt Kit was a bit sweet on you. She always baked her special cake if she knew you were dropping by."

"Please don't make this any harder, Fiona."

"Make what harder? What are you talking about? Are you retiring or something, Faron?"

He took a deep breath. Stood straighter. It wasn't that hot yet, but I could see the front of his white shirt sticking damply to him. "I'm so sorry, Fiona, but even after our long history, Findlay Insurance will no longer be able to insure your home."

Tolstoy snarled and lunged. I grabbed him by the collar and marched him into the house. A minute later, I returned. "I must have misunderstood."

"You didn't. Please understand that I have tried everything to see if I can change that, but…"

"Why not? Why can't you insure it? You've insured it for at least fifty years."

"The house is unsafe."

"It is not."

"You had a problem with your wiring. Had an electrician in."

"Yes."

"We've been informed that this place is a death trap. You probably shouldn't even be living here, Fiona."

"Wait a minute," I said. "The electrician told you that?"

He nodded.

"But he didn't tell me that it was unsafe."

"Are you sure?"

"He said it needed work. And he said he'd fix it. But he never said it would affect my insurance. He never mentioned death trap. That sort of thing sticks in your mind."

"You're a writer. Sometimes you're caught up in your work. A bit vague, forgetful."

"Death trap, Faron. Not so forgettable. But my point is, why would the electrician tell *you*? Why did you ask him about my house in the first place? Why wouldn't you ask me?"

"I didn't ask. He just volunteered the information."

"He walked into your office and told you about my house?"

"Fiona, please. This is hard enough."

"I want to know what's going on. The electrician seemed like a nice guy. I didn't realize he had anything against me."

"I don't think he does. He's probably doing you a favour. Maybe this could save your life. That was the impression I got. I was standing in the Chez waiting for my Chinese take-out, and we got to talking. He knew I was in insurance, and he started telling me about this house that he'd been working on.

Said he was worried. Said…"

"He said he could fix it. He was going to give me a price. He didn't mention to me that I shouldn't be living here, that my life might be in danger. So I don't believe this."

Faron Findlay opened the door of his car. "I have no choice. I have to cancel your policy. But I can reinstate it the minute you get the work done, bring the place up to code. You just call me, and I'll drop everything. I feel terrible. But not as terrible as I would if I was at your funeral."

He reached over and handed me an envelope. "You'll receive an official notice of this by registered mail, but I felt I had to tell you face to face first. After all…"

I stood frozen in the driveway and watched Faron speed off. I found I couldn't even move as he rounded the bend and disappeared down the green and leafy road. I opened the envelope and read the cancellation notice. I'd just raised my head again when Jean-Claude cruised by, slowly, in his silver Porsche Carrera.

He gave me a jaunty little wave.

*   *   *

Josey had spent the night back at her own cabin. Uncle Mike had needed a bit of help, apparently, and her burn seemed to be healing nicely. But she managed to get back to town before I left. She listened with horror to the insurance news.

"It's so not fair, Miz Silk. You can't let him get away with it."

"What choice do I have? I don't have the money to get the wiring fixed yet, although I am working on it. I didn't think it was so bad. The house isn't really worth anything anyway, you know that. But I really don't want it to go up in smoke. Tolstoy doesn't either. And you spend a lot of time here too. You're not going to be able to spend the night until we get this all settled."

"I bet that electrician's in his lordship's pocket."

"Obviously, he must be. Hélène certainly wouldn't be behind it. I can't think of anyone else. Everyone in town knows who Faron Findlay is. But even so…"

"We can't let him get away with it. He's trying to intimidate you into selling to him."

"I realize that. And I'm not going to sell to him, but it doesn't change the fact that I now have a big problem."

Josey scowled. "I'm going to find that electrician to tell him what I think of him."

"You think he's going to admit that he caused me to lose my insurance coverage for a few under-the-table bucks from Jean-Claude? That has to be illegal. Even in St. Aubaine."

"Leave it to me."

"No, Josey. Jean-Claude plays dirty. You know that. We have enough trouble without looking for any more. Promise."

"Okay, but I'm going to find you another electrician, one who will run a tab. So if you don't mind, I'll start packing up the kitchen stuff. I'll find someone to fix your wiring. I'll move the stuff in your office too so he can get at the panel."

"Sure," I said, feeling too distracted to argue. Anyway, it seemed like a good idea.

"Okay. The guy's name is Tom, if he shows up. He might say Mike Thring sent him. Don't worry. He'll be sober."

One of Uncle Mike's buddies? Oh well, it wasn't like I had anything worth stealing.

It was just before nine in the morning. Josey went off to pack everything not nailed down while I answered the door with a cup of freshly brewed coffee in my hand. It was still early enough to swallow hot liquid, although according to the weather guy, that window was about to close. Should I have been surprised to see Sarrazin on my doorstep so early? In retrospect, perhaps not.

Sarrazin perused the river view, then flicked his gaze to the trees and to my little garden patch, where my Asian lilies were making headway because of the hot weather.

"Hello," I said.

He checked out the passage of a pair of cardinals swooping toward the feeder.

"Something wrong?" I said.

"Why do you ask?"

No eye contact, for one thing. Shuffling feet, for another. Not typical of Sarrazin, a cop who wears the easy confidence of twenty-five plus years of service.

"No reason," I said. "How about coffee? Before it gets too hot to drink it."

Sarrazin accepted the offer, and we took it outside on the porch, not to interfere with the packing.

"So," I said, after a long while. "What brings you here today?"

He cleared his throat. I smiled encouragingly. Never make the big policeman angry has always been my motto.

"We've had a complaint."

"What now?" I had no idea where we were going, so I decided not to get unnecessarily unsettled, at least until I needed to.

"It could lead to the laying of charges."

"Oh."

"Do you have any idea what I'm talking about?"

I shook my head. "You'll have to tell me."

"It's from the staff at the rehab centre."

"Oh, for heaven's sake. That crazy residents' aide, Paulette? I'm heading over there today to set the record straight."

"There are allegations that you attempted to fraudulently obtain money and goods from a patient."

173

"I don't believe this. They can allege all they want. It didn't happen. I was visiting Marc-André Paradis. I foolishly told him about the trouble I was having. He wanted to help."

Sarrazin watched a blue jay swoop down to the bird feeder, scaring off the cardinals. I hoped he was at least listening.

I continued. "He offered me the money to pay my back taxes."

"A loan?"

"Yes. I told him I couldn't accept it, and he insisted, and we were going around and around that mulberry bush."

"You didn't accept?"

"How could I take money from him? He's brain-damaged. He's helpless. He might not even know what he's saying, really. Although I think he did yesterday. But he might not remember it today. Anyway, it's a matter of principle."

"So you never said you would take any money, nor did you lead him to think you would?"

"That's right. I was trying to explain to him that I couldn't do that when this Paulette burst in. She may have been listening from the hallway or something, but she got it wrong anyway. She called security and made a big fuss. I'm not allowed back there."

"Huh."

"I know, it sounds weird, but that's the way it went. I believe she has a bit of crush on him. Marc-André is very attractive to women, you know." I felt a puce blush racing up my neck as I said this.

"I guess so," he said.

"I never thought she'd call the police. Isn't that a bit extreme?"

"They claim you were trying to extort money from a seriously disabled individual. That is a crime."

"But it never happened. Either she misinterpreted, or else she just wanted to get me away from him. You can ask Marc-

174

André what happened. He'll tell you."

"We will. I just don't know if that will be enough."

"My word against hers, you mean."

"Pretty much." He put down his coffee cup. "I think those lilies over there are going to need a bit of water," he said before he rumbled off, leaving me to face my ruined morning.

Before I left, I headed into the office, where Josey was packing with single-minded concentration.

"Please leave out the stuff for my cookbook project, Josey. I'm going to get at it full steam as soon as I take care of a bit of business this morning."

"Sure thing, Miz Silk. I already put them on the kitchen table with the rest of the library books and the recipes that people have given you."

"Thanks. Do you really have to take everything off the wall?"

"Don't want this new electrician to do any damage, do we? Sometimes they have to go behind the walls and up in the ceiling."

"I guess. I've got a really crazy day, but if you're free later, I'd like you to come back with me to Hull before the staff changes to the afternoon shift. I'll stay outside the rehab, but I'd like you to go in and explain to Marc-André why I won't be able to visit. Right now, I'm headed out to do a lot of stuff I should have done a long time ago."

*   *   *

The manager at the Caisse Pop was not understanding about the wiring situation. Something about taking a loan against a house that might burn down before the day was out. Even when I explained that he had nothing to lose, as the lot was

175

probably worth more without the house, he still gave the mortgage the thumbs down. Of course, he did golf with Jean-Claude. I added "find a new bank" to my list of things to do.

Next I made my way to the Wallingford Estate in search of the elusive Harriet Crowder. At least this time I was able to talk my way past the security folk. Maybe I seemed harmless without my eyebrows. Maybe they felt sorry for me because of my red and blistered forehead. Who knows?

Once inside, I found Chelsea Brazeau, the very chilly Anabel's lovely, warm executive assistant, fluttering about in the office. She was wearing a sharp yellow dress and jacket that set off her lustrous honey-brown hair and hazel eyes. She smiled in welcome. For a brief second, I wondered why I hadn't been born with lovely, smooth, rich chestnut hair like that. Hair that would always look great. And the confident personality that seemed to go with it. Of course, it would have been nice to be twenty-five again too. Except for egotistical trophy hunters like Jean-Claude who preferred blonde and Botoxed, I thought most men would fall for her at the first sign of that melting smile.

"You get full marks for getting past security," she said with a grin. "Unfortunately, Harriet's not available. I don't even know where she is. But you can often find her sitting in her vehicle with the motor running to keep cool while she makes her phone calls out of earshot. She's very secretive."

"Huh," I said. "Well, please pass on this message. I'm out most of the day, but I'll be home tonight. And she could leave a message for me, if that's not convenient. Here's my address, here's my phone number. If I haven't heard from her tonight, I'll send the wallet by registered post tomorrow, to the address I found in her ID."

"Ooh," said Chelsea. "Good luck. Just keep in mind that she's very vindictive."

"It's not going to be my problem any more. She can sue me if she wants."

Chelsea grimaced. "Well, she's no Miss Congeniality, but she probably won't really sue you. Very likely no one's told her. I tried to after we first spoke, but she was already on the warpath, and she cut me off. She's her own worst enemy. I left her a note in her pigeonhole." She turned and pointed to a large wall of boxes with names on them. The one marked HARRIET was crammed with paper and yellow messages.

A voice behind me made me jump. "There's plenty to do here without providing message services to the villagers." I turned to face Anabel Huffington-Chabot. She strode past me to the far side of the desk. She scowled at me and ignored her EA.

Chelsea interjected mildly. "But Anabel, Fiona is just trying to help. Couldn't we…?"

Oops. Apparently not. I pitied Chelsea working in that environment.

"Thanks, Chelsea. Sorry to disturb." I felt I could trust Chelsea to deliver the message. I got the impression she'd be happy to help me, but it would have to be behind Anabel's cold, hard back.

I stepped into the hallway and nearly knocked over pudgy little Brady, still wearing his cowboy boots. He made a sympathetic face, ran his hand over his fauxhawk, and pretended he hadn't been listening at the door.

A pattern was emerging. It reminded me of how glad I was to work for myself, despite the setbacks.

*   *   *

Philip was still not returning calls. No big shock there. But I'd decided I was finished with his BS at this point. When I reached his office in the old Hull sector, I was ready for war. This time, no matter what, I intended to come away with a cheque. He could deduct it from the settlement. He could charge me interest. He could wreck the knees of his Harry Rosen suit while he hid under the desk, but I damn well didn't plan to leave empty-handed.

I pulled up in front of the impressive historic home on Rue Laurier that housed his legal office. For the record, Phil owned the building and rented out the second floor to a notary public and the third to an interior designer. He owned the building next door as well, and two or three others in the neighbourhood. I parked on the street and trotted up to the door. The first part of the battle would be getting past Irene. But I was prepared. I'd given myself one long pep talk all the way down from St. Aubaine.

I hadn't left a message to say I was coming, because that would have eliminated the element of surprise. I stomped up the stairs and yanked at the door. It failed to open.

I checked my watch. Just before noon. Prime business hours. Philip might have been in court or at a meeting or even on one of his preferred golf courses, but where was Irene? As long as I'd known her, she'd taken her lunch and breaks in the office. Not at her desk, of course, but in the tiny staff room in the rear of the office.

After five minutes of banging on the door, I stood back. Fine. I ignored the amused glances from two people heading upstairs. I tried the second floor office, then the third. Even when I asked nicely in French, no one could tell me anything about Philip or Irene. The usual shrugs and a *"désolé, madame"* or two. The back door had a tiny window into the small staff room. No Irene there. No Philip either. Neither car was parked in the reserved spots.

What was going on?

                    *   *   *

It felt very odd parking in front of the home that I'd shared
with Philip. I hadn't been near it since my stormy departure
more than three years earlier. It was a beautiful place set on
immaculate lawns. You might expect that I would have a pang
of regret. I was pangless, although I did notice that my fingers
were white from gripping the steering wheel.

I pulled up by the front stairs. I looked around. Philip had
treated himself to a brand new BMW M5-E60, perfect for
driving a single lawyer from home to work to golf club.
Especially perfect for someone who hadn't settled with his ex-
wife. The Beamer was nowhere to be seen. I tried the doorbell.
No answer. I strolled around to the back of the house. No
Philip. He was still a creature of habit, though. I extracted the
spare key from the hiding place under the back porch and let
myself in. First, I checked the garage. No car.

Of course, I felt furtive and even slightly criminal. I had to
remind myself that I was still a half-owner of this house. I
hurried into the kitchen to leave him a note. I stood still,
shocked. A few dishes lay scattered around the counter. A half-
full cup of cold coffee waited on the table. Papers had been
tossed in disarray onto the ceramic tile floor. What was going
on? I headed upstairs. His book-lined study was in its usual
immaculate order. I stopped and peeked through the bedroom
door at the king-size bed we'd shared. Unlike me, Philip had
always been a neat sleeper. His side of the bed had obviously
been slept in. The sheets were tossed back in a tangle. The
pillow lay on the floor.

My heart raced. Philip could no more stand to leave the
house with his bed unmade than he would tolerate a family of
rats residing in his imported German toaster.

It didn't make sense.

I felt a bit shaky as I made my way down the stairs, out through the kitchen towards the back door. This time I saw something I'd missed before. Near the phone in the kitchen, a glass lay shattered on the ceramic tile. On the way out, I stooped and felt the soil in the droopy flower pots on the shady side of the patio. Bone dry. Wherever Philip was, he hadn't been home for a while. And he must have been in a state when he was last there. Unmade bed, dirty dishes, broken glass. I never thought I'd see anything like that in Philip's house.

I turned around and checked out the main level again. Had he been kidnapped? Had a burglar broken in? Or a vandal? Had he been tied up and locked in a closet while some thief made off with his car? I headed back upstairs. I checked each storage area. All were prime examples of the anal-retentive personality. Philip's own walk-in closet was in its usual impeccable state. But in the bathroom, towels lay on the floor. Dirty water stagnated in the sink. It seemed to me that these things were the mark of a distracted person rather than a struggle. Had Philip been too distressed about something to make his bed, sweep up the broken mug and water the dying plant?

When we'd last spoken, he'd been upset by Danny's death, for sure, but he'd still sounded like the same old fusspot. Something else must have precipitated this. Something worse. I asked myself what could be worse than finding out that your friend and business partner had been killed?

I opened the bathroom linen cabinet and checked. As usual, a year's supply of toilet paper, neatly stacked. Extra toothpaste for sensitive teeth, boxes of tissues, hair products to keep baldness at bay, Egyptian cotton towels. Everything you might expect and lots of it. But his leather toiletry kit was gone.

In the study, I searched for something that might give me

Irene's home address. I had a vague recollection of where she lived, but not enough to do me any good. Despite my best efforts, I probably left the study worse than I found it. Luckily, I turned up a spare set of keys to the downtown office. I stuck those in my pocket.

Before I headed out, I picked up the phone and called Sgt. Sarrazin. Oddly enough, I knew his phone number by heart. I listed the things that had bothered me about Philip's departure in a message and asked him to follow up. I left my cell phone number, explaining I was on the run. Before leaving, I checked the call display on Philip's phone. He'd had a lot of calls from Danny Dupree and one from a blocked number. That was all. Phil's social life definitely hadn't improved.

I watered the droopy plant on the way out. I kept the key.

Piña Colada Popsicles

Contributed by Dr. Liz Prentiss

The ultimate tropical drink.

2 ounces rum (light or dark)—chilled
5 ounces pineapple juice—chilled
2 ounces coconut cream—chilled
3 ice cubes

Pour the rum, pineapple juice, coconut cream and ice cubes into a blender and whir for several seconds until well mixed. Better yet, get someone else to do that for you. Pour mixture into popsicle forms overnight or until frozen (may take longer).

Or just forget the freezer part, put in a glass, top with a maraschino cherry and chug away.

Twelve

My cell phone was out of range just long enough to miss Sgt. Sarrazin's response to my call.

"About your call," his message said. "Your husband's an adult, and he's been separated from you for nearly three years, unless I hear wrong. We don't usually follow up over broken coffee mugs and unmade beds."

I hoped he was right.

The cell phone buzzed. "Sgt. Sarrazin?" I said. "It's just that you don't really know Philip. Honestly, this is so out of character—"

"Fiona, forget the police for once. It's me. Liz."

"Oh, Liz. Something's wrong with Philip. He left the—"

"Who cares about that tightwad? I don't have all day, Fiona. But I do have a recipe for that book you keep fussing about."

"What?"

"Piña colada popsicles."

"I'm sorry. Did you say *you* had a *recipe?*"

"Very funny. I'm doing you a favour. No need for sarcasm. I'll drop it off next time I'm by the house. I have to go now. I have patients waiting."

On the way home, I stopped off at L'Épicerie to pick up something to eat. Josey was chewing the fat with Woody when I walked in. They both wore expressions of barely contained glee. I tried to suppress my alarm.

Woody said, "Hoo boy, wait'll you hear this."

Josey's freckles stood out almost three-dimensionally. "Guess what?"

"Just tell me."

"That aide? The one where Marc-André is?"

"Yes. I know who you mean. Paulette. What about her?"

"Uncle Mike drove me in to Hull, Miz Silk. Remember you said you would drive me in, and I would tell Marc-André what happened and why you couldn't visit him. You were real busy today, and it would have been a waste of your time to wait outside. So Uncle Mike and me worked together like a team. Family, eh?"

My head buzzed briefly.

"You want to know what we found out?" she said.

"Sure."

"Paulette just recently arranged to transfer into that area."

"Who told you that?"

"I have my sources. I know somebody who was able to find out. Uncle Mike helped. He's real good with people. He has a contact in Personnel at the rehab."

Woody guffawed from his wheelchair. "Like to hear how that would hold up in court."

"Okay, I no longer want to know how you found out. But I think you can get into trouble doing things like that."

"Things like what?"

"Like whatever you did. Personnel records. Privacy issues. I hate to even think about it."

"We were just people talking to people. And there's more."

"Come on, Josey. I don't think…"

"So you don't want to know about the Jean-Claude connection?"

Damn. "Connection?"

Woody was chortling away. "I think she's got you."

Josey said, "It's okay. I'd hate to compromise your integrity or however you say that."

"Go ahead. Just this once. Compromise my integrity. What connection?"

She took a deep breath. Woody continued to chuckle and twirl all through this exchange.

Finally, I snapped. "Josey!"

"She's his lordship's cousin," Josey shouted triumphantly.

"Well, hell," Woody said, stopping. "That *is* news."

Josey said, "I bet your tame cop will want to hear that."

"I don't actually have my own cop. Tame or otherwise. Anyway, everyone in this entire region seems to be related to everyone else. There's no law against being someone's cousin."

"You think? She was working for him until just last week. Before she became a resident's aide."

"Oh."

"He put in a word with someone high up at the rehab. And that word came down to Personnel. She wanted to work in that same section where Marc-André is. Although nobody mentioned his name. And why do you think that was?"

"To undermine my relationship with Marc-André? But that's horrible. Marc-André needs help and support, and I need to be there for him. That whole situation at the hospital was so stressful. Not to mention, I could be charged with trying to extort money from him."

"Bingo," Josey said. "He's chipping away at you. I told you he's a cruel man."

"I believe I will mention this to Sgt. Sarrazin. I'll tell him I heard a rumour. He can follow up legally."

"It's okay," Josey said. "I already let him know."

"But he won't believe you."

"Come on, Miz Silk. I didn't make the call myself. Let's just say he got an anonymous tip."

"Oh, my God."

"Don't thank me, Miz Silk. What's the good of having an executive assistant, if I can't help you out of trouble?"

Of course, it explained the second message from Sarrazin on my cell phone: "And the other thing? You might want to rein in that Thring girl. Maybe if you just encouraged her to go to school, she might stay out of trouble for a day or two."

I supposed he'd recognized Uncle Mike's voice and unique ability to slur his words. The problem was, he didn't indicate how he would react to the information.

I was so distracted I almost forgot about the appointment with the V-E-T.

*   *   *

I popped home to pick up Tolstoy and passed the mail truck. I raced for the mailbox. Sure enough, a small XpressPost envelope from Lola. I opened it with shaking hands and found a cheque large enough to settle the tax bill, fund the rewiring project and a new bottle of Courvoisier. Maybe even a few frozen diet dinners. Yee-haw!

I was busy bribing Tolstoy to leave the basement when Josey arrived, notebook in hand. She glanced at her watch.

I said, "When did you start wearing glasses?"

"They're not real. I got them at the Roi du dollar. They make me look more serious. That's important for an executive assistant."

There was no value in telling her she looked like a kid with cowlicks and freckles wearing dollar store specs with clear glass. Why ruin her day?

She said. "I'm glad you're dressed up a bit. Rafaël is making time to see you right after they finish shooting. This is great news for us."

"But I have to take Tolstoy to the V-E-T for his S-H-O-T-S,

so I can't do it right away. And I have to dress down a bit for that. You know there's always a bit of wrestling involved. Plus I have to pay my taxes today. The tax wicket is open late today, and so is the Caisse, so I can get that off my mind."

"Oh boy, Miz Silk. I didn't know you had an appointment you know where for you know whats."

"I never thought to mention it."

"Well, how am I supposed to be your executive assistant if you keep me in the dark about things?"

I was about to protest my innocence when I realized what a waste of words that would be. I said, "Good point. I'll get Tolstoy ready. You take care of the cheque. I don't want to forget it and have to come back."

"Sure, right away," she said, calling over her shoulder. "Hey, this is great! I'll clean out your car to celebrate!"

Tolstoy had been lured up the stairs by a dog biscuit, and I had the leash behind me, ready to snap it on, when she returned. "All your junk's in the garbage can, Miz Silk. The car looks much better. The cheque's in the glove compartment. But getting back to Rafaël, the problem is that he's a big star, and it wasn't easy getting an appointment with him. Everyone wants to see him and talk to him. There are food groupies all over, and they'd turn green if they knew."

"I understand, but I can't cancel the vet this late. Oops."

Tolstoy bolted out of the hallway and into the living room. It took the two of us five sweaty hard-breathing minutes to finally corner him. I gave him a treat and caught my breath. "I hate V-E-T day."

Josey said, "It's just a matter of time until he learns to spell it."

A few more treats got the usually amiable Tolstoy into the Skylark. Josey and I hopped in too.

"Just remember," she said, "act natural. Don't be intimidated.

When we see him, don't let the fact that he is a huge star in the food biz throw you off. He's just a normal human being, even if he looks like a movie star, and his show is a mega hit and he has magazines and cookbooks and…"

"I'll try to pull myself together," I said. Privately, I thought it couldn't be nearly as stressful as the V-E-T.

I turned the key. Nothing. I tried again. Still nothing.

I should be used to non-performing cars, but I'm always caught by surprise when they let me down. Hélène would have given us a lift if we'd asked, but she had a regular manicure scheduled every Thursday at this time. Liz would be tied up with patients, and Tolstoy's not good on a bike. No choice but to call a cab.

"Want me to check under the hood?" Josey yelled out as I called Cyril Hemphill on my cell phone.

I shouted over my shoulder, "Just make sure you-know-who doesn't escape."

"Right," she said, "before we get to the you-know-what."

Five minutes later, Cyril sprayed gravel as he spun his cab into the driveway. He opened the passenger door. Tolstoy hopped in right away. He still loved Cyril, in part because we have never been known to take a cab to the you-know-what. As Cyril is paunchy and bald with quite remarkable ear hair, he accepts affection where he finds it.

I waited until I cut a deal with Cyril. "I'll have to run a tab," I said. "Until a cheque clears."

"Oh, sure. That the one from the dirty book?"

"What?"

"Whole town's talking about that, all right."

"I bet it is."

"Never mind. Yer credit's good with me. You know the terms. I bet this one will make you a mint. Even if your ex is

hanging you out to dry. You can show him a thing or two."
Cyril turned to leer at us as we climbed into the back of the cab.

Josey leaned forward and said, "What terms?"

"Not your business, girlie."

"Yes, it is. I'm her executive assistant."

"That a fact?" Cyril barely suppressed a snicker.

Josey snapped. "Yes, it is. What are the terms?"

"Interest and all that. It's between me and Mrs. Silk."

Josey narrowed her eyes. "Not any more it isn't. Everything goes through me."

I could have leaned forward myself at this point and established my personal sovereignty. However, in the face of having someone else deal with the slippery, usurious Cyril, a little loss of autonomy was a small price to pay.

"Twenty-eight per cent."

"Too high."

"Same as Visa."

"Not our problem. Ten per cent, starting at the end of the month of the debt. Nothing if the debt is discharged first," Josey said. For some reason, she always sounds like a forty-year-old accountant when discussing money. I attributed it to business programs on the damn satellite service.

"Don't insult me, girlie."

Josey shrugged. "It's not like you're the only game in town."

This was a nervy bluff, because, in fact, Cyril was the only game in town.

"Take it or leave it," said the only game in town.

"We'll leave it. Come on, Miz Silk, Tolstoy. We're calling my Uncle Mike."

Cyril's bald head turned a peculiar shade of crimson. "What are you talking about, girlie. Your uncle Mike's probably having a siesta in the slammer."

"Not today, he isn't. Got out early. Released on his own recognizance. And he's sober as a judge. He'll be happy to drive Miz Silk. Won't charge her anything, never mind interest." Josey swung open the door.

I imagine that Cyril and I were equally astounded by this development. Still, there's no point in having an executive assistant if you're not going to take advantage. Of course, if the bluff failed, I would have to cancel the appointment, because I was pretty sure that Uncle Mike never really sobered up, recognizance notwithstanding. Still, I slid back out of the car. I knew what team I was on.

"Eighteen," Cyril said.

"Eight," Josey said.

"What? That's not the way it works."

Josey narrowed her eyes at him. "It is now."

They sawed off at nine. No interest for the first thirty days. It worked for me. Tolstoy hopped back in and licked Cyril's ear in an expression of solidarity.

"We have an appointment with Rafaël up at Wallingford Estate after the V-E-T," Josey said haughtily. "We'll need you to wait to take us home."

"Sure thing, Mrs. Silk," Cyril said, making eye contact with me. "I'll be waiting."

"With the meter off," Josey said.

*　　*　　*

Tolstoy was not in a forgiving mood after his rabies shot, but I figured some takeout fries from the Chez would fix that. I planned to take care of that the minute we finished with Rafaël.

Jean-Claude showed up at the Wallingford Estate just ahead of us. He buttoned the middle button of his silk suit and curled his lip at us as we approached the house. He'd already vanished from sight as we entered.

Brady was passing through the foyer. He clutched his clipboard in front of him and shuffled his cowboy boots nervously.

A siren sounded along Rue Principale, drowning out what he said.

Josey said, "What?"

"He's not available," Brady said, looking miserable.

"Are they still shooting?" I interjected.

"No. They finished a while ago, and I'm afraid he had to leave."

"Well, we'd like to reschedule," Josey said, whipping out her agenda.

It was time for me to act like a functioning adult. Not my best thing, admittedly, but I had to try.

"Thank you. We were very happy to have this appointment, but things do come up. Could you thank Rafaël for making room for us in his busy schedule and tell him I hope we can get together for a few minutes when it's convenient for him." I smiled, almost sincerely.

Josey looked like she might self-combust. Brady, on the other hand, seemed grateful. "It's not his fault," he whispered. "Someone *else* has a bee in her bonnet. I'll let him know what you said. He probably has no idea what's going on."

"What about Marietta?"

"She's not available either."

Josey said, "Does this have something to do with Miz Huffington-Chabot and a certain local big cheese?"

Brady flushed to the top of his fauxhawk. He turned to leave.

"One last attempt to track down Harriet."

"Harriet? Good luck if you find her. She didn't even show up for the shoot today. Or yesterday. That's unheard of, even for the Red Devil. Anabel's having a hissy fit over it. It puts a lot of stress on everyone. Lucky for us, Rafaël and Marietta are easy to deal with. Sorry, I've got to go."

He turned and scurried off down the hallway toward the kitchen area. Josey's blue eyes were narrowed and stormy as she came stomping out of the Wallingford estate.

"Something's going on, Miss Silk. I smell a rat."

I smelled the same large, silk-clad, hyphenated rat. As we headed for the car, Jean-Claude passed us in the Porsche. He waved and gave us one of his custom-made humourless smiles. The ones that make your spine snap.

Tolstoy gave his opinion by lifting his leg and sprinkling the decorative juniper outside the house.

I didn't bother trying to shout over the noise as a pair of fire engines roared down Rue Principale, drowning out all other sounds. I was wondering about Harriet Crowder and what would possess a producer to miss a shooting day.

Apparently Josey had places to go, people to see and things to do, and I was happy to toodle about the village without an executive assistant. I planned to pick up a bit of food at Woody's, deposit the advance cheque, then settle my tax bill by post-dated cheque, since the Caisse always holds my cheques until they clear. But Jean-Claude's silver Porsche was now parked right in front of the Caisse, and I also planned to avoid him. I headed for City Hall, or Hôtel de Ville, as we call it in these parts. This was the one day of the week when they had late hours for the convenience of the locals wishing to have their taxes squeezed out of them.

The middle-aged clerk at the tax wicket took my post-dated cheque and handled it as though it contained anthrax spores.

"A post-dated cheque?" she said. "That account is in serious arrears."

My familiar puce blush raced up my neck and across my face. "I realize that," I said, "and I'm very sorry. I've been waiting for a payment to come in, and it has finally arrived. I'm going to deposit it now, and in five days it will clear. Because it's a large amount, and they..."

She sighed. "I don't know. I'll have to get authorization for this."

"No problem," I said. "I'll talk to your supervisor." Hey maybe some of Josey's qualities were rubbing off on me.

"He's not here."

"Ah."

"You'll have to come back."

"When will he be in?"

"Next week. He's sick."

"I'm just trying to avoid an extra trip back in order to pay you the money that I owe you. I'm quite far out of town and—"

"Chemin des cèdres? Just a couple of miles."

"Well, my car's not working very well."

"That's not our problem. You need to settle your tax account."

"Well, I'm trying to pay it."

"I've already explained that I am not authorized to accept postdated cheques."

"Everyone else does. I've done it in the past." Was this woman connected to Jean-Claude too?

"Sorry, you'll have to come back."

"I'd like to speak to your supervisor's supervisor."

She wrinkled her unattractive nose. "You're not allowed to have dogs in here, you know."

"Fine, I'll put the dog outside, but then I'd want to speak to your supervisor's supervisor."

"I'm not sure if she's here."

"Look, you can deal with me or you can deal with my executive assistant. *I* am a wimp. *She* has a tendency to contact the media. So please get authorization to accept this cheque, and the dog and I will be on our way."

I succeeded after a couple more conversational loops like that. I felt such relief at getting the post-dated cheque accepted that I decided to drop in and share the news with Woody. He was in a fine mood and agreed to bridge funding for my few purchases. He advanced me a few dollars for a bottle of Courvoisier. I got some hummus and tabouli from him, plus a bit of almond butter and a loaf of the artisan bread that he sells. It is definitely to die for.

After a quick trip to the Régie d'alcool, I headed to the Caisse to deposit the advance cheque. Jean-Claude had moved on. How can someone who is such a wheeler-dealer spend so much time idling in his vehicle yakking on his cell? When did he work? At any rate, I felt relaxed as I pushed open the door and waved to Giselle, my favourite teller. This was indeed a happy day. As I went to fill out the deposit slip, the happy fell right out of the day.

Where was the advance cheque?

Ah. Right. In the glove compartment of the car. Of course. I'd left the piece of paper that was going to save my bacon in the non-performing Skylark.

"Listen," Giselle said, "I hear you're writing a cookbook that's supposed to be pretty—"

"Darn. I forgot the cheque."

"But I have a recipe for you! Perfect for a special evening by the river."

"I'll be back." I fled.

Of course, it would mean finding Cyril and burning through a few more bucks returning to get the cheque, then roaring back to town.

Cyril was a whole lot happier about the situation than I was. I couldn't spot Josey on our way back to the house. I figured we'd get her the next time around.

Sex on the Beach

Courtesy of Giselle from the Caisse Populaire

1 ounce vodka
3/4 ounce peach schnapps
Cranberry juice
Grapefruit juice
1 blanket

Add vodka and peach schnapps to a highball glass. Fill with equal measures of cranberry juice and grapefruit juice, and stir.

Enjoy on secluded beach with someone special.

Thirteen

As soon as Cyril careened onto Chemin des cèdres, I spotted the plumes of smoke funneling high over the cedars and spruces. I shouted, and Cyril yanked at the steering wheel just in time to pull the cab over to the shoulder. A fire truck barrelled past us, sirens wailing, a firefighter swinging from the back.

"Pumper," Cyril said. Another fire truck rocketed by in its wake. "Tanker," Cyril added.

From the passenger seat, Tolstoy barked a piece of his mind at the fire trucks. He hates sirens almost as much as he hates being hot.

I knew from the direction of the smoke, there was only one place the truck could be headed. Cyril revved the engine and followed. As we screeched to a halt in the road, I gasped. Two other fire trucks were already there, and a half-dozen fire-fighters were hard at work. Soot rained down from the air. But that was the least of it. One end of my small house lay smouldering as three firefighters uncoupled the hoses from the pumper and started to spray. The powerful spray was aimed toward the living room end of the house, which was still standing, at least. In the face of it, defiant bursts of red-tinged flames shot up through the remaining part of the roof.

"Good thing they got respirator packs," Cyril said. "Smoke's bad."

I'd never experienced a smell like that. The faint scent of slow-smouldering cedar was overlaid with the stench of burning drywall, wire and roof shingles. A reek of melted plastic told me that I'd just lost my computer. Or maybe it was coming from the Skylark. It had taken me a minute to process the idea that the burnt-out metal skeleton next to the house was all that remained of the little car. I scrambled out of the cab. A firefighter wearing a respirator lumbered toward the house. An unfamiliar police officer in the blue uniform of our local force gestured for us to back away from the property.

Cyril parked on the other side of the street. I hooked Tolstoy up to his leash, and we stumbled to the perimeter of my lawn. Cyril puffed behind us. We watched as my own history and Aunt Kit's burned. Tolstoy whimpered.

Firefighters wearing masks rumbled toward the woods as the fire jumped from the house to the trees on the edge of the property. The tanker had roared across my lawn and down to the edge of the river.

"Gonna use the river water," Cyril said. "Probably too late for them trees."

I held my breath and watched as the hoses turned from the house to the cedars and maples, trying to stop the spread of a forest fire that could wipe out this side of St. Aubaine.

We watched, open-mouthed, as two firefighters aimed a stream of foam at what was left of the house.

"See that? That stuff is so powerful, one guy's holding the other guy to keep him steady," Cyril said.

I could hardly hear, the foam made so much noise. Tolstoy whimpered again. I stroked his silky white head. My heart was thundering. This was one of the few days that Tolstoy wouldn't have been hiding out in the basement crawlspace to escape the heat. "Just this once you can be grateful to the V-E-T."

A firefighter approached and pulled down his face mask. "Is there anyone in the house?"

I shook my head. "Just lucky my dog was with me."

"That's good," he said, "because—"

A horrible thought froze my brain. I opened my mouth, and nothing came out. No, it wasn't possible. The fire seemed to have started in the office. Where was Josey? Could she have come back from the village and let herself in? I grabbed his sleeve and tried to speak.

"Maybe," I croaked, "maybe there's a girl."

I could tell by the look in his eye that if she was in the raging fire, it would be too late. He turned and shouted to his colleagues. Over the shout, I heard something. Tolstoy barked and lunged backwards. A red pickup careened onto the lawn, and Josey jumped out. Uncle Mike waved from the truck. Possibly in no shape to walk.

"It's okay," I shouted to the firefighter. I pointed toward her. "She's here."

He raised his gloved hand and waved before turning back to the blaze.

Josey raced forward, cowlicks waving. I wrapped my arms around her and wept sooty tears. My life might have gone up in flames: my work and possessions and my few family heirlooms. But I wept more for what I hadn't lost. Josey and Tolstoy. I couldn't even chew her out for driving with Uncle Mike, although we'd have that discussion another time.

From the end of the house, a sharp bang issued.

"Oh, boy, Miz Silk," Josey said. "Maybe that's your Courvoisier."

I whirled as I heard my name shouted. Hélène Lamontagne was running across the grass toward us. Somehow she managed to look graceful, even moving quickly in her stylish wedge-heeled espadrilles, the jacket of her linen suit flapping in the sooty breeze.

She gave me a warm hug. Tears streaked her perfect make-up. "Oh, Fiona, *comme c'est affreux!* Are you all right? You look...*oh là là.* How could this happen?"

She turned to give Josey a matching hug, but Josey pulled away. I was just as surprised as Hélène by this.

"What is it, Josée? Are you hurt?"

The cornflower blue eyes blazed. Sooty tears ran down her freckled cheeks. "How can you live with yourself?"

Hélène and I said, "What?"

"You know what! And you do too, Miz Silk."

Hélène stared.

I whispered, "She must be in some kind of shock." No wonder; my home had been a refuge for her when Uncle Mike was in the slammer and even when he wasn't.

But Josey was staring straight at Hélène. "First he wrecked our appointment with Rafaël. Now his lordship has burned down Miz Silk's home and everything in it. She could have been killed! And Tolstoy too—"

Tolstoy whimpered and nuzzled Josey's hand. For once, she didn't stop what she was doing to stroke his fur. "… and he's your husband, and you know what he's like, so what kind of a friend does that make you? The kind that shows up at the funeral?"

I said, "Josey!"

She sobbed, "It's true, and you know it's true, and we're always just pretending that it's all right for her to be with him, taking orders and being afraid to stick up for what's right. And why? For a fancy house and an expensive car?"

Hélène stood, her lovely face white beneath the perfect make-up, her freshly manicured hands pressed against her mouth. Soot settled on her cream-coloured linen jacket and dress. She stared at Josey as if she'd been struck.

None of us noticed the looming arrival of F.X. Sarrazin until he cleared his throat loudly. Well, Uncle Mike might have spotted him, because the red pickup reversed and sped off.

Josey wasn't letting Sarrazin off the hook either. She reached him first, and by the time I got there, she was in mid-tirade. "And he'll get away with it because he uses his money to get a handle on everyone in St. Aubaine. The tax department wouldn't have been pushing Miz Silk if it hadn't been for him. They don't threaten other people like that. The insurance agent, he couldn't even give her a chance to get her wiring fixed. You know that he's behind that too. He got his cousin to work at the rehab and make false charges against Miz Silk. You're not going to do anything about that either."

"Josey!" I called out. But there was no stemming her words.

"And that woman he was holding hands with at Café Belle Rive, she's the one who made sure Miz Silk couldn't get her interview with Rafaël. He was just laughing at us all." She glared at Sarrazin. "And now this. Everything's ruined. And maybe the cops are in his pocket too, and that's just great, isn't it? There's no justice for anyone but Jean-Claude Lamontagne in this village."

She turned and stumbled toward her beat-up bicycle. I rushed after her and touched her arm. She pushed me away. "You let it happen, Miz Silk. You let everyone walk all over you like a doormat, and now look."

Tolstoy threw back his head and howled.

I watched as Josey pedalled the old bike furiously down Chemin des cèdres until THE THRING TO DO sign vanished around the bend. I stumbled over to join Hélène and Sarrazin. Hélène still stood staring. I put my arm around her, wordlessly.

"Not your fault," I managed. "She knows that, deep down. It's the shock. We're not ourselves."

Sarrazin was busy wiping smudges of soot from his face. He said, "Well, that sure was informative."

Whatever you could say about him, François Xavier Sarrazin was way too big to fit in anyone's pocket. Ever.

*   *   *

No matter how dramatic the events in your life, you are still going to need a safe place to sleep, a toothbrush, clothing, and access to a bathroom. I had a few choices, all of them untenable.

Once she'd regained the power of speech, Hélène had offered her luxurious guest suite, complete with marble ensuite bathroom, soaking tub and spa towels, but I couldn't bring myself to stay under Jean-Claude's roof. My old friend Kostas O'Carolan was out of town on a wool-buying expedition, or that might have been an option. Liz offered, and despite the temptation to drink her booze for a change, I wasn't sure how long either of us would survive in her one-bedroom "loft" condo. As much as I missed my chairs, I knew who'd end up sleeping on the floor. There was always Marc-André's empty house up the river. I had been keeping an eye on it for him, and it was clean and comfortable. But after the fracas at the hospital, I couldn't chance doing that. Josey's cabin was a no-go zone for so many reasons, all of them directly related to Uncle Mike.

Philip had the sprawling home we'd shared for years, but even though I had the key, it would only remind me that if Philip had settled up when he was supposed to, I would have paid my bills and updated my wiring. I wouldn't have been in this wretched situation.

I had not a cent toward a bed and breakfast or hotel.

That left Woody. I figured if I could survive standing outside my burning house, I'd live through the cigarette smoke for a few days. A can of Jolt cola or two probably wouldn't kill me either. Best of all, Woody had a giant air conditioner and not an environmental bone in his body, so his digs were always nineteen degrees. Normally I am mildly disapproving, but I knew that Tolstoy would be in heaven. I wouldn't have to worry about him. I would be right in the middle of the village, so not having a vehicle wouldn't be quite so much of a problem.

I spoke to Sarrazin. "If you need to talk to me, I'll be at Woody Quirke's place. If I'm not there, Woody will probably know where I am. Or try my cell."

Sarrazin seemed less than convinced. "You sure that's the place for you?"

He'd probably raided Woody looking for dope or something. Not that I would know anything about that.

"I'll be fine," I said. He raised an eyebrow. The unspoken words hung in the air. "If it doesn't work out, I'll find something else. It's the least of my problems."

"Yeah, I can see that."

"Thank you."

"I'm not such a bad guy, you know."

"I never thought you were," I fibbed.

*   *   *

It took a while to get the soot out of my hair and the stench off my body. Woody had installed a capacious shower, designed for a wheelchair. Tolstoy got a shampoo in there and was happy to cool off. Woody doesn't really subscribe to germ theory, so he had no problem with a large dog in the shower. I chose the soaker tub in the guest bathroom. Hélène had been kind enough to pick up two bras and two pairs of matching panties for me. The bra and panties were perfect, but the cotton sundress she'd brought was too small. I borrowed a T-shirt from Woody and a pair of baggy shorts. I tossed my own clothes into the washing machine.

203

Woody's renovation was quite wonderful: the smell of cedar was everywhere, plus light, fresh walls and comfortable window seats with cushions. The guest room had a handmade quilt and high-count cotton sheets. I don't know who he'd been expecting, but I was sure glad he'd done such a good job of it.

"This is great, Woody," I said, towelling my hair dry. "It looks so comfortable."

"Glad I can help, kiddo," he said. "You and pooch can stay here as long as you want."

"Thanks. I'll be able to take care of myself soon as the cheque clears."

"What? What is it? Why are you so pale? Here, you better sit down, kiddo."

I slumped into the nearest chair.

Woody said, "A bit of a delayed reaction to losing your house? You've had a big shock."

"The advance cheque," I croaked.

"What about it?"

"It was in the Skylark."

"That's rough."

"I wrote a post-dated cheque against it for the taxes."

He stared at me. "Oh crap, kiddo."

"I'd better make a call."

*   *   *

Lola's line rang on and on. Finally, the answering machine kicked in. "Hi, this is Lola. I will be at BookExpo Canada making things happen this week. Please leave a message, whoever you are, darling, and I'll get back to you as soon as I can."

Damn. I knew how busy Lola could get during the big trade show for the Canadian publishing industry. She'd be on the floor all day and out for dinner or industry parties until whenever. Then a round of breakfasts would start. She usually stayed in the conference hotel. Would she even pick up the message before the show was over? I left a babbling message talking about the fire and the cheque and the need for a replacement ASAP. I hoped she'd get it. I hoped she'd understand it if she did.

When I hung up, Woody was looking even more serious than before.

"Trouble, kiddo," he said. "That big cop wants to talk to you. He's not coming here, though. Wants you to meet him at the tea shop. Better than the cop shop, but don't you trust him any further than you can throw him. Listen, Tolstoy's okay. Leave him with me. He'll keep the customers in line."

*   *   *

I blinked at Sarrazin, amazed. I was used to him asking tough questions at the Sûreté and even at the Chez. It seemed just plain weird to be interviewed by the police in the cozy tea room atmosphere of Thé Pour Deux, surrounded by china teapots, delicate cups, lace-edged napkins and the subtle scents of imported teas and homemade shortbread. Sarrazin blinked back at me. It might have been because I was wearing Woody's shorts and Marijuana Party T-shirt.

It felt wrong to be there in the evening; it's definitely a morning kind of shop. But with *En feu!*, the proprietors weren't going to miss an opportunity. I guess that was a good business decision, because the place was jammed.

"I didn't know you felt that way," he said, referring to the T-shirt.

"I borrowed it. It's not a political statement." I didn't disagree with the sentiments on the shirt, but I did regret that I hadn't picked one of the Grateful Dead ones.

"Glad to hear it. I have a pretty good idea who you borrowed it from. At least it looks a lot better on you than it would on the original owner. Now, you'd better sit down."

I sat. He had already ordered iced tea for both of us and homemade lemon shortbread cookies.

"I don't want to beat around the bush, but there's no doubt about it," he said.

"About what?"

"Didn't Woody tell you what I wanted to talk to you about?"

I shook my head.

"I figured you'd want to hear what I have to say in some kind of privacy."

I glanced around the tea shop. Everyone was busy pretending not to gawk at us. It seemed fairly obvious they were listening intently.

I said, "Privacy?"

"Best I could do. Even though we don't have the full report from the Fire Marshall, all the indications are that an accelerant was used in your home."

"An accelerant?" I blurted.

Heads turned.

I lowered my voice. "What are you talking about?"

"People use them to start fires," he said.

"Well, I know what an accelerant is, of course. It must have been used on my car too."

He cleared his throat. "We're pretty sure that the car was torched separately. As a rule, in cases of arson—"

"So it's arson!"

Heads around us snapped.

My voice rose. "But I'm usually home at that time of day. My car was parked by the house. Tolstoy could have been killed. And Josey might have been there."

"We don't know that anyone intended to kill you. As a rule, it's either the owner wanted insurance—"

We both looked up as a shadow fell over the gingham tablecloth. Josey stood there with her hands on her hips. I hadn't heard her come in, but then she had perfected the art of arriving without warning.

She snorted. "Well, Miz Silk doesn't have any insurance. So you can just forget that."

Sarrazin glanced at her and furrowed his eyebrows. He turned back to me and said, "Does this Thring kid have to be everywhere?"

I nodded. "Yes. I'm always glad to see her. She could have been killed in the fire. I think you should be happy too." Mainly I was hoping he would forget her words at the fire.

"Everyone's glad she's alive, not that there was any question about that. It's not the point. She's a juvenile for one thing, and for another, she never seems to be in school."

"Exam prep, all week," Josey said. "Plus it's the evening, if you haven't noticed."

"Is that so? Then maybe you better go prep for your exams."

For a fleetingly admiring moment, I thought I could learn a few lessons in hardball from Sarrazin.

Josey met his eyes. "I'm prepped."

"I could check with the school."

"Trust me."

Sarrazin hauled out his tiny cell phone. "Not so much. I think I'll just verify that."

"Go right ahead. See if you can get anyone this time of night, but if you do, they'll tell you I always get straight As."

So much for hardball. I would have given up after the first lob back at me. Not Sarrazin. He smiled. "It's good that you're free. You might want to check at home. I hear the boys are about to pick up your uncle Mike for dealing in stolen goods. Second time in a week. They say it's a big screen plasma television this time. Over five thousand, he's facing serious time. Never mind that released-on-his-own-recognizance crap."

Josey's eyes widened. Her freckles stood out. Her cowlicks quivered. She turned as white as the crisp linen napkins in Thé Pour Deux. "You're bluffing."

Sarrazin said, "What's that you said before? Oh yeah. Trust me."

As I watched Josey explode through the door and head for her bike, he cleared his throat.

I turned back to him. "I'm pretty sure he's just a drunk."

"He handles some stuff that falls off trucks."

"This is St. Aubaine. Who doesn't? Surely you're not going to raid their cabin just because of what Josey said."

"Maybe I'm mistaken about that raid. Got a lot on my mind lately. Now," he said, "what's all this about M. Jean-Claude Lamontagne having reason to burn down your house?"

"Don't you think I did it?"

"No, madame, I do not."

"Oh. I was sure you suspected me."

He shook his head. "And I would have good reasons. Our murder rate went sky-high when you moved in, but I have learned to see past all that."

"Glad to hear that you're open-minded." I stirred an extra teaspoon of sugar into my tea and nodded. "I've learned to see past things too. I had trouble believing that Jean-Claude would go far enough to burn my house down. Really. He's my neighbour and my friend's husband. Josey suspected him all along. I kept reminding myself that Josey and Jean-Claude have a history of mutual dislike."

"They sure do. That Thring girl got her drunk uncle to call

the station with the information that the residents' aide who made the accusation against you at the rehab centre was Jean-Claude's cousin. He said she set you up."

"And was she Jean-Claude's cousin?"

"Afraid so."

"And did you talk to her?"

"She's making herself scarce, but don't worry, I'll catch up with her. That's a serious accusation she made against you. Some people might have believed it."

"I'm glad you didn't."

"Making that kind of false accusation is serious too. In more ways than one. That fellow there, Marc-André Paradis, she deprived him of the one thing that gave him a little bit of happiness."

"I thought she was jealous."

"According to the people I did talk to, there's more to it than that. Apparently she was asking around, trying to find dirt to use against you. Other staff members spoke in your favour. I thought you might like to know that. Since everyone knows Jean-Claude wants your property, I intend to find out if he was behind this too."

"I have no trouble believing he would arrange a stunt like that at the rehab. He's not in the least bit sentimental, and he's cold and calculating, but to think that he would torch my house. That's a shock."

"I don't care how rich and important he is, if he did this, we will get him, and he will go to prison. But I need to know if he threatened you."

"Not threatened, no." Here was my chance to do the dirty on my old enemy, the man who had bullied his way to the top of the West Quebec heap. The man who had done his best to intimidate Aunt Kit and to steamroller me. But I couldn't lie about it.

Sarrazin shifted in his chair, folding his arms and staring at me.

"People are funny. He tried to get you charged after that fire in his kitchen. Madame Lamontagne put her foot down on that."

An idea flashed through my brain. "It was after that fire that Faron Findlay dropped by to tell me he had to cancel my insurance policy."

Sarrazin plopped two sugar cubes into his tea. "Just before this fire?"

"That's what Josey meant. Faron Findlay had to cancel my policy because of the wiring. The electrician told him about it."

"So you won't be able to replace anything?"

"Nothing," I croaked through the lump in my throat. "A lot of it was irreplaceable anyway. My manuscripts. My computer files. Family heirlooms. I lost a valuable painting."

Sarrazin slipped another shortbread cookie onto my plate. "Everyone in the village knows you're broke. I've heard over and over again about your stalled career, the back taxes, the final notice from the Hydro, the broken down car, the tab at L'Épicerie."

It was my turn to shrug. "It's the price you pay for living in a small town where everyone knows everyone's business." I didn't mention that Sarrazin's relationship with coroner Dr. Lise Duhamel was also a topic that inspired much speculation from Le Nettoyeur to the Chez.

"They're getting a lot of conversational mileage out of the new project with the cookbook."

"That's gone too. My computer. The contract. The advance cheque was in the car. Pffft. I guess that can be replaced."

"You could have sold this artwork."

"I would never have sold it. It was an Alex Colville. And it wasn't properly insured even when my policy was in effect."

"But the arsonist might not have known that."

"So?"

"If someone thought you could sell that painting and pay

your taxes and all that, and they wanted your property, they might want to get rid of it." It made sense, in a horrible stomach-clenching way. "Was that the big painting in your office?'

Sarrazin didn't mention that he was well-acquainted with my office because he'd once done a crime scene investigation there. I appreciated that.

"Yes."

"Interesting, because it looks like the office is where the fire started. Maybe they weren't trying to kill you."

"Just keep me from having my home and my livelihood and the things I loved." I picked up my iced tea with a shaking hand. I put it down again before I sloshed it over Woody's shorts. "Somebody must hate me."

Sarrazin nodded. "Sure looks like it. And one name comes to mind."

*   *   *

I don't know why I got Cyril to drive me back to Chemin des cèdres to see the house. Although it was the longest day of what seemed like the longest week of my life, I couldn't see myself sleeping otherwise.

It was after nine by the time we got there. It had turned into a dusky June evening, but the rising full moon was enough to light the area. I blinked at what used to be my home, the burnt shell of the Skylark, and the singed grass and trees. The smell of scorched plastic, drywall and textiles stung my nostrils. I walked around the remains, pausing to stare at my trampled flowers and herbs. The birdfeeder lay broken on the ground. The sound of the cardinals' cheer-cheer-cheer was probably gone from this place forever. The only thing I owned that had escaped damage was the garbage can at the end of the driveway.

Someone had done this to me deliberately. I needed to get my head straight, because there was a good chance it wasn't over yet.

Cyril did all the talking on the drive back.

*   *   *

Of course, I would have preferred to arrive in the village without drawing attention to myself. However, Cyril Hemphill does not suffer from any of the symptoms of a wallflower. He leaned out the window and waved at everyone.

"Howya doin'?"

Not that he ever waited for an answer, but few would be unaware of his presence on Rue Principale. I suppose his proximity to me might mean that he had new information for the gossips. Tolstoy was picking up some of this in-your-face behaviour and barking greetings.

When we reached the end of Rue Principale, we noticed Anabel Huffington-Chabot gliding up the stairs to the most exclusive restaurant in town. Her blonde hair glinted in the moonlight, her face remained untouched by emotion, not even pride in her latest designer suit, a metallic shade this time. Several members of the production team seemed to be joining her for a fashionably late dinner. Rafaël and Marietta followed, strolling together, maybe a bit closer than work might demand. Rafaël smiled and waved and returned his obviously besotted attention back to his cooking co-star, or perhaps her capacious cleavage. In turn, Marietta pirouetted on her red spike heels, blowing sexy kisses to people on the sidewalk. With her dizzying curves and her white skirt swirling in the wind, it was all very Marilyn Monroe, except Marietta's curls were dark and shoulder length. The fans applauded. Brady pulled up at the rear, still holding his clipboard and still wearing those cowboy boots. He'd added a jaunty little orange neckerchief to his outfit and perked up his fauxhawk. It went well with the diamond stud in his nose. Chelsea Brazeau, the only normal-looking person in the group, hurried behind to catch up. She was more casually dressed in an ankle-length Indian print skirt and a simple blue tee. She was laughing and holding on to a pretty straw hat as the wind picked up. I wondered how long she'd survive in that zoo. I decided when I had a bit of cash again, I'd take her to lunch to thank her for trying to help. And Brady too.

Cyril spotted the production group heading into the restaurant, and he stopped the cab. "Good evening, ladies and gentleman," he beamed.

Chelsea smiled back and waved. Anabel looked down her aristocratic nose and glanced away, in disdain I suppose. I couldn't say I blamed her.

I slithered down on the seat to avoid being associated with whatever Cyril would do next. Luckily, I didn't have to worry. The group continued up the restaurant stairs and vanished from view.

Cyril made eye contact with me in the rearview mirror.

"Hubba hubba," he said.

I said nothing.

"Damn good looking woman. What do you think?" he said.

"Huh," I said.

"She's a hell of a good tipper too." He wiggled his eyebrows quite salaciously. "Picked her up out of town the other day, and she made it worth my while, if you know what I mean."

"I can get out anywhere around here," I said. A little bit of Cyril goes a long way.

Ménage à Trois

Contributed by Rafaël

Place scoops of passion fruit, mango and raspberry ice in a meringue nest with a splash of Framboise and a sprig of mint.

Very easy, and you will have more time to savour it with your lover.

Fourteen

It was one of those middle of the night revelations. That blinding insight that we've all experienced at three a.m. I sat upright in Woody's spare room. The question was clear in my mind. And I knew damn well if I went back to sleep and waited until the morning, the thought would evaporate.

I turned on the light and got out of bed. I fished my notebook out of my bag and retrieved the pen. This was more of an achievement than it sounds, given that I was emotionally exhausted and sleeping in an unfamiliar room.

How had that good-looking electrician, Arlen Young, known that Faron Findlay was my insurance agent? And what had made him walk up to Faron while he was waiting in the Chez for Chinese take-out? The last I'd heard was that the wiring was fixable, he'd order the part for the stove, and he'd give us a quote for repairs. Then he'd pulled that stunt. A coincidence that it was just before the fire that took everything I owned? I didn't think so. If he would admit that it was Jean-Claude's doing, then Sarrazin would have something to go on.

Since I had nothing better to do, I decided to pay Arlen a visit in the morning. Tell him what I thought of him. I lay in bed for the next hour practicing plain speaking.

*   *   *

Woody in the morning is pretty hard to take. For starters, he gets up very, very early and sings Grateful Dead songs off-key. Today it was "When Push Comes to Shove". He whirled around the kitchen in his custom-built wheelchair. I wondered where you could buy an apron with Jerry Garcia's face on it but decided against asking.

"Coffee's on the counter," he said, stubbing out a cigarette in the nearest ashtray.

"It smells wonderful," I said, not fully recovered from lying awake half the night mentally shouting at Arlen.

"Fresh ground. So, clog your arteries, kiddo?" he said, slamming the fridge door, slapping a pound of bacon on the counter, followed by a dozen eggs, which he handled with a bit more care. Woody'd had his kitchen counters custom-made so he could work at them. They were low enough for someone in a wheelchair, and the curved work surface allowed him to get up close. Even the stove top was located at Woody's height.

"Need any help?"

"Don't tick me off," he said.

I said yes to artery clogging, filled a large mug with fragrant coffee and watched Woody go to work. He's a whiz with butter and a frying pan. There is never a scrap of granola in Woody's home.

"Did you ever meet an electrician named Arlen Young?" I asked.

Woody slid the frying pan onto the cook top and turned on the burner. "Arlen Young. He's a musician, guitar."

"That's right. He said the group was called No Where To Go But Oops. You know them?"

"They're not bad." That is high praise coming from Woody. "Opened for Sue Foley the last couple times she played at the Britannia. Why are you asking?"

"You know about my insurance being cancelled."

Woody glowered. "I guess we can figure out who was behind that."

"Yes, but Faron Findlay said the electrician told him."

"So why would this Arlen Young tell Faron?"

"That's what I'm asking myself. There's nothing in it for him."

"You said Hélène found him for you."

"Yes, but Hélène wouldn't ever do anything to hurt me. I know that."

"Agreed. But she must have asked Jean-Claude for the name. And that would mean that the bastard knew you had some wiring issues."

I bit my lower lip. "That's what I think. Hélène probably mentioned it to him, inadvertently."

"So then Jean-Claude asks the guy what the story is, gives him a bit of cash under the table to tell your insurance agent. You think Jean-Claude would know who insures your property?"

"Of course, he does. Faron's their agent too."

"Writing's on the wall, kiddo. Hey, maybe you can sue Jean-Claude's silk-covered rump. It'll make a real good story if people find out he did that. Then your house mysteriously burns down and you lose everything, and hey, here's the guy with something to gain who tries to do you the dirty. Cops might be interested."

"I mentioned it to Sarrazin already. I'm not sure if he knows Arlen's name. He didn't ask me for it, so I guess he does."

"You got to talk to this guy. Find out if Jean-Claude put him up to it."

"That's the plan, but his business card burned up with everything else in my house."

"There's always the telephone book."

"I checked. He's not in it. I could ask Hélène, but I don't want to give Jean-Claude a clue that I'm going to talk to this guy."

"Good thinking."

"Well, except I still don't know how to reach him."

"You like your bacon crispy? Or extra crispy?"

I voted for extra crispy. "I guess I could go over to the Britannia when it opens and ask if anyone knows how to reach him or one of the other guys in the band."

"No one at the Britannia's going to give you anyone's number. They know you've been talking to Sarrazin a lot lately. After breakfast, I'll call my contractor. He knows every trade around these parts. So, kiddo, want some extra cheese on these eggs?"

* * *

The dirt road off the 366 North was long and bumpy and unsigned. Clouds of dust rose in our wake. No wonder Arlen Young's pickup had been covered with mud. I closed the windows of Liz's Audi, even though I usually love the scent of wildflowers and wild grasses.

I said, "Lucky that Woody's contact gave good directions and landmarks. I don't know my way around this area."

"Boy, I wonder if Dr. Prentiss would have lent you her new car if she knew we were coming up here."

"She won't know. We'll take it to the car wash before she gets it back."

"Come on, Miz Silk. I'll wash it. We don't have money to waste on the car wash. Hey, did you notice? There are no phone lines down this road," Josey said. "No Hydro either. Maybe he's living off-grid. He's an electrician, I bet he's got all kinds of gear rigged up. Solar-powered batteries for his fridge and television. Maybe propane stove and stuff. Let's ask him to show us."

"It's really lonely. We've only passed one other vehicle. I can't imagine living way out here," I said, struggling to keep the car out of the giant potholes that peppered the road. I had planned to use this errand as a quiet time to talk to Josey about her accusation against Hélène, something we really had to deal with.

"He's mostly a musician. This would be a really cheap place to live. I'd be surprised if he even gets cell phone reception up here. Too many trees." Josey fished out her own cell phone and shook her head. "Told you so. I got the best coverage there is around here and look, no service. He must just check in every now and then and get his messages. A lot of people up this way do that."

The log cabin appeared in a clearing. Josey said, "Told you. Look at those solar panels. And he's home." She pointed to the dusty pickup angled near the woodpile.

We found no other sign of Arlen as we glanced around the house and yard.

"Arlen!" I called out.

"I bet he's avoiding us," Josey said.

"You're probably right."

"You can run but you can't hide, Arlen Young," she yelled.

"Talk to us or talk to the police," I chimed in cheerfully. But there was nothing except the soft wave of the thigh-high grasses.

"The door's open," Josey said.

"We can't just go in."

"Speak for yourself."

"No, Josey, it's trespassing. Hey, what about his dog? Do you think they're out on the river?"

"He can't walk to the river from here, Miz Silk. We're half-way up a mountain."

219

"Right. Well, I'll just check around and look in the outbuildings," I said as Josey strode through the open front door bellowing, "You're in big trouble, mister."

"Don't do that," I said, rushing after her. It belatedly occurred to me that Arlen was a huge man who might also have a hunting rifle or two, in addition to the German shepherd.

"The police know we're here," I shouted. It was as good a lie as any, and it seemed like a wise prevarication. If there'd been cell phone service, I'd have called Sarrazin at that moment.

Inside, the log cabin was basically one room, furnished mostly with guitars. There was a battered futon, a rustic coffee table that had been made out of several sections of a tree trunk and a huge, soft dog-bed for Sweetheart. On the coffee table lay a pair of plates with half-eaten sandwiches, back bacon on Kaiser buns, unless I was mistaken, and four empty bottles of Sleeman, one of them knocked over. You could still smell the perfume of the bacon. The scent of spilled beer wasn't quite so appealing.

"Miz Silk!" Josey whispered.

I bumped into her and stared. Sweetheart, the big shepherd, lay to the side of the futon. I touched her chest. She was still warm, and there was an infinitesimal movement in her chest. I thought I heard a moan from upstairs.

"Josey, go call for help," I whispered back.

The blue eyes were wide and panicked. "No reception. Remember?"

"I mean get to a place where there is reception. Run out onto the road or up on a high point. I'll try to find Arlen."

"I don't want to leave you, Miz Silk."

"Something bad happened here. There's no sign of an injury. I think the dog has been drugged. Go call 911, then try and reach the vet for the dog."

"But—"

I thrust the keys into her hand. "Get in the car and drive out to the road. We don't know who did this."

"Dr. Prentiss won't be too happy if she finds out you let me drive her car."

"She'll just have to cope. Don't argue. Stay on the main road until the police arrive. Lock the car doors until they come. Give them a landmark and wait by that landmark. They might not find this place otherwise."

I had a bit of plan. For sure, Arlen hadn't harmed his own dog. What if the person who had was still there? If they were, I wanted them to think that both Josey and I had left. I whispered this to her.

She nodded. Eyes like saucers.

"Let's go," I said loudly, as if we both were leaving,

As she headed toward the door and banged it behind her, I grabbed one of the guitars, the only weapon I could find, and ducked behind the futon.

Minutes after I heard the roar of the car engine heading back down the dirt track, I emerged from my hiding place and moved quickly toward the steps to the loft. I heard a muffled groan. I crept up the stairs, clutching the guitar by the neck and trying to keep my breath under control. A buzzing sound became louder as I advanced.

I stuck my head up through the hole in the loft floor. I saw the bed, the tangle of greyish sheets and a smashed guitar. A bloody walking stick lay on the floor by the end of the bed. A pair of bare feet poked out of the sheets. Big feet, size fourteen minimum. I lurched toward the bed with its tangle of sheets. Arlen Young lay face down, naked, his long, dark-blond hair spread around him. A pool of blood surrounded his head, probably from the wound in the back of his skull. A cluster of flies explained the loud buzz.

I gagged but moved forward. Could anyone survive that? The pool of blood was spreading slowly. I knew I shouldn't touch him. It was obviously a crime scene. He couldn't be alive, but what if he was? I reached over and touched his wrist. A faint pulse, but for how much longer?

Everything else seemed very, very unimportant. I knew if I didn't do something, Arlen would bleed to death. I grabbed the sheets from the bed, wadded them together and pressed them against his wound, waving away the flies.

Time ticked by.

I sat cross-legged on the floor, avoiding the blood, and kept murmuring to him, soothingly. "It's okay, you're going to make it. Josey has gone to call 911. Sweetheart's going to be all right, and so are you. But try to fight. Please try to fight."

With my free hand, I held his limp hand and squeezed, hoping that it wouldn't increase the blood flow. "Don't go," I said. "The world needs musicians."

It felt like hours crouched there, mesmerized by the buzzing of the flies and the slow seeping of Arlen's blood. I was still trying to murmur encouragement when I heard the sound of sirens in the distance.

"Hang on, Arlen. Hang on."

Garlic Shrimp for Two

Contributed by Marietta

13 shrimp, peeled, deveined, but with tails intact
2 tablespoons olive oil
2 crushed garlic cloves
1/4 teaspoon red pepper flakes
1 teaspoon steak seasoning
1 teaspoon lemon zest
2 teaspoons lemon juice
1 tablespoon chopped parsley
1 tablespoon chopped chives

Pour two glasses of chilled white wine. Heat a large skillet over medium high heat. Add olive oil, garlic, red pepper flakes and shrimp. Season with steak seasoning or salt & pepper. Cook shrimp 3 minutes or until just pink. Toss with lemon zest, juice, chopped parsley and chives. Taste one. You know you can't resist it. Remove the rest of the shrimp to a serving plate, pour liquid in pan over.

Surprise your lover!

Fifteen

Any folksiness that Sarrazin had been projecting had pretty well evaporated by the time he lumbered in to see me in the interview room at the St. Aubaine Sûreté.

I jumped to my feet when he finally showed up. No ice tea this time. Just the low hum of the tape recorder noting Interview with Fiona Silk, June 11, five p.m. Present Sgt. F.X. Sarrazin and *Agent* Viau. Somehow *agent* seems much more menacing than the English equivalent rank of constable. I'd never seen Viau before. He was a wiry man in his early thirties, with hair buzzed close to his scalp. He gave off a "don't mess with me" vibe. I forced myself to make eye contact. His eyes were black, beady and accusing. Mine were most likely red-rimmed, matching my forehead. Not that I'd been near a mirror to know.

"Okay, madame," Sarrazin said gently, "I just need you to tell the truth."

I blinked. "But I always tell the truth."

I may have looked a bit shifty at this point, because I didn't always tell Sarrazin the truth. At the moment, I was so rattled I couldn't really remember what fibs I'd told. Mostly white lies to protect Josey, I decided.

Viau cleared his throat. "I hope you realize how serious this is."

I bleated, "Of course I realize it. I spent what seemed like hours worrying that Arlen Young was going to die in my arms. Is he okay?"

"Let's deal with the interview."

"Listen, I held him. I have his blood all over me. I have a right to know if he's alive."

"Yes. He is alive, but we don't know if he is going to make it. He's still in intensive care. So why don't you explain to me how you came to be in the bedroom with a naked bleeding man that you say you hardly know."

"But it's true."

Viau said, "Were you having an affair?"

My jaw dropped. I was starting to hate this man. "I only met him the one time when he looked at my wiring."

Agent Viau smothered a smirk. Sarrazin swivelled and faced him. The smirk vanished. Viau squirmed in his chair until Sarrazin turned back to me.

I stared straight at Sarrazin. "I've told you what happened there. Arlen said he'd give me a quote, and then he talked to my insurance agent. I told you all about it in the café."

"But why were you in his cabin?"

"I wanted to find out why he told Faron Findlay that my home was unsafe. You must be able to understand that. I lost everything I have ever valued in my life. I could have lost Josey and Tolstoy. You yourself said accelerant was used. Arlen was connected to that somehow, and I just—"

Viau interjected, "—hit him with your stick when he didn't tell you. Or maybe he did tell you, and then you hit with the stick. Which one is it?"

"It's neither," I said in a wobbly voice. "I didn't hit him. I found him. The stick was just lying there, on the floor. It had blood on it. I never touched it."

Sarrazin took over again. "Okay, we're having a bit of trouble with that too. The guy was naked and *upstairs* in his cabin. You told me you hardly knew him. Yet you walked in the front door when he was, as you claim, already unconscious and bleeding."

Viau added, "You do that kind of thing all the time?"

Sarrazin rubbed his temples. I guess it wasn't easy being the good cop.

"Of course not. Josey and I went to talk to him. We saw the truck outside. We knew he was there. The front door was open, and Josey took a look."

Viau snorted. "Right. There's a name for that. Trespassing. That kid will answer for that."

"Please, leave her out of this. If she hadn't gone for help, he would have died alone. She could see Sweetheart unconscious by the table. She called to the dog, and it didn't move."

"That dog is a shepherd. Weren't you scared he would attack you, since you were intruders?"

"She. Of course, she would have barked if she thought we were intruders. Or she would have come to greet us, if she recognized us. When she didn't move, we knew something was wrong. That's why we went in. Then I sent Josey to call the police."

Sarrazin said, "And you stayed behind because?"

"I knew Arlen wouldn't hurt his dog. When I heard moaning upstairs, I figured that something had happened to him."

"So you went upstairs, even though you thought there might have been an intruder? Was that smart?"

"It was pretty stupid actually. Impractical. Idiotic. But it turned out to be the right thing to do. Arlen would have died if we hadn't gone to that cabin and if Josey hadn't gone for the police and if I hadn't checked upstairs. I wish you would try to understand that. I am not the bad guy here."

Sarrazin puffed out his cheeks.

"Look," I said, "why would we call the police if we'd committed a crime?"

Viau leaned forward and said, "People who commit violent acts

227

aren't always thinking straight. They do things that don't really help their case. Maybe this was one of those times. You didn't mean to hurt him. You certainly didn't mean to kill him. You just wanted information. Then when you were talking to him, you became enraged because this man had caused the loss of your home and your livelihood. We wouldn't blame you. You couldn't help yourself. You raised your walking stick, and you smashed in his skull."

I flinched. "No."

"And then you hit him again and again. You couldn't stop yourself. He had it coming."

"No. I didn't." I turned to Sarrazin. "You know that isn't true."

Viau wasn't buying it. "Afterwards, you were overcome with remorse. You hadn't wanted to hurt him. You didn't want him to die. Just tell us, and we'll try to help you."

"Oh, absolutely. That's what this is all about. Helping me. And what are you talking about, *my* walking stick? I had one something like it. It burned up in the fire like everything else."

"No, madame. Apparently, it didn't. We know it was yours, because guess what we found on it?"

My heart constricted. "What?"

"Your fingerprints and those of that Thring girl."

"It's not possible. Josey didn't go upstairs. And I didn't touch it. The murderer must have—"

Viau help up a hand. "Another thing—you keep saying the Thring girl called the police."

I stared at him. "She did. I sent her out to the road to make the call."

"Right. Getting a minor to steal a car."

"It was an emergency." My head was beginning to throb. "We've been through that, over and over."

He shook his buzzed head. "But the Thring girl didn't call 911, did she?"

"Of course she did. You came, didn't you?"

Viau snickered. "We did. But not because of her. Didn't you think we got there pretty damn fast?"

I blinked. "It seemed like forever. I lost all track of time. It was like a nightmare. All that blood, those flies. Why are you saying that Josey didn't call?"

Viau leaned back in his chair and put his hands behind his head. "She claimed she couldn't find a spot with service before we arrived. And then she left the scene before we could question her. Must have hitched a ride back to town."

I probably looked pretty murderous right then. That's the problem with wild, curly hair, it can give you a deranged appearance at a moment's notice. And it doesn't help your image if your clothes are covered with blood. "But why would you send patrol cars up to a cabin in the middle of the woods if it wasn't for Josey's call?"

Sarrazin and the agent exchanged glances.

My mouth felt dry. "Oh, let me guess. You got a tip."

Sarrazin said, "That's right. Crime in progress. But not a tip about a seriously injured person. That's why the ambulance came later."

"Well, ask yourself, who could tip you except the person who committed this crime?"

Viau had a way of smiling without a tinge of humour. "The tip said that you had said, and I quote, 'Arlen Young knows who is behind my fire, and he is going to tell us if he knows what's good for him.' Is that true? Did you say that, madame?"

"No." I had thought it, though, but there was no way a tipster could know my thoughts.

Sarrazin said sadly, "And then things got out of hand."

Things were very definitely out of hand. I said, "I suppose I better have a lawyer. I don't know what to do."

Viau said, "Why don't you just tell us the truth, and then the lawyer can help get you the best deal."

"I didn't do it, and I don't want a deal. You need to find out who is committing these crimes."

What had my wussy little world come to when I was yelling at the police in an interrogation room?

At that point, Sarrazin and Viau started all over again, back at the beginning, every detail of the morning and the events up until they arrived at Arlen's cabin. By the time we'd gone over it for the tenth time, I was beginning to understand how a normal person could confess to anything at all, just to get them to shut up.

There was a knock on the door as Viau was asking once again with feeling, "So did you bring the walking stick along just in case you needed protection from Young or from the dog? Was that it? Maybe you didn't plan to kill him, but you were a bit nervous around him. We could understand that."

"It doesn't matter how many times you ask, I didn't take a weapon to Arlen's house. I didn't attack him."

I heard the knock again.

Sarrazin held my eyes while Viau ambled over cockily to open the door. A fresh-faced young female officer whispered something into his ear. He made a face like he'd just found spinach in his chocolate sundae. He beckoned to Sarrazin. Sarrazin heaved his bulk out of the chair and joined them. They stepped into the hallway, closing the door behind them. I sat there, heart pounding. I'd heard the word hospital. I knew what had happened. Arlen Young must have died. Now I was done for too. And so probably was Josey. Wherever she was.

A century later, the door opened. Sarrazin loomed in it.

I stared at him. "I didn't do it."

He nodded. "You're free to go."

I staggered to my feet. "What? I mean, that's good, isn't it?"

"Yes, madame. That's very good."

For some reason, my knees wobbled. "Why? What happened?"

"Good news, madame. Arlen Young regained consciousness."

"That's wonderful. He didn't deserve to die."

"No, he did not. And he was able to answer an important question for us."

I held my breath. "He told you it wasn't me?"

"That's right."

"But who did it?"

Sarrazin shrugged. "He didn't give us a name. He said he didn't know the person. We'll have to wait for that. He didn't stay conscious long. But it looks like he'll make it."

I was still clutching the table for support. My knees appeared to be on strike.

He added, "Go back to your friend's place and get some rest."

"And the small matter of Josey driving the vehicle. You'll drop that?"

He produced one of his major league shrugs. "Dr. Prentiss insists she'd given her permission for the Thring kid to practice on the vehicle as long as it was on a private road."

"And Arlen's road was private."

"Appears to be. And I think we have more important things to concern ourselves with. So it turns out to be a good day for you, madame."

"Oh, absolutely. Splendid."

"You're not the only one with problems. Keep it in perspective."

"What do you mean?"

"You remember that woman who lost her wallet?"

That damn wallet had completely slipped my mind what with the fire, Arlen, the interrogation and all.

"You can stop searching now. A couple coming back from

Montreal found her last night, parked in their driveway, by the river. "

"What do you mean, found her?"

"Car was out of gas, windows closed. She was sitting inside and running the air conditioning, not that you can really stay very cool like that. Coroner said looks like carbon monoxide poisoning. The woman had been there a couple of days."

"That explains why she didn't call me back. And why she didn't show up for the shoot."

"That would do it."

"Why didn't you tell me this before?"

He scratched his five o'clock shadow and glared at me. "Let me see. Hmmm. Maybe because we were interrogating you about an attempted murder?"

"For heaven's sake, you knew all along I didn't do it, even if your colleague didn't."

"You need another reason? How's this? Not everything that the police are working on is your business. Even if we approach you and ask you questions and expect you to be fully disclosing, it doesn't work the other way around. I know it's hard to grasp, but there you go."

"Did anyone report her missing?"

He shook his head.

"That's sad. The whole *En feu!* production was terrified of Harriet. No one would even give her a message about the wallet. Now she's dead."

"No question it's tragic, but we're pretty sure it was accidental."

I thought about that for a couple of seconds. "But don't you think it's strange that Harriet Crowder accidentally dies of carbon monoxide the same week that Danny Dupree is killed, my house burns down and Arlen Young is found attacked?"

Sarrazin stood up and towered over me. "It was an accident.

That's what Coroner Duhamel says, that's what I say, that's what you are going to say."

"But I can *think* what I want."

"Go ahead, think. But don't go running around the village stirring everybody up with your idea that this accident is not an accident, because right now, we've got more than enough to deal with, and all of it somehow seems connected to you."

"You'll just have to get on top of the situation then, since I can't," I said with as much dignity as a person with out of control hair, bloody clothes and tear tracks down her dusty cheeks can have.

After all, a big chunk of what my unpaid taxes were supposed to pay for went to police services.

*　　*　　*

I found Josey much later in front of the Chez. I had managed to get cleaned up at Woody's but otherwise wasn't feeling much better. My clothing was back in the washing machine again.

"I hope you can express your appreciation to Liz," I said to Josey. "I told you she's a worthy friend, even if it's not always obvious. We both could have faced charges."

Josey snorted. "I think pretty much any judge would dismiss those charges. But anyway, I've already thanked her. She *is* your friend, and she came through when you really needed her."

"Told you."

"You got to admit, she's pretty hard to take." Josey glanced over at me. "Good thing she came up with that whopper just in time. The cops were at my place looking for me and giving Uncle Mike the gears. Lucky I wasn't there."

Of course, I should have realized that any executive assistant worth her salt wouldn't choose to hide from the law at her own address. "You shouldn't have take off like that. Where were you hiding out? Oh, never mind. Don't tell me. I wouldn't want to betray your position if anything like this ever happens again, which I really really hope it doesn't."

"If we don't catch whoever's doing this, it could."

"We have to leave it to the police. I've learned that lessson. We don't really understand what's going on and why."

"You know what, and you know why, Miz Silk." Josey nodded her head toward Jean-Claude's silver Porsche Carrera, ostentatiously blocking the pedestrian walk in front of the Chez.

I said. "We're out of our depth here, Josey. This has gotten way too dangerous. It's a good idea for you to stay away from the Wallingford Estate too." I told her about Harriet Crowder's death.

"Harriet Crowder? You're kidding. What happened?"

"She was found in her car. Carbon monoxide. Remember, she used to leave it running because of the air conditioning?"

"Oh boy."

"The police say it's accidental, but I'm not so sure. Too much of a coincidence, these deaths. Promise me you'll just stay away from that place."

She shrugged. "Sure. I'm just going down to the vet's to see what's happening with Sweetheart."

*   *   *

Cyril Hemphill is inclined to haunt you, except when you really need him. I finally located him parked outside the Britannia, waiting for some unwary tourist to have one too many and require transportation, plus tip of course.

"Heard the cops let you go for now. That's good. Where to?" he said cheerfully.

"Nowhere. I just have a question."

He hesitated. I suppose he was trying to calculate a reasonably extortionate rate for questions.

"Well, I guess," he said.

"Remember you said you picked up Anabel Huffington-Chabot?"

"Who?"

I repeated it. "You know, that tall, beautiful lady. We just passed her in town, and you said she was a good tipper."

He lit up. "Oh yes, she is that."

"Okay, so when was that?"

"What?"

I took a deep calming breath. The kind you so often need to take in dealing with the good folks of St. Aubaine. "When did you pick up Anabel?"

Cyril licked his lips. "Is that her name?"

"Try to cooperate, Cyril. When? What day and what time?"

He scratched his combover. "Let me think…hmmm, it must have been…"

I stood there, prepared to outwait him.

"…last Monday."

"Really?"

"Pretty sure."

"What time?"

Cyril rubbed his nose and thought hard. "Must have been just before three."

"Where?"

"Down near Tulip Valley. That's a good fare."

"And she just called you from the highway?"

"Nope. She arranged with me ahead of time. I was expecting her call. I was waiting nearby. I'm pretty fast, you know."

"I do know." I might have added that I'd learned it the hard way, but it wasn't the time to alienate Cyril, not that he's the most sensitive flower in the garden. "What was she doing there?"

"Well, ma'am, I didn't ask her that. Wasn't any of my business." First time that ever stopped Cyril.

"What did she tell you?"

"Nothing. Just paid the fare without making a fuss."

"Didn't say why she was getting picked up in the middle of nowhere?"

"Said it was a little joke on someone. She tipped me a twenty, and I dropped her off at the Wallingford Estate as soon as we got back to town here."

"I'm surprised, Cyril, because usually you chat with your passengers."

"Puts them at ease."

"But not her."

"No, ma'am."

"So she just sat there, not saying a word for the twenty-minute drive back to St. Aubaine."

His brow furrowed. "Well, not exactly not saying a word. She kept talking to someone on her little phone and poking out messages. Busy little gal."

"For sure. Did you notice what she said."

"Hard to hear up here in the front seat."

"What about the accident that day? The Cadillac Escalade where the guy was killed."

"What about it?"

"Did you pass that scene?"

"Oh, sure. That was a bad one. You could see where that Caddy hit the guardrail as it went over. Cops had part of the road blocked off coming home. Funny too that happening right there in that straight bit of road. I know it's a hill and there's a ravine, but that's a good stretch of road and it was dry.

I don't mean funny ha ha, but weird."

"So your passenger didn't seem upset by the accident?"

"Nope. Didn't bother her. Why are you asking?"

"Thanks, Cyril."

"So listen, I hear you're collecting recipes for that dirty book of yours."

"No, I'm not."

"I got a good one for you."

"That's okay."

"Nothing beats a nice big, rare steak and a couple of bottles of reds to get a lady in the mood. I got a special way to make it too."

I shuddered as I got the hell out of there.

Romantic Steak Dinner for Two

Contributed by Cyril Hemphill

- 2 16-ounce rib eye steaks
- 1/4 cup Guinness
- 2 tablespoons teriyaki sauce
- 2 tablespoons brown sugar
- 1 teaspoon salt
- 1/2 teaspoon fresh ground pepper
- 1/2 teaspoon garlic powder

Preheat grill for high heat. Use a fork to poke holes all over the surface of the steaks, then place steaks in a large recloseable plastic bag. In a bowl, mix together beer, teriyaki sauce and brown sugar. Pour sauce over steaks and let sit for twenty-four hours. Sprinkle both sides with the seasoned salt, pepper and garlic powder. Let marinate another few minutes.

Remove steaks from marinade. Pour marinade into a small saucepan, bring to a boil, and cook for several minutes.

Open first bottle of red wine to let it breathe. Lightly oil the grill grate. Grill steaks to desired doneness. Baste steaks with boiled marinade.

Serve with a couple of bottles of good red wine. Loosen belt.

Sixteen

The next morning, Sarrazin was standing in L'Épicerie, staring at the bins of buckwheat and rolled oats and bran with a perplexed expression, when I trotted by with Tolstoy. I know it was my imagination, but I could almost detect a small black cloud over his head. He said, "Do you want to go somewhere private?"

Over in the corner, Woody watched us from his wheelchair, small black eyes gleaming, waiting for informational crumbs to drop. Woody might have been my good buddy for many years, and he'd been great about putting me up and keeping Tolstoy, but gossip was always his first love. I'm pretty sure he could read lips. And I was equally certain that whatever Sarrazin had to say, he didn't need Woody blasting it around town.

"Good idea. I was just about to try to walk off breakfast. How about the river path?"

The door of L'Épicerie jingled behind us as we left. I was probably biting my lip. Whatever Sarrazin wanted, it wouldn't be good. Was Josey in some kind of trouble? Had Arlen died? Had they found Philip? Was he all right?

Five minutes later, we were strolling by the banks of the Gatineau. Sarrazin kicked at stones. I worked at being calm.

"The suspense is killing me," I said. "You've told me that you don't think I set fire to my own home. And you don't think I attacked Arlen. Have you changed your mind about either of those?"

"No, madame. I'll cut to the chase. Do you believe that your ex-husband would have burned down your house?"

"What? You're kidding, right?"

"Let's see, arson investigation. Nope, not kidding."

"Philip? Committing arson? Boy, are you off-base with that theory."

"And why would that be?"

"For one thing, Philip is equal parts vanity and anal-retentiveness. There's no way he would ever risk getting any stinky accelerant on his hands. The man gets regular manicures. Are you getting my point? To say nothing of the angst if some noxious substance splashed on his Harry Rosen suit."

"Maybe he'd wear casual clothes for an arson outing."

"His casual clothes cost a bundle too. He favours Egyptian cotton, silk, cashmere. Trust me, Philip did not torch my house."

"He could have had an accomplice."

"An accomplice?"

"Common practice. Get someone to do your dirty work. If that happened, I'd like to get both of them."

I gave this some thought. "Did I mention that Philip's a bit of a control freak? Here's an example. He always recalculates his accountant's figures. He'd reload the dishwasher every time I filled it. Do you need to know any more? There's no way he could trust anyone to set a fire that would meet his high performance standards."

Sarrazin chuckled. I figured that was good.

I kept talking. "That means he'd have to have been there, issuing instructions, corrections and general personal slights."

Sarrazin said, "Maybe he *was* there."

"I refer you back to my previous point about soiling the wardrobe."

"I still want to talk to him."

"Go right ahead. I am sure you think I'm nuts because I don't think he did it. And I have thought about it, but honestly, if he wanted to harm me, maybe even kill me, he could certainly do it, but he'd find a neat and tidy way to do it. That's my point. Nothing messy, nothing smelly, no need to cooperate with others. I'm glad you're looking for him, and I hope you find him, because I sure couldn't. Please, feel free to make him absolutely miserable."

Sarrazin didn't completely buy my theory about Philip, but then the detective hadn't spent all those years stuck in the same house with my ex and his neuroses. He said, "Maybe he just wanted revenge. We see it all the time in divorce cases. Wife leaves. Husband does something vile to get back at her. Keeps us busy."

"I suppose, but I think he was glad to get rid of me. I never did do much of a job on the laundry. I couldn't really cook well, and my housekeeping fell way below standard."

"Sexual jealousy then."

"That's hilarious. The spark went out of our marriage before Philip even finished law school. And it was mutual."

"Then why did you stay together?"

"Who knows? He was building a practice. I was busy with other things. I suppose I really lacked the confidence to leave." No point in telling Sarrazin how Philip could chip away at my self-esteem. For a long time, I'd been short of the guts to take action and the brains to know I should.

He shrugged. It was the first shrug of this entire conversation. I wasn't sure what it meant. "You may have a natural bias."

"Please don't think I want to spare him inconvenience or embarrassment. Everything I owned was lost in that fire. So my net worth actually declined when the house burned. There's nothing to subtract from his assets when the settlement is concluded. I think this fire is going to cost him money."

"Humph."

"May I ask what triggered your desire to talk to Philip? It seems to be coming from out of the blue. You refused to follow up when I asked you to find him."

"Never mind."

I slapped the side of my head. "Oh, wait. Let me guess."

He narrowed his eyes at me.

"You got a tip!"

"Yes, a tip with some really good information that directly implicates him in the arson."

"That's just ducky. I'm glad that you'll be hunting for him, because as I told you, his disappearance is worrying me. Try to ask questions before you shoot. And while you're asking, maybe consider that Jean-Claude may have sent that tip."

*　　*　　*

I borrowed Liz's car again and drove back to Chemin des cèdres to see Hélène. Face to face seemed better than by phone.

She gasped when she opened the door. *"Oh là là,* Fiona! Look at you."

"What? I thought I got myself cleaned up a bit. You think this is bad, you should have seen me before."

"But what are you wearing?"

"I had to borrow another T-shirt and shorts from Woody. I already ruined one of his at Arlen Young's place. The bloodstains didn't even come out in the wash."

"I heard about the electrician. *C'est épouvantable!"*

"Yes, it is terrible. And that's why I'm here, Hélène."

"Let's sit outside. The painters are in the kitchen now, repairing the damage from our little disaster. You know, I would be happy to lend you some clothes, Fiona."

"Not sure how that would work. You're a lot smaller than I am."

"You have lost weight. I am sure we will find something. Let's have some lemonade first."

"I really need to talk about Arlen." Of course, I had to wait until she'd arranged a tray with a pitcher of lemonade and some truffles.

"I am so sorry about that poor man," Hélène said. "And I feel as though I brought you *beaucoup de misère*. I know Josée is very angry."

"You're not responsible. I know that, and Josey does too, deep down. I hope you realize that. She didn't mean to hurt you."

Hélène nodded slowly. "She is just a child. I don't blame *her*."

"That's good. So please tell me about Arlen. Where did you get his name? From Jean-Claude?"

"No. I would never ask Jean-Claude anything in connection with you. He was very angry about the kitchen and, *voyons,* you know what he is like."

"I do. So where did you get the name?"

"Well, I asked at the Wallingford Estate. They used all the local trades and even had to bring some people in."

"Who did you ask?"

She narrowed her eyes. "Madame Huffington-Chabot, of course. She managed all that. Her assistant helps a bit, but really, she is the one in charge."

Her facial expression told me that Hélène had heard and understood Josey's comments about Jean-Claude and Anabel.

I said, "Right. And she gave you Arlen's name?"

"Yes. She left a message for me the day after I asked her. She's *très efficace.*"

"You have no idea just how efficient." My suspicions were being confirmed, and high time too.

"I feel responsible."

"Don't."

"Let me buy you something to wear. You've lost all your clothing. You cannot walk around in Woody's clothes. How can you talk to television stars if you look like that? And we need to get some make-up for your eyebrows and forehead. It must be painful."

"No make-up. Liz said the burns can become infected if I'm not careful. They're getting better, and they look worse than they feel. And anyway, I feel guilty taking so much from you."

"Don't turn me away because of my husband, please, Fiona."

"It's not because of your husband. I'm just not comfortable with handouts."

"When your other friends offer help, do you think of it as handouts? Liz's car? Woody's shorts and horrible T-shirts? Everything that Josée does for you?"

I nodded. Hélène needed to help me more than I needed to stand on my own two feet. I said, "Okay, thanks. But I can't shop right now. I have something I have to take care of."

Hélène smiled. "Leave it to me."

*   *   *

"Did you hear that, Miz Silk?" Josey burst through the door of L'Épicerie, seconds after I got back from Hélène's. She let the door bang behind her.

Of course, I am always the last person to hear anything in St. Aubaine. "Hear what?" I said.

"Cyril wiped out on the 366."

"Oh, no. I was just talking to him last night." As much as I like to gripe about Cyril and his money-grubbing and garrulous ways, I never wish him ill.

"Oh, yes."

That's another thing about people around and in St. Aubaine. They love to gossip, but, even more, they relish having you struggle to extract information from them, once they have piqued your interest.

"What happened?"

"Apparently, he drove his old cab right off the road. Forty-five minutes ago."

"Is he all right? Don't make me drag it out of you. If he's not, tell me now."

"Nobody knows yet. They took him to the hospital down in Hull. I'll try to get an update."

"Go find out, please."

As Josey scampered off to put the thumbscrews on some hapless health care worker, I stood there, heart thundering. Cyril had driven his cab right off a familiar road in broad daylight, just like a certain Danny Dupree.

*   *   *

I hustled along the main street to the Sûreté, hoping Sarrazin hadn't left to hound Philip yet. I was in luck. He was filling out forms. "You have to listen to me," I said.

"You sound hysterical."

I lowered my voice. "Maybe so, but hear me out and try not to think I'm absolutely crazy."

"I'll try. How about you do your best not to *sound* absolutely crazy. Because that will help."

"You know that Cyril Hemphill was in a car accident too. We need to compare toxicology results with Danny Dupree's. And Arlen's. Check out Sweetheart too and see if it's the same stuff that—"

Sarrazin held up his hand. "We? Who is this we?"

"Fine. You. *You* need to."

"Hmm. And why do I?"

"Because the accident was so similar to the Escalade. Cyril

could practically drive in his sleep. He's not a drinker, and he knows every inch of road around here, yet on an ordinary stretch, he drove right off the road. And Sweetheart was drugged, and I bet Arlen was too, or how would a big guy like that get attacked without a fight? There was no sign of a struggle, except for the busted guitar. That just occurred to me."

He took a breath.

I said, "Plus, it wouldn't surprise me if they find the same stuff in Harriet Crowder. It's a pattern."

"Really? A pattern? I think I've heard of them. Speaking of patterns, something tells me that you're about to inform me of who you suspect of doing this."

"Yes, I am. Anabel Huffington-Chabot, possibly in cahoots with Jean-Claude."

He rolled his eyes. "Madame Huffington-Chabot is a very important businessperson in our community. We can't accuse her of serious crimes like this because it's your latest wild idea."

"Cyril had a previous arrangement to pick up Anabel on the highway on the day of Danny Dupree's death. Have you forgotten that she locked me in the toilet cubicle. All right, I realize that that is trivial. But her feud with Harriet Crowder wasn't, and Harriet's now dead. Then there's the fact she knew Arlen Young would check the wiring in my house. She has a relationship with Jean-Claude, and he knows Faron Findlay is my insurance agent and where I live, of course."

The tally was: dead, dead, burned down, nearly dead and maybe dead, but that was not enough to get more than a shrug out of Sarrazin.

*   *   *

To recap: I had no settlement, no house, no car, no money, no computer, no insurance and now, no cab driver. There was nothing I could do about most of it, but why should I have all the fun. I decided, for once, to go on the offensive and find Philip, wherever he was.

Liz lent me her car again, and I had the keys to Philip's office. I didn't think for one minute that he had burned down my house, but he had made me miserable for years, and I was looking forward to telling him that the police thought he was implicated in arson.

Five minutes after I let myself into Philip's downtown office, I had a sick feeling in my stomach, but I also found Irene's home address in the files. If his office dragon didn't know what was going on, no one would.

*　　*　　*

Irene answered the door of her condo apartment just off Montcalm in old Hull. Her eyes were red and swollen.

Finally, he's gotten to you too, I thought.

"Fiona," she said.

"Irene," I answered. I almost felt sorry for her.

She let out a slow muffled sob. Oh, crap. The last thing I needed was to have to comfort the very woman who'd made it her job to "protect" Philip from me, the wicked ex-wife.

I stepped past her and into the condo. "Come on. I'll make you a cup of tea."

"Too hot," she shuddered.

"Fine. Why don't we just sit down, and you can tell me what's going on."

"I can't."

"Philip's in a lot of trouble."

She snuffled. "He's lost everything."

I sat stunned for a full minute. "What? But what went

wrong? His practice was busy. He was on the go all the time. Too busy to take my calls, for sure."

She reached for a tissue. Her hands were shaking. Somehow, even given her relationship with Philip, it seemed too much. "Investments. They went bad."

"Investments? You must be kidding. But Philip's so…"

She was sobbing now.

And it hit me. "Did you invest too?"

"I cashed out my RRSPs. My savings. Everything. I even took out a new mortgage."

I stared at her in horror. No wonder Philip had been so slow to pay. "What did he invest in? He's so cautious."

"He said Danny Dupree was handling everything. All the money. They were going to flip this big property. They had the seller. They had the buyer. They needed to have the money up-front. It was going to make them a fortune."

"But Danny's dead."

"Of course. Do you think I don't know that? Not everyone's as stupid and self-centred as you."

I controlled myself. "How much was it anyway?"

"Three hundred and fifty thousand from me. More from Philip. He had a lot more money to invest." The tears welled up again.

"Why cash?"

"It was to avoid some kind of tax or something. Philip feels terrible. He's ruined, and I am too."

"But in this day and age, no one needs cash for transactions. Let alone huge transactions. It's all done through banks."

She snapped. "Philip knew what he was doing, although you never gave him credit for that."

"Apparently, he didn't know what he was doing, Irene. Or you wouldn't be sitting here bawling your eyes out, and Philip wouldn't be…where is he anyway?"

"I have no idea where he is. None! And do you think I'm going to tell you? Never! If you hadn't been endlessly badgering him to get an unfair share of his assets, he probably never would have taken a chance on Danny's idea. You have been nothing but trouble for the poor man." Flecks of froth formed on Irene's lips.

"Spare me," I said, standing up. Even though I felt sorry for her, I knew that one benefit of all this would be never seeing Irene again. "And by the way?"

She sniffed.

I said as I headed for the door, "You might not want to tell me where Philip is, but you won't have the same flexibility with the police. I believe they're on the way."

I dialed Sarrazin before I was out of the building.

*   *   *

I thought fast. Philip might have been a lot of things, but for sure he wasn't an embezzler. Too messy, too dangerous. He might have been a jerk and a bully, he might have been a pompous ass, but he was not a criminal. But even so, it explained why he would act out of character. He'd panicked. I needed to talk to him. And although I wasn't foolish enough to betray this to Irene, I even had an inkling about where he'd take shelter from the world when the going got rough. The main plan was to get there before Irene tipped him off. *No idea where he is, my fat fanny.*

I got that same fat fanny in gear, along with Liz's car. Luckily, Liz had filled the tank. I broke a few laws heading up the line. I stopped on a quiet back country road in Rupert and parked out of sight. I sidled along the driveway and approached the immaculate grey farm house with the freshly painted white gingerbread trim. Every blade of grass in the acres surrounding appeared to be exactly the same height. Philip doesn't come by his obsessions by chance.

249

I liked Grandma Silk even less than Irene, and it was mutual. I was pretty sure she was the source of Philip's personality quirks. Maybe it skips a generation, because his parents were both relaxed people. I'd had a warm and jovial father-in-law and an affectionate mother-in-law. I'd been very sad to lose them both. While they were alive, they'd spent a lot of time scratching their heads about the way their only boy had turned out, although they'd been far too loyal to admit it. Granny Silk was another story. She and Philip shared the fusspot gene for sure. We had managed to avoid each other for most of the years of my marriage and for all of the years afterwards. Now that she'd hit ninety, there was always the chance she might have mellowed, but I wasn't counting on it. Sometimes you just have to straighten your spine and march off to war. I checked the garage. Sure enough, a shiny new BMW M5-E60. Not Granny's, I was betting.

I ducked around the back of the house, to the kitchen entrance. The inside door to the house was open, the Victorian style screen door keeping the bugs out. A shadowy figure loped around the kitchen. I whipped open the screen door and stepped in. A small matter of unauthorized entry was nothing compared to the rest of what I'd been dealing with.

Philip whirled and almost dropped his glass. I put a finger to my lips. He pursed his.

I said, "Don't alert your grandmother, and no one will get hurt. Step outside. We need to talk."

He blanched. He was already pasty, so that was something. "Did anyone follow you?"

"Absolutely not." I had no idea and hadn't thought to look. I wasn't accustomed to being followed. Of course, I wasn't used to having my house burned down either.

He hesitated.

"Fine," I said, "we'll stay inside, but I don't want to deal with you-know-who, and if you betray me, I'll shop you to the cops."

He said, "You wouldn't."

"I would," I said, "and what's more, I'll tell your grand-mother everything you've done. Every single, vile, messy thing. I will use words like bankrupt and bailiff and prison."

He fell for that. Which was good, because I actually didn't know the vile, messy details. This bluffing business was going pretty well. I felt I'd learned a good deal from my executive assistant. "She won't hear us. She sleeps for about an hour every day at this time. Nothing wakes her."

I followed him into the parlour, which was the place where blindingly white starched doilies live out their days. He sat on the sofa, and I sat on a chair that felt like it was made of concrete. I knew from memory that the sofa was just as unyielding.

"I want to hear everything from your viewpoint, Philip. And if you know what's good for you, you'll do that without a single criticism or dig at me."

Too late. "What are you wearing? You look like a goat herd. Is that a Grateful Dead T-shirt? I hope you didn't run into any of my colleagues dressed like that." He just couldn't resist.

"And you," I said, "are wearing two different socks."

"I am not," he huffed.

I pointed to his feet. I kind of liked this mean stuff—on a purely temporary basis.

He stared down at his mismatched socks and deflated a bit. "I have a lot on my mind."

"What was Danny up to?"

"A deal. An amazing deal."

"Maybe you mean an amazing death. What happened?"

"I didn't know everything. It's not my fault."

"Jury's still out on that."

"I didn't know he'd signed your name too."

What? Well, that came from nowhere. Of course, if I asked all the questions that were about to leap from my mouth, especially if I shouted them, Phil would clam up. Trust me, no one clams up like Phil.

"Didn't you?" I said, with great restraint.

"Well, no. I'd hardly condone forging your name on a legal document, would I?"

Forging my name on a legal document? What could that be? A loan application? Hardly. No one in the world could get credit based on me as a co-borrower or collateral or anything else.

It hit me. I probably turned pastier than Phil. "No. Not possible," I said. "Not the house. Not our house. He couldn't have done that."

One look at Philip's face, and I realized he'd thought I already knew. I said, "You sold the house?"

"Not sold. Mortgaged. I mean, you hadn't lived in it for three years. Don't get all sentimental on me."

"*Sentimental?* You were party to a scheme to defraud me of my share of the house I worked to pay for, and you are calling my reaction sentimental?"

"Danny did it. I didn't know."

"You're a lawyer, for Pete's sake. How could you not know? Did he forge your signature too? Oh, my God, he did."

Philip managed not to meet my eyes after my outburst.

"Spill," I said.

"I confronted him when I found out he'd forged your name. I couldn't believe it. He kept saying that house was half-mine, and the deal was going to make us a fortune. We couldn't lose. It was just a couple of days, and then I'd get my funds back and pay off the mortgage with a nice profit, and you'd never know."

"I guess I got mine, all right. So now, even my property is mortgaged."

252

"That didn't come out right. What I'm trying to say, Fiona, is that he duped me too. And Irene. And who knows who else. He was crazy. Nuts. Out of control. He could be so charismatic. He convinced me that if he had access to cash and a bit of time, he'd be rich. And so would I."

"If I remember correctly, he was more of a jerk than a charismatic businessman. Anyway, now he's dead, you'll have to go after his estate to recoup our funds. What's that look on your face, Phil?"

Phil stared down at his feet. The bags under his eyes matched the navy sock, and his skin tone was equal to the grey one. I realized that he was hyperventilating.

"Breathe!" I said. "Then talk."

"He had it with him."

"The money?" I have always prided myself on not being a slave to money. This might have been less true than I thought.

"Don't shout, Fiona. You'll wake my grandmother."

I lowered my voice. "He had the cash with him when his car incinerated?" I didn't have to hear the answer to know that it was true. I said, "But why?"

"He was about to make the big transaction. He was very excited about it. He told me like it was good news."

"You actually knew that he was driving around like a maniac with our money in his oversized status symbol?"

"Please keep your voice down. It's not like you to shout."

"I never had anything this big to shout about before."

"I found out just before the accident. I tried to meet up with him. But I didn't get there in time. The road was blocked off, and he was..."

Okay. Big exhale, as they say in yoga class.

"It's all gone, Fiona."

Tolstoy's Temptations

Peanut Butter Dog Biscuits

2 cups whole-wheat flour
1 tablespoon baking powder
1 cup, less one tablespoon, chunky peanut butter
1 tablespoon liquid honey
1 cup milk

Preheat oven to 350°F. In a bowl, combine flour and baking powder. In another bowl, mix peanut butter, honey and milk, then add to dry ingredients and mix well. Place dough on a lightly floured surface and knead. Roll dough to 1/4 inch thickness and use a heart-shaped cookie cutter to cut out cookies. Bake for 18-20 minutes on a greased baking sheet until lightly brown. Watch carefully, they burn! Cool on a rack, then store in an air-tight container.

You should check with the V-E-T before you serve these to your canine companion.

Seventeen

I was halfway to St. Aubaine when it hit me: how had Philip found out that Danny Dupree had the money with him? I did a U-turn and headed back. This time I wasn't lucky enough to avoid the grandmother. She blocked the screen door.

I raised my voice and bluffed. "Get out here, Phil. I don't have much time."

Philip slunk to the front door. "We can't talk here." Meaning in front of his grandmother.

"How did you find out about that situation we were discussing? With Danny, the other day."

"He texted me."

"But I was trying to reach you. Irene insisted you had your Blackberry turned off that day. Was she lying?"

He shook his head. "I was at the hospital having a test. They make your turn them off."

"So when was the text message sent?"

"I don't know. I never looked. "

"Even I know that there will be a record of the call. Now would be a good time to check."

Philip handed me the Blackberry. I clicked around until I found it. But that couldn't be right. "Is your clock wrong on this?" I said.

He bristled. "Of course it's not. What are you talking about?"

"I saw that accident. I know what time it happened. At the time that this message was sent, Danny Dupree was already dead."

*　　*　　*

I took a detour past my late home, for once glad to see the garbage can. Then I drove to see Sarrazin.

Sarrazin took the offence. "Were you planning to tell me that you have been in contact with your husband?"

"I just spoke to him. Now I want to cut a deal."

He massaged his temple and sighed.

I said, "Remember that cigarette butt?"

"Remind me."

"The one I told you about. The one that the woman in the Escalade flicked out at me. The same woman that Cyril must have picked up in Tulip Valley. I still have that butt. It didn't burn up in the car. Josey cleaned up the car and put the trash in the garbage can."

Sarrazin sighed dramatically. "I thought I'd already explained the importance of chain of evidence to you."

"Fine, I understand that, but there will be DNA on that butt, no? And you could find out who the person is, since you don't believe it's Anabel. I know a bit about this stuff. I watched television the odd time when I still had one, you know."

"DNA? Don't make me laugh. Leaving aside the backlog at the lab, you can only match DNA when you have someone to match it too. There is no database called EBWIQ."

"What?"

"That would be Every Blonde Woman in Quebec."

"Very funny, but…"

"And don't start again with Anabel Huffington-Chabot either. I want to talk about your husband."

"Ex-husband."

"Right. The one you're shielding."

In the end I gave Philip up, with the minor concession that

Sarrazin would agree to send the butt to the lab. No guarantees.

*   *   *

I hit the Hull hospital as soon as Josey provided me with the good news that Cyril was conscious. Luckily, I wasn't *persona non grata* there, although I still was in the rehab centre. As I tiptoed in, he lay sleeping, snoring gently. There was black bruising around both eyes, his nose had been broken, and judging by the bandages and stitches and IV hookups, he still had a way to go.

"Cyril," I whispered. "Cyril."

"He's sleeping. As if you didn't notice." Cyril's fellow patient in the semi-private room looked to be about a hundred. Wicked little blue eyes sparkled at me.

"I thought he might be just resting," I said. *"Cyril!"*

The eyes opened slowly. He croaked something, but I couldn't really make it out.

"Shhh," I said. "Listen to me. Did Anabel Huffington give you something to eat or drink before you had your accident?"

"Who is…?"

"You know who she is, Cyril. The good tipper."

He shook his head, but that caused him pain. The other patient said, "That didn't sound good. They can up his painkillers."

"Okay," I said, "I'll call the nurse." I pressed the button by the side of the bed. "But tell me about Anabel. It's urgent. It could save your life."

"Don't know."

"Sure you do. You waved to her. Blonde. Tall."

It was painful to listen to Cyril's breathing. "No."

"What? Sure it was. You picked her up."

"Didn't."

"Yes. Did."

"Pain."

"The nurse will be here. I'll get help. Hold on. What is taking her so long?"

The roommate said, "Spend much time in hospitals, lady?"

"More than I want to," I said, heading for the door.

Cyril croaked out. "The other one."

"The other nurse? The other buzzer? What?"

"Pretty, smile. Hair. Different." Then nothing but erratic breathing. Eyes closed.

"You lost him again." The roommate seemed to find that quite satisfactory. Probably needed a bit of drama in his life.

I headed down the hall and snagged a nurse. "I can only be in one place at a time," she said, crisply.

"Oh, right. I'm glad you're here now. He's in bad shape."

"Yes, we're getting used to him," she said, striding up to his bed. "Can you wait outside, please?"

"But—"

"Won't be long." She whipped the curtain around the bed. With all the violations of personal privacy that routinely take place in hospitals, such as the catheter quite obviously displayed by the side of the roommate's bed, I wasn't sure why Cyril's nurse was so uptight.

I paced in the hallway, while Cyril's roommate positioned himself to send me lascivious looks. It's good to know when you reach your nineties, not all the sparks are out. By the time I got back into the room, the morphine had hit the target, and Cyril was sleeping.

"He'll sleep for a couple of hours. You can wait here with me," the roommate said.

"Sorry, other plans."

I was already running when I left the room. Cyril hadn't been talking about Anabel, as I had thought. He must have been talking about Marietta. Marietta with the wavy chestnut hair. The pretty, flirty lady who'd been an actress before she became a cooking sensation. Marietta, who was rumoured to be setting up a corporation to market her own unique "brand". Had she been in cahoots with Danny Dupree to get the money to finance the next step of her meteoric rise? Marietta, who'd had a problem with Harriet, Marietta, who liked to sneak a cigarette, and Marietta, who was around the Wallingford Estate and who could easily have learned that Anabel provided the name of an electrician for me. And what electrician wouldn't do whatever Marietta wanted? Who wouldn't let her in if she came knocking?

*   *   *

I used my cell phone as I trotted along the hot Hull sidewalk to Liz's car. Josey had left a message.

"Good news, Miz Silk. I got word that Marietta is going to give you a choice of recipes, and she's agreed to a photo for your book. I'm going up there to make arrangements now. Can you try to keep your schedule clear for me? This is important. It could make or break us."

"Oh, no, Josey. Whatever you do, don't go to the Wallingford Estate." Of course, I was talking to the air. I dialed her cell phone with shaky hands and left a message. "Stay away from Marietta! I think she's the killer. Promise me you won't go there."

Next, I phoned Sarrazin and reached his voice mail.

"You were right, I was wrong. It's not Anabel Huffington-Chabot," I said, panting. "It's Naughty Marietta. You should get someone over to the Hull hospital to talk to Cyril and to protect him. And you could show Marietta's picture to Arlen too, if he regains consciousness. I'm searching for Josey. She was trying to connect with Marietta on my behalf. Oh, and get Marietta's DNA too."

I tried not to imagine the look on his face. Instead, I got into Liz's car and floored it all the way back to St. Aubaine.

*   *   *

Damn. As I pulled into the village, I picked up the phone and realized I'd missed two messages. That's the problem with the reception cutting out on the rural highway.

Sarrazin's was quite clear. "Do not, I repeat, do *not* go anywhere near Marietta or the Wallingford Estate. Do you hear me? I will follow up on this latest batch of allegations, but I want you to go to Woody's and stay there. We, that is to say the *police,* will follow up. We will find the Thring girl."

Josey's message was not so clear.

"Miz Silk?" she squawked. "We got a big problem. It's not—"

The line went dead.

Obviously, Josey hadn't received my message in time. I spun gravel as I gunned Liz's car up the hill to the Wallingford Estate. The foyer was deserted. Chelsea was on her way out. She looked more sophisticated than usual in a black linen suit, perhaps a clue to the splendid woman she would no doubt become by the time she hit thirty. "Oh, hello," she said. "There's no one here. They've finished filming."

"I need your help. I'm looking for…"

"Sorry. Anabel wants me to make arrangements for Harriet's memorial before everyone leaves town. I have an appointment at the funeral home, and I'm a bit late. She'll have my head on a spike if I miss that."

"Do you know where Marietta is?"

"Marietta? I think she went into the village with Rafaël. They're quite the team, those two. I feel terrible, but I have to ask you to leave now."

"But my assistant is here somewhere."

She lit up. "Josey? She's so funny and cute. Executive assistant, she calls herself. I wish we could give her a job. She seems really on top of things. She was here, but she said she had to go down to the village. She seemed a bit panicky. Anyway, no one's supposed to be on site except staff. Sorryeee. Anabel's orders again."

I followed Chelsea out the door and waved goodbye. I drove down the hill ahead of her and parked at Woody's. Woody was tied up with a couple of suppliers. He shook his head when I asked if he'd seen Josey.

I checked

No Josey there. I checked out all the restaurants and shops. No Josey, which was to be expected, but no Marietta either. I hurried along to the Britannia, but Uncle Mike had no idea where Josey could be. I left a new message every couple of minutes.

Finally, I marched back up the hill to the Wallingford Estate. The foyer was empty. I thought I heard a thump and ducked into the office quickly, since I'd been told I wasn't supposed to be on the premises. Across the room, I could see Anabel's golf bag. What if she came back to get that? I couldn't get tossed out before I found Josey. I decided to duck behind the desk. As I moved, I tripped over a suitcase, protruding from under the desk. I sprawled forward and knocked down a framed photo that had been propped behind the door. I glanced at it as I got up. It was just a standard boring PR group shot, one of many that had been taken outside the Wallingford Estate main house. Why was it stuck there instead of the wall? I picked it up. Everyone was smiling broadly at the camera. A local realtor whose face was on every second FOR SALE sign grinned wider than anyone. No wonder. The Wallingford Estate, even in its derelict days, must have meant a hefty commission. Jean-Claude seemed pleased with himself, while Anabel looked haughty, but happy. The man I took to be her husband had his hand on her shoulder and seemed blissfully unaware that he would soon be put out with the trash. My heart jumped when I saw Danny Dupree, cocky and cavalier, in the photo too. I did another double-take at the woman standing next to him. Chelsea Brazeau was showing her pretty white teeth too. But that wasn't what I noticed.

What a fool I'd been.

Things were quiet in the foyer, but just as I stuck my nose out, Brady came clattering down the stairs in his cowboy boots. He whirled and clutched his clipboard when he spotted me.

"You scared me," he gasped. "I thought no one was—"

No time for chatting. "Have you seen Josey? My assistant."

"Yes, she was here earlier trying to find Marietta. They had an appointment, and apparently Marietta didn't show up."

"Is that like her?"

"No. She's actually a sweetheart and a real pro. But now that the shooting's over, maybe she told someone to send a message, and it didn't get sent. Chaos rules when a production is breaking up."

"Where did you see Josey last?"

"She was heading toward the kitchen."

"And Marietta?"

"She was in the kitchen earlier too. That's what I told Josey. I also told her that the site's still off-limits. We have to let people know that."

"Who told you?"

"Anabel."

"Or was it Chelsea speaking on her behalf?"

"Same thing, isn't it? One is the friendly face, the other the harsh reality?"

"Not this time. One other question, Brady. When did Chelsea change her hair colour from blonde?"

"That new honey-brown colour rocks, doesn't it? I was blown away that she could get a colour job that good at a little salon in *this* village on such short notice. She decided just like that!" He snapped his fingers. "It shouldn't have been a surprise. People will do anything for Chelsea. I wish I had half her personality. Even having brown hair doesn't hurt. Although I loved the blonde highlights she had before too. I guess she thought her 'do was too much like Anabel's, and she wanted to make her own style statement."

My head spun slightly. "I need to know when she had it done."

"Around the time they started production. Monday night, I guess. Yeah, I noticed it Tuesday morning. Wasn't it blonde the first time you came up here looking for Harriet?"

"I didn't see Chelsea that first day. She was in the office, and Harriet had just reamed her out."

"Ooh. I remember that fight. And you're right. Chelsea was blonde that day."

"Okay. And I'm guessing that although I didn't see her, she saw me."

Brady stared at me. "This is one really strange conversation."

"It's about to get stranger." I struggled to sound rational. "Josey is in danger. Chelsea is trying to kill her. She murdered a man called Danny Dupree for his investment money, she burned down my house, she killed Harriet, and she attacked Arlen Young and a cab driver. She's very dangerous, and she's getting rid of anyone who can tie her to murder and fraud involving a very large sum of money."

Brady squeaked in alarm. "Are you joking? But I haven't done anything to her!"

"This is serious. Start running down the hill. Use your cell phone, call 911 now and tell them there's a crime in progress. Tell them to hurry."

"But Chelsea couldn't..." As Brady stood there, I could almost see the light bulb go on over his head. Some small memory told him Chelsea was not what she appeared to be.

"Please do what I ask before the body count goes up."

I raced along the corridor as soon as Brady scampered down the front stairs.

I pushed open the heavy swinging doors into the kitchen. The vast food preparation space was full of gleaming stainless and high-end cooking equipment. The show was over, the sound and lighting equipment had been packed up and removed. All that remained of the gifts of food was one large green can of olive oil and a decorative glass jar of balsamic vinegar. I stared at the twelve-burner stove top, the shelves of white china. I thought I heard a muffled noise, but perhaps that was my jittery imagination.

Again, I heard a sound. Was it coming from outside? Had Brady decided I was nuts after all and come back to tell me so instead of calling the police? I moved through the kitchen, checking here and there. I kicked a crumpled piece of blue paper in front of the walk-in freezer. The freezer door had been secured with a padlock. A soft thump, thump, thump came from inside. I flipped open my cell and dialed Sarrazin one more time, just as I heard the click of heels behind me.

I whirled, whipping the phone behind my back.

Chelsea stood there, behind the door, smiling and holding a golf club as if it were a fashion accessory. I hoped she was too far away to hear the sound of Sarrazin saying "Leave a message after the beep."

She didn't seem to notice. "So, you just couldn't give up, I see."

"I couldn't," I said. "And I haven't."

"I'm afraid you have to now."

"Not much chance of that, Chelsea. What have you done with Josey?"

Best not to let Chelsea know that I had a good idea where Josey was. And I planned to rescue her, not join her.

I hustled myself around to the far side of the huge centre prep island. Chelsea approached, swinging the golf club.

I said loudly. "Very clever of you to use Anabel's golf club, Chelsea. She'll get the blame. I notice you're wearing gloves, so of course, no prints. Are those her golf gloves?"

"You won't need to worry about that, because you'll be dead."

"But you know, prints aren't everything. The cops have that cigarette butt you tossed out at me from the Escalade. They'll find your DNA. Did you mean it to fly right into my car? They should find the same DNA on one of those Sleeman bottles at Arlen's place. Maybe even on the sheets. Who knows? I suppose there will be some trace in Harriet's car too." I hoped that Sarrazin would be able to hear at least some of this on his voice mail. And preferably while I was still alive.

I kept on. "Yes, I can see where Harriet would have been a real handful. She was on to you, for sure. What was it? Some kind of fiddling with funds or cheques? No wonder she was so angry, but of course, everyone felt sorry for poor little you, being picked on. That was a terrific performance. I'm guessing you couldn't resist chiselling the production company, even if it wasn't the big bucks. Even though you did have the big score with Danny Dupree. I'm sure there were others. Then what a great idea to fleece the fraud artist, although killing him seemed a bit excessive. I suppose he had no clue that you'd slipped him some kind of GHB drug. And Philip and Irene believed that their money had burned up in the Escalade. Genius. I'm sure it must have been satisfying. Then I show up, and that annoying little Harriet comes along raising hell about this and that."

"She's out of the picture now. And you will be too."

"You're really clearing the field," I said. "Danny Dupree, what did you do? Stage a fight just before you figured the drug would kick in? Did you switch briefcases on him? For sure you knew he was a reckless driver. Chances were he'd be killed? No big deal, because you had arranged for Cyril to pick you up ahead of time. Did he try a bit of blackmail when he figured out who you really were? He likes extra cash, that Cyril. But he likes his beer too, so it wouldn't be hard to slip him something. Terrible drivers in these parts. So many accidents on that highway."

She watched me with slitted eyes. The girl next door look had vanished, leaving behind someone else, someone hard, calculating, and dangerous. How calculated had that look been? And how many people beside me and Josey had fallen for her warm, friendly smile and soft, pretty face? Chelsea was still swinging the golf club, just out of range.

I kept backing away to make sure of that. "He's still alive, but under police guard, of course. He'll talk. They'll trace something to you there. Maybe the drink you used to drug him. I don't know what, but they will. They've sent a lot of samples to the lab for comparisons." I was making it up as I went along and lying like a rug. I could only hope that she fell for some of it.

"Arlen too, of course, he's in and out of consciousness. But he's already been able to tell them I didn't do it. There's a cop by his bedside, and it's just a matter of time until they show him your picture and he says that's her. So I'd say the best thing is to let Josey and me go. You can take your suitcase from the office and make a run for it."

I stumbled backward as she lunged, swinging the club. I stared around wildly, looking for a weapon to defend myself. There are many dangerous items in a commercial kitchen, but nothing that protects against a golf club. Chelsea stepped closer. I backed further and further away, until I felt the doorknob at my back. I grabbed it and tried to open it. Would I be better off in the side garden of the house? Chelsea's smile said no. She raised the club and advanced. I feinted to the right then ducked toward the far side of the giant kitchen island as she swung toward where I'd been.

"You won't get away," Chelsea said, laughing.

"It's a game to you, isn't it? The scams. Outwitting people. Tricks, disguises. But this game is over. The police are coming. You don't want to add another murder to your list of crimes. You'll be caught in the act this time."

"What do I have to lose?" Chelsea said. "If they have the evidence you claim, I'm done. But this way I have the satisfaction of getting you first. And I'll probably still get away."

"But they'll find you."

"The police are idiots. They've never found me before."

"Well, I agree with you about the police. Absolute fools. They're looking for my ex-husband, Philip, now. Why don't you pin the killings on Philip? Have you thought of that?"

She hesitated. "Don't be stupid."

I tried to keep my voice from shaking. "He was Danny's business associate. He was angry at Danny. I'll tell them."

She laughed. "Sure you will, and then you'll change your tune as soon as we're out of here."

Here was my last panicky chance to play a bit of her own

deceitful game. I needed to stay alive until help arrived.

"Are you kidding? I hate the bastard. I'd be happy to tell them he burned down my house so that he could get half the money from the sale of the property. But mostly, he did it for spite. He could easily have killed Danny if he thought Danny was stealing the money from him. And he is perfectly capable of attacking Arlen to implicate me. He's always hated Cyril. They've had public battles. I'll say that you're lucky he didn't get you."

A smile flickered at the corners of her mouth. She obviously liked the idea of Philip being charged with the arson that she'd committed. The same arson where she'd stolen the walking stick to frame me when she attacked Arlen. She said, "I don't trust you."

"Trust this. Philip will go to jail. You'll go off to do whatever comes next. I'll get access to what's left of his property, and I'll have the pleasure of revenge. We'll both win."

She tapped the golf club against the floor, just to remind me who was really in charge.

"And the best thing is that the police are already looking for Philip for the arson. They won't want to start again. With my testimony they'll get a conviction. How good is that?"

She narrowed her eyes, thinking.

A dim noise reached us from the front of the house. She whipped around toward the entry door at the far end of the kitchen. Just for a second, but it was long enough. I reached onto the counter and snatched the big green tin of olive oil. Lucky for me, it had been opened.

She swivelled to face me. "Thanks for the kind offer," she said. "But I think I'll go it alone. I don't want to have you holding anything over my head for the rest of my life. Like I'm holding this golf club over yours." She raised the club and slashed. I shook the container and spewed oil as far as I could. Chelsea slipped, fell and swore. I made a dash for the other end of the vast kitchen island. Chelsea struggled to her feet and turned around.

"You're never going to make it," she shrieked.

"Watch me!" I turned the container upside down and spread the rest of the oil over the stretch of floor between us.

"You can't stop me." She stood up, raised the club with one hand and grabbed the side of the island with the other. I used every scrap of strength I had to heave the empty can of oil at her head. It made a very satisfying thunk. The tin crashed onto the floor as I raced to the end of the kitchen and flung open the swinging doors. I heard a resounding *"Tabernac!"* as the door smacked Viau on the forehead. I collapsed against Sarrazin. Viau, holding his head, staggered ahead, along with several armed officers.

From the sounds in the kitchen, Chelsea put up a good fight. The officers had some challenges with the oily floor. But they also had weapons.

Sarrazin growled as he stepped past me to join the fray. "Okay, madame, exactly what part of 'don't go to the Wallingford Estate' was unclear?"

"The Josey part. I think Chelsea stuck her in the walk-in freezer. It's been padlocked. Watch out for the oil on the floor. Oops."

Corpse Reviver

Contributed by Woody Quirke

1 1/2 ounces aged brandy
1/2 ounce bitters
1 ounce white crème de menthe

In a mixing glass half-filled with ice cubes, combine all of the ingredients. Stir well. Strain into a cocktail glass.

For emergency use only.

Eighteen

There was something fitting about our gathering that night at Hélène's. Not only were there special guests, but the kitchen refinishing had been completed, and Jean-Claude was nowhere to be seen. The heat wave had broken, and Tolstoy was able to wag his tail again. Oh right, and Josey and I were alive. We'd had a few hours to recover and get our adrenaline levels back to normal.

"His lordship must be in the doghouse," Josey whispered to me. She was still a bit pale after her ordeal in the freezer.

Hélène glided around the patio serving hors d'oeuvre. Bottles of chilled Pinot Grigio stood open next to a fresh pitcher of her signature sangria. Woody had parked his wheelchair at the poolside bar and was busy mixing himself something he called a "corpse reviver". He claimed it could work wonders for anyone's sex life. Not that anyone had requested this information.

He chortled. "That Hélène is one classy broad. No other bar in this village would have ten-year-old brandy, bitters and white crème de menthe. You want one, kiddo? These suckers are seventy proof. Knock you right on your keister."

Liz snorted from a deck chair. She had beaten Woody to the bar and discovered that the Lamontagne household had an excellent supply of Courvoisier.

Hélène approached us with a plate of smoked salmon canapés. She reached down and offered one to Tolstoy. He likes the finer things in life too. Josey's new project, Sweetheart, was resting near her feet. She had her own steady source of treats. Of course, her presence was purely temporary, because Arlen was expected to recover.

"Josée told me that Jean-Claude's cousin, Paulette, interfered with your visits to Marc-André at the hospital. Is that true?"

"Of course it's true," Josey said.

"It is so very serious that I need to hear it from Fiona, Josée."

"Yes," I said. "She called security on me and claimed I had tried to defraud Marc-André."

"Very painful and embarrassing for you," Hélène said. "And it must have hurt Marc-André terribly too."

"Yes. And also robbed us of some time together, because who knows—"

"C'était épouvantable!"

"Sure was scary," Josey said grimly.

"Josée and I have had a nice discussion," Hélène said.

"Oh, good. I've been worried about…words that were said. I wanted to talk to you about it again, but…"

"You had other things on your mind, Miz Silk."

"You mean like murder," I said.

"And your book!"

"You know what? I'm not sure I ever want to set foot in a kitchen again."

"You don't need to, Miz Silk. Marietta and Rafaël said they'd do the recipes for you, as many as you want. They said it's a piece of cake for them, although that's like a joke. Your name will still be on the cover. Here they come now."

Marietta and Rafaël strolled toward us, hand in hand. Marietta swooped in for a pair of air kisses. "I am so grateful," she said. "Poor Harriet did a lot for me. I know that no one else cared much for her, but she was unique. Thank you for finding who killed her."

Rafaël put his arm around her shoulder.

I said, "Huh."

That little bit was the most dramatic moment of the party, up until Jean-Claude appeared. For once, the smug superiority was missing. His lordship was definitely subdued.

Hélène clinked on a glass to get our attention. *"Mes amis, écoutez!* Jean-Claude has a happy announcement to make."

Conversation lulled, but I could still hear murmurs and giggles here and there.

Jean-Claude cleared his throat and frowned. Something told me this happy announcement was going to hurt. Hélène nodded encouragement.

"Our neighbour, Fiona Silk, as you know, has suffered a serious personal setback in the loss of her home," Jean-Claude said, his voice cracking.

The group fell silent at that, except for Josey, who muttered, "And whose fault was that?"

"My company, Les Entreprises Lamontagne, will reconstruct the house at no cost to Fiona, as a gesture of community support. Work will begin as soon as the arson investigation is complete."

"You can go ahead any time," a bearlike voice said. Jean-Claude turned and did a double-take at the sight of Sarrazin.

Josey whispered, "Who invited him?"

"I did. The sergeant has been very helpful to me. He has given me a *lot* of useful information," Hélène said, with a sly look at Jean-Claude.

Jean-Claude paled. I was too flabbergasted by this news to utter a single word.

"We're done with the site," Sarrazin said. I noticed his eyes were focussed on the plate of smoked salmon canapés. "Just thought you'd like to know that Arlen Young was able to identify Chelsea Brazeau as the woman who attacked him. So has Cyril. And we have been able to confirm that she is wanted on fraud and extortion charges, under various names, in other jurisdictions. We'll get her for both murders and for the arson too. So that's good news for you, Jean-Claude."

"What about locking Miz Silk in the ladies room so she wouldn't recognize her from the Escalade? Before she got her hair dyed?" Josey said. "That was just plain mean. I guess now we know what Chelsea was really like, we shouldn't be surprised that she'd do something like that to embarrass a person."

Sarrazin seemed to be having some trouble with his mouth, a twitch or something.

"It's okay, Josey, we'll let the past go," I said. "Some people are naturally malicious. Chelsea enjoyed all the trouble she caused, big and little, I know that now."

"She will go to prison for a long time, I am sure. *Mais, c'est merveilleux, n'est-ce pas*, Jean-Claude? And is there something else you want to mention, *chéri?*"

As Sarrazin edged his way toward the smoked salmon plate, Jean-Claude recovered his composure. He smiled his familiar shark smile. "As part of this goodwill project, of course, we will provide Fiona with new appliances, furniture and housewares."

"Whoa. Really must have been in the doghouse," Josey said in another non-whisper.

"That's terrific," Liz said. "Does that mean you don't need your old chairs back, Fiona?"

"No, it doesn't," Josey snapped. "They have sentimental value. Those snifters and the good dishes do too."

"Thank you, Hélène," I said. "I'm completely overwhelmed. I don't know what to say."

"This is all Jean-Claude's doing," she said, with an angelic smile. "From now on, things are going to be much better on Chemin des cèdres."

I didn't have the heart to tell her that Faron Findlay had contacted me and explained that my insurance company might have to pay out anyway, because I hadn't received the official notice of termination by registered mail before the fire. Time would tell how that would play out. But Jean-Claude could dangle in the meantime. It was the least I could do to thank his wife.

Scampis in Love: An Appetizer for Two

Contributed by Marietta and Rafaël

1 tablespoon melted butter
1 finely minced garlic clove
1 tablespoon finely chopped green onions or finely minced fresh chives
pinch of salt and pepper
6 large shrimp
2 tablespoons white wine
Crumbled feta cheese, enough to cover shrimp

Mix together butter, garlic, onions, salt, pepper and shrimp. Put three shrimp each in small (4 ounce) ovenproof dishes or ramekins, add tablespoon of wine to each dish, and cover with enough crumbled feta to make a nice crust.

Put pots on baking sheet and bake in 400°F oven for 10-12 minutes or until shrimp are pink and cooked through and the feta is slightly browned.

Share with someone you love.

paramour

Nineteen

It ain't over 'til it's over. One month later, my house rebuilding was coming along nicely, I had learned to cope with living in Woody's spare room, and some of my nineteen lost pounds had found their way home as a result of his breakfasts. A book of sorts had been submitted to Lola for Bixby and Snead's fall list, mostly due to Marietta and Rafaël. I still blushed when I thought about that particular book, but you do what you have to. Plus, Josey kept hinting at a big surprise. Naturally that made me nervous.

"What kind of surprise?"

"I can't tell you, Miz Silk, or it wouldn't be a proper surprise. You should know that."

"I hate surprises. And you should know that."

Tolstoy gave Josey a nuzzle. He loves surprises, especially if they involve food.

"Boy, Miz Silk, I think you'll like this one. Just keep driving. It's not far from here."

"But where are we going? You know I have to get Liz's car back to her before too long, or I'll never hear the end of it."

"I already spoke to Dr. Prentiss, and it's okay. She said that we could take our time."

By that point, we were ten miles from the village, heading along the highway in the opposite direction from Woody's. What could Josey want to show me?

"But—"

"No buts, Miz Silk. You're not making this easy for any of us."

I sighed. "I suppose you're right."

"Good. Try to go with the flow. And listen, do you think you could pull over and fix your hair a bit and maybe put on some lipstick? It's a good thing your forehead's healed." She squinted at me. "Your eyebrows have grown in not too bad."

I took my eyes off the road long enough to stare at her, but not enough to get us killed. "Isn't that out of character for you, Josey?"

"I got my reasons for asking. It's not like I bug you about beauty stuff all the time."

I pulled over and tried to arrange my hair using the rearview mirror. I managed to get it under control with the help of a scrunchie that Josey had brought along. She'd produced my one all-purpose lipstick too.

"Don't ask, Miz Silk. Just humour me, please," she said. "Hey! Isn't that Marc-André's house?"

"Of course it is. I've been up here once a week until last month." I slowed to a crawl as we approached the property I'd looked after for so many months. In all the hassle with the rehab, I'd hesitated to step on his property in case I got arrested. Not seeing Marc-André had been the worst of the whole crazy series of events. "I can't believe the rehab centre is still investigating those allegations, especially after Paulette blabbed about her part in it."

"I guess they had to be sure, Miz Silk. But someone's there now. We should go see."

"Maybe not, Josey. We have to wait until everything's cleared up."

"Miz Silk. Stop the car."

The car seemed to stop itself. Josey opened the passenger

door and hopped out. Tolstoy hopped out with her. Together they trotted down the driveway to Marc-André's house and auto shop. The sign still said: *MA Paradis: Specialisé en voitures européennes.* Every time I saw the dusty FERMÉ sign, I felt a catch in my throat.

The door to the house was ajar. Was someone inside? That was too close for comfort after our disastrous discovery at Arlen Young's house. I didn't want Josey coming face to face with a burglar. Or worse, some government official sent to take charge of Marc-André's affairs after the rehab fiasco? I climbed out of the driver's seat.

Josey and Tolstoy had already arrived at the front door. I hustled down to try to minimize whatever bad stuff was going to happen. The front door stood open. "Josey," I said. "Maybe we should… Josey? Josey?"

Josey and Tolstoy had dashed though the kitchen to the living room. I squared my shoulders and followed, prepared to meet some local thug who was planning to clean out Marc-André's property.

Tolstoy set up a riff of barking. Too hell with it. If there was a price to pay, I'd just have to pay it. I marched through the small neat kitchen and squealed to a halt at the door to the living room. I didn't even notice that the place was dust-free, and the dropcloths that I'd used to cover the furniture had been removed. My eyes were on the man on the leather sofa.

"Hello, madame!" With the help of a cane, Marc-André rose to greet me. He wobbled slightly and sat down again. But the triumph remained.

Josey's grin consumed her face. "Are you surprised, Miz Silk?"

Surprised didn't quite cover it. I wobbled a bit myself as I moved toward him.

"I have so much to get used to," Marc-André said.

"Why are you here?"

"I am a free man, madame."

"Isn't that great, Miz Silk?"

"I understand that Mademoiselle here is your new executive assistant. She is a very good one. She is responsible for this freedom."

Josey beamed.

"But how did you get here from the rehab centre?"

"Luc brought him!" Josey said.

I turned to find my favourite nurse grinning sheepishly. By this time, I had decided I was probably having one of many dreams about Marc-André, and any minute Woody would wheel through the door, waving a can of Red Bull and shouting for me to get up and face the afternoon.

Josey said, "Isn't this great? Marc-André is coming home. Luc arranged for a lawyer and an assessment. Luc's partner is going to come in every day and help him with exercises and nursing stuff. We cleaned the place up, and we'll move his bed down here so he doesn't have to take the stairs."

I was hardly listening. My eyes were glued to Marc-André. He was still pale, but he looked so much better than he had when I'd last seen him.

He smiled. "Sit here, Fiona."

"And no wonder he couldn't remember," Josey said. "That last couple of weeks, Paulette was slipping him drugs before your visits."

Luc said, "Can't prove it yet, but we believe that's why he was having more memory troubles."

"Josey didn't mention it to me."

Marc-André said, "I asked her not to."

"But why?"

"Because we can't prove it, and if the problem turned out

to be my brain instead of drugs, then I didn't want you to be disappointed."

"You mean heartbroken," Josey said. "You know, Miz Silk, if you got your hopes up that he was really all right, and then…" She cast a quick glance in Marc-André's direction.

He leaned forward. "Things weren't looking good. You know, I might have slipped back into a coma."

Josey said, "But now, it's all good. And I bet that Paulette person is going to jail."

In that moment, everything else seemed unimportant. The wait for my home to be rebuilt, my bankrupt ex-husband, even the heartbreaking loss of the Colville, who cared? Marc-André was back, and he was going to be fine. Better than fine, and he was already wonderful.

Well, deep in my heart, I knew I would always mourn for the Colville a bit, but this was hardly the time to dwell on that.

"And another good thing, Miz Silk. Marc-André will need someone to stay with him. To keep him company. Just until your house is finished, in case there's an emergency in the night. Purely platonic. Do you think Woody would mind if you stayed here instead of with him?"

Marc-André smothered a grin.

I said, "Woody will be glad to get rid of me. Better smoking conditions."

Josey wasn't finished. "And Tolstoy will be happy here. Plus Marc-André will need someone to drive him, because he's still not really a hundred per cent. Sorry, Marc-André, but it's a fact."

Marc-André shrugged. "I will be a lucky man."

Josey said, "So you can get your old Beamer out of storage. And I'll get my 365 in September, once Miz Silk can pay her tab, and then I could take you places too."

He paled slightly but rallied. A prince among men.

I said, "What will you do now, Marc-André? Will you re-start your business?"

"I will have to see how I do," he said. "My hands do not necessarily listen to my head. And vice versa."

"You're a licensed mechanic. You could hire someone, if you wanted to keep it going."

"Even an apprentice," Josey said. "Part-time."

"Right now, I want to enjoy every minute spent outside the walls of the hospital."

"Josey, I'm sorry I resisted. This is truly the best surprise I ever could have had."

"But Miz Silk, this isn't the surprise!"

"Well, it's the most surprising thing that's ever happened to me!"

"Me too," Marc André said. "And I was part of it."

Josey's cowlicks waved as she shook her head. "It's *surprising*. And it's the happy ending. But, I have to tell you, it's not *the* surprise."

"Okay. I'll play. What is *the* surprise?"

"You want to close your eyes?"

"All right, Josey, I'll close my eyes."

"Keep them closed."

I heard her footsteps crossing the hardwood floor.

A swish of fabric and "Ta da! Okay, Miz Silk. You can look now."

It took a second for it to make sense and longer than that before I could speak.

I said, "What's going on? How did the Colville get here?"

"Please don't be mad, Miz Silk. I was worried about it. I knew how much you loved it and how it belonged to your aunt and how that husband of yours wanted to take everything from you. And I was afraid that the electrician would damage it. Or steal it. So when I packed up the stuff for electrical panel repairs,

I put the painting in Uncle Mike's truck. He didn't know anything about it."

"Right." Otherwise my beautiful painting might have sold for the price of a couple of bottles of Johnny Walker at the Britannia.

"But the police routinely check your cabin for, um, stuff, Josey."

"I told Uncle Mike I had to deliver something to the new tenant here."

Since there'd never been a tenant at Marc-André's place, I figured I wasn't the only one who didn't trust Uncle Mike one thousand per cent. Some people shouldn't be made aware that a nice house like Marc-André's remained unoccupied for nearly ten months. Josey may be loyal, but she's also practical.

"And you kept it with the furniture under the dust covers?"

"No. I hid it in the attic. Just in case. I was going to tell you, but then when everything burned up, I thought it was better if your ex didn't know. In case the cops never got all the money sorted out, he might still come after it."

I said, "The Colville looks great in this room. It should stay here."

"Well," Josey said, "I have to get going. I'll call my Uncle Mike. Gotta get to school. I have an exam in about an hour. Hope he's sober."

Luc looked alarmed. Of course, he was new to Josey's ways, "I'll take you, Josey. My car's parked behind the garage. We'll be in touch, Fiona, about the home care schedule. I'm glad you used the oyster recipe in your book. Good luck, you three."

Tolstoy's tail thumped the floor.

As they pulled out of the driveway, Marc-André turned to me. "I was disappointed to hear that our relationship was purely platonic."

"Is it really?" I said. "I had no idea."

In addition to the Fiona Silk books, Mary Jane Maffini is the author of five Camilla MacPhee mysteries published by RendezVous Crime, the recently launched Charlotte Adams series (*Organize Your Corpses,* Berkley Prime Crime) and nearly two dozen short stories. She's a charter member of The Ladies Killing Circle and a former President of Crime Writers of Canada. Before turning to a life of crime, she had a lot of mysterious fun as a librarian. She lives and plots in Ottawa with her long-suffering husband and two princessy dachshunds. Find more clues at www.maryjanemaffini.ca